AFTER THE SHOW

The Mays are a theatrical dynasty. From Gilbert, and his wife Madge, the gift for putting on a show passed to their children—even to the mentally handicapped Toby, given to flamboyant parades through the town in one of Gilbert's old costumes.

But not to Emmy. Emmy, 'the other one', the sensible, non-performing May.

So when Toby dies in a re-enactment of another, long ago death, nobody's *really* worried that Emmy might start opening cupboard doors. Letting out the clearsighted malice of Toby's artistic vision, the shadow on Gilbert's past, the truth about Harvey Persky, the one startling scandal in her own life...Emmy wouldn't do that. Would she?

AFTER THE SHOW

AFTER THE SHOW

by

Margaret Hinxman

Magna Large Print Books
Long Preston, North Yorkshire,
England.

British Library Cataloguing in Publication Data.

Hinxman, Margaret
　　After the show.

　　A catalogue record for this book is
　　available from the British Library

　　ISBN 0-7505-0715-4

First published in Great Britain by Orion Publishing Group
Ltd., 1993

Magna Large Print is an imprint of
Library Magna Books Ltd.
Printed and bound in Great Britain by
T.J. Press (Padstow) Ltd., Cornwall, PL28 8RW.

CHAPTER ONE

It was, she decided afterwards, quite right and proper that the precursor of the most dramatic change in her life should have been the younger Burstyn boy. No blinding flash of lightning truth, no searing decision, not even a knock on the door from a sombre priest, just an impudent, acne-ridden hobgoblin of a boy who was never up to any good.

You had to believe in a comical God who would choose such a bearer of momentous tidings. And Emmeline May firmly believed in a comical God. The idea of a deity with a sense of humour had comforted her through most of the arid reaches of her fifty years.

Apart from one youthful folly it had on the surface been a responsible and ordered life: so responsible, so ordered, that it was common knowledge in Clifton Coombe that Wednesday was her day for Sunny Hill nursing home. It seldom varied and, if it did for some reason or another, that was common knowledge in Clifton Coombe too.

'Run up to Sunny Hill and get Miss

7

May. Tell her it's her brother. He's at the old Adelphi. And *stop* that, you dirty little devil!' Betty Burstyn, who managed the newsagent's next door to the derelict Adelphi, had interrupted her son in the process of quietly masturbating on his bed before a poster of Madonna.

Caught in the act, the boy caressed a juicy rash of pimples blooming in the crease behind earlobe and chin and reluctantly dragged himself away from his contemplation of Madonna's pointy breasts. 'What's the looney been up to now?' he muttered under his breath but loud enough for his mother to catch it. 'Never you mind that. Just be quick about it. Get your skates on!' Which he did: new state-of-the-art skates which he'd saved up for from his paper round. His mother had sounded urgent and, as he left, he'd heard her telephoning the emergency services. All in all it promised to be a livelier Wednesday than usual in the idle midweek wasteland of the summer holidays.

Emmy May (only her family called her Emmeline and then only in moments of extreme provocation) was in the middle of guiding old Mrs Richmond's clumsy fingers through the intricacies of a pattern for a multi-yarn Kaffe Fasset jerkin that she would never wear and probably never finish but had obstinately insisted on tackling.

'I know. I know. You don't have to tell me. I'm not daft, like some in here.' She dabbed ineffectually at Emmy's hovering hand, a hint of malice in her watery eyes. The gentle sweetness that is supposed to be the redeeming grace of dependent old age had found no home in her prickly nature.

She was a crusty old girl whom Emmy, alone among the voluntary helpers at the home, found bearable, even endearing. She liked a show of spunk in the elderly. Mrs Richmond would never become a vegetable like so many of the others. *She'd* go raging into the dying of the light, all right. And woe betide God on that day!

'How's that mad brother of yours?' It wasn't a conversational question: rather, a sly dig at the May heritage. The Mays were famous in Clifton Coombe, but not unflawed, she was reminding Emmy. She meant mad: not wild or mischievous or funny, but mad.

Emmy smiled, quite amiably. Evil old thing! 'Toby? Toby's fine.'

'I suppose you'd know,' Mrs Richmond grumbled, cross at getting no rise out of Emmy. Three or four hopelessly tangled balls of yarn attached to a shapeless bit of knitting slid off her lap on to the floor.

'Damn! Blast! Shit! Bugger!' Mrs Richmond aired her repertoire of swear words

9

very deliberately and very loudly for maximum effect.

'Language!' said Emmy mechanically, although she couldn't think why the old should be denied a good healthy explosion of expletives on occasion as if they were children. Manners had a lot to answer for.

Mrs Richmond kicked the balls of yarn across the communal sitting room with surprising vigour and pursued her chosen topic of conversation.

'I suppose you'd know,' she repeated. 'But, then again, maybe you wouldn't. That Mrs Barnes who comes Monday told me she'd seen him directing the traffic up by the war memorial on Saturday afternoon.'

'That's right,' Emmy agreed. ('Who's been the naughty boy?' the police constable who had brought him home had said, not meaning to sound patronizing but sounding it just the same.)

'All done up, straw hat, bow tie, striped blazer, cane, white gloves,' Mrs Richmond persisted. 'Directing the traffic. Making an exhibition of himself. And singing he was. She said. That Mrs Barnes. Singing. And directing the traffic. You ought to have him put away. For his own good.' She nudged Emmy quite sharply in the ribs with her bony elbow.

Maybe, thought Emmy, it gave her some comfort to imagine someone else being put away, immobilized from life.

'He does no harm,' she sighed as she picked up the errant balls of yarn. How often she had fielded that same unconsidered argument over the years since she'd assumed responsibility for Toby after her parents' death. She shivered slightly at the painful memory of the one time she'd been persuaded to broach the subject with her brother, the agitation in his eyes at the mere thought of being parted from the familiar boundaries of his limited life: Emmy and their sprawling Victorian home and the workshop where he laboured at the one skill he possessed, painting those brilliant, fevered impressions of a fantasy world that triggered his imagination and mystified everyone else's.

All the time he was tucked away out of sight he was secure, safe, loved, on his best behaviour when the rest of the family visited. It was the occasions when the fancy took him and her shy, inoffensive brother escaped into the persona of an extrovert *boulevardier* about town, wearing their father Gilbert's old music hall costume, that bothered people, even those who charitably regarded him as a character, not really unhinged, just extravagantly eccentric.

'But he might. Do harm.' Old Mrs Richmond was still at it. Emmy had thought that, too. But she wasn't about to put him on a leash, restrict his life even more than it was already restricted by the accident of his mental handicap. 'He'll always be a trial,' their doctor had warned her. Well, all right, he was a trial. She admitted it. But he'd be more of a trial in a home, however caring and comfortable, leaving her feeling guilty and worrying endlessly about his well-being.

'He just likes to dress up and put on a show—now and then,' she explained patiently as she had so often before, realizing as she said it how absurd that must sound to anyone who wasn't a May.

After all, that's what the Mays had always done. All except her, that is. Emmy. Emmeline.

Maybe that's why her parents had chosen such an unfrivolous name for her, evoking stern images of suffragettes chained to railings and force-fed in prison cells. Maybe even at birth it had been apparent that she would never grow into a true May. 'The other one' they used to say in the town when she was little, to differentiate her from Penny and Cissie and Val and Reggie and even poor Toby who could only ape the flamboyant showmanship of those other gifted Mays.

Memories! So many memories! Some good. Some bad. Some...she shivered again. 'Let's see if we can sort out this mess,' she said briskly.

She rescued the knitting needles from Mrs Richmond's faltering fingers and purposefully tried to change the subject, to concentrate the old lady's attention on something other than Toby's erratic behaviour. The effort was short-lived.

At that moment Trevor Burstyn was being admonished by matron to take off his skates, wipe his feet and wait quietly in the hall while she fetched Miss May.

When Emmy arrived at the Adelphi in her tacky but serviceable hatchback, the Burstyn boy and his skates bundled in the back, the police and the fire brigade were already there. A sprinkling of curious shoppers and holiday-makers, scenting a happening out of the ordinary, was congregating on the pavement outside the dangerous rickety theatre.

It was long overdue for demolition, beyond restoration. The out-of-town property developer who had bought it was still wrangling with the council over permission to build a block of offices in its place and with conservationists who wanted to preserve the old theatre's façade. Although why the town needed a new block of offices in the depths of a recession was beyond comprehension, the local paper editorialized, hinting darkly at ulterior motives in influential quarters, favours given for favours received.

Meanwhile the subject of the controversy sat reproachfully on its prime town site, unkempt and uncared for. A half-hearted attempt to erect scaffolding around the structure habitually fell victim to vandals.

Try as she might, Emmy could never summon up the same affection for it as others in the town who would rather have it remain an increasingly neglected eyesore than allow it to be consigned to the debris of history where it rightfully belonged.

But she realized she was biased. She'd ceased to care about the Adelphi after her father had sold it to a cinema chain that had had no luck with it either as a cinema or, later, a bingo parlour. She had watched the spirit drain out of it through its successive new guises, like a star performer reduced to playing inferior roles in third-rate productions. Buildings, she thought, were flesh and blood, living entities: they knew when they were being degraded and deprived of purpose.

Briefly, she'd hoped that some rich theatrical entrepreneur might race to the rescue and restore it to the glory it had

14

known under Gilbert May's management, when every show—musical, drama or variety—had played to near-capacity houses. But no white knight had taken up the challenge. And the hope had died along with the Adelphi.

These days she averted her eyes as she passed it. Above the once elaborate porticoed entrance the letters 'AEPHI' clung lopsidedly to the wall. The 'D' and 'L' had been wrenched off during the near-hurricane that had swept the south of England in 1987. The scarred stucco and dome, its intricately assembled glass panes long shattered by high winds and well aimed stones, were like a rebuke. We were yours and look what you've let them do to us! But you were never mine, she'd mutter to herself. You belonged to the Mays and the Mays deserted or died on you and I was never a genuine eighteen-carat May. I was the other one.

But today she was forced to look at this wreck that was once the Adelphi.

How often had she warned Toby not to go near the place, explained that it wasn't the Adelphi they remembered, but old and hazardous and sorry for itself?

And yet, at the back of her mind, she'd been fearfully anticipating this day: the day when he wouldn't be able to resist inspecting the May legacy for one last time, not cautiously like an intruder, but in appropriate proprietorial style. Like a May.

She identified herself to the young constable outside although there was no need. 'He's in there, Miss May. God knows how. The entrance was boarded up.' She sensed the reproach in his voice, that if-she-can't-look-after-him-properly-she-should-have-him-put-away voice to which she'd become resigned.

'That didn't stop the vandals,' she said in what she fancied was a reasonable tone but apparently wasn't.

'I didn't mean...' He sounded bullish, his uniformed status affronted. He was, she thought, awfully young. How quickly one took offence when one was young!

'Oh yes you did,' she said mildly and marvelled at how calm and unflustered she felt. 'Now perhaps you'll let me in to see my brother.'

They escorted her through the sightseers and the battered doors. The gaping windows flanking the upper foyer reminded her of eyeless sockets: she'd never noticed that before. The Burstyn boy, who understandably considered himself a principal player in the drama, didn't see why he should be left out now and followed behind. Then she was standing in what had once been the auditorium: in the glory days all gold and frescoes and scarlet plush and polished brass and plaster cherubs tooting trumpets. Now it was gutted of seating. All the theatre's finery had been dismembered. The pillars supporting the dress circle and gallery were perilously shaky.

A cluster of police and firemen with ladders were conferring, their eyes fixed on the uppermost gallery, the 'gods'. They greeted Emmy with a mixture of relief and resentment: relief that she might help to solve their problem and resentment that she was partly responsible for it in the first place.

'We don't want to risk the ladder in case it panics him. Maybe you can talk him down. He must have shinnied up those supports somehow. It's a wonder he didn't break his neck.'

The fire officer who seemed to be in charge was joined by a police inspector who looked dapper and sounded superior. 'We'll tell you what to say,' he instructed Emmy. 'There are ways of dealing with these people. We've had a lot of experience —multi-storey car parks...' It was on the tip of his tongue to mention suicides but he stopped himself in time. 'He knows you and that would be useful. You mustn't worry, we'll get him down,' he added almost as an afterthought.

'I'm not worried,' she murmured. I'm not behaving properly, she thought. They'd rather I were weeping and helpless and desperately grateful for their massive male authority in a crisis.

Only then did she look up at the point upon which their eyes were focused. And the sight she saw made her smile, a broad, unmistakable smile.

'Good God, what's the matter with the woman? She must be in shock,' she heard the inspector grumble behind her.

No, this wasn't the right response at all. But she kept smiling because she couldn't help it.

Toby was poised on the narrow railing skirting the gallery, one leg suspended like a dancer's over the dark mass of what had been the dress circle and beyond down to the auditorium, a crushing drop of a hundred feet or more. The sun shining through the domed ceiling skylight played on his slight figure like a theatre spotlight singling out a show-stopping entertainer, centre stage. His prematurely wizened face was turned toward it with an expression of exultant triumph, acknowledging perhaps the clapping and cheering of an audience only Toby could see and hear.

He was dressed in that old costume her father had worn every year for the Christmas pantomime when he'd performed the spectacular stunt he'd learned in the circus and later incorporated into his music hall act, suspended on a trapeze from the gallery to the stage.

It had been the annual highlight of the production and it had always brought the house down. As children they'd watched him with awe and dread until he'd landed lightly and safely on stage to gasps and roars of approval.

'Toby!' she called just loud enough to be heard but not so loud as to scare him off his perch. 'That's wonderful, Toby.'

'Christ, woman, get him *down!*' muttered the inspector.

Her brother peered down at her into the gloomy crater below, shading his eyes. He looked happier than she'd seen him in years, since he was a little boy mimicking the father he worshipped.

'I'm flying, Emmy. Just like dad. I'm flying. I'm Gilbert the filbert. How am I doing, Emmy?'

'You're doing fine, Toby, just fine.'

'Why don't you tell the damn fool to get down off that rail?' someone hissed.

'Why?' she said. 'There's enough of us down here. Only one of him up there.' What am I saying? she thought. How can I be so casual? It's death we're dealing with here. Like that other death. Suddenly, she was overcome by the same terror she'd

19

experienced watching her father, only far, far worse.

'It's time to come down, Toby.' She tried to keep the fear out of her voice, but it was there and it communicated itself to her brother. She watched the smile freeze on his face, the excitement drain out of his eyes. He looked around him, conscious of where he was. Slowly, he lowered his extended leg back on to the rail.

'Easy does it, Toby. Step down off the rail. Someone's coming to get you,' she said soothingly, gesturing as she did to the firemen with the ladder behind her.

'I'm frightened,' her brother whimpered.

'There's nothing to be frightened of, Toby. Dad would have been proud of you.' Then, in a whisper to herself, 'Hang on, Toby, hang on!'

Her reference to his father gave Toby a renewed surge of confidence. As the ladder shifted into place against the gallery railing and a fireman began to ascend, he turned once again towards the sun pouring through the skylight and bowed with enormous dignity.

Then he braced himself, like a majestic performer approaching his big, climatic scene, and dived gracefully off the railing, arms outstretched. For a moment his slim body seemed to defy gravity, hanging in space, before it bounced off the side of the dress circle and down to the floor of the theatre. It lay there, crumpled and lifeless, in a cloud of dust inches away from Emmy's feet.

A smile of sweet fulfilment was still pasted on his upturned face. And she felt an irrational gratitude. At least he'd died joyously, doing in death what he'd always longed to do in life. Putting on a show. No more suffering. No more frustration. No more memories of that day none of them mentioned and none could forget. The day of that other death.

'Is he dead?' The Burstyn boy had been making himself scarce on the fringe of the action, rightly guessing he'd have been told to buzz off if he'd been spotted. But he could contain himself no longer. This was the real thing, not video or TV. And he'd actually seen it happen. He shoved himself forward to the centre of the group surrounding Toby's still body.

'What's he doing here?' cursed the inspector. 'Out!'

Trevor Burstyn looked enquiringly at Emmy. 'Is he dead?' he repeated. 'He doesn't look dead.' He cocked his head sideways, studying the face that still reflected the moment of blissful triumph. 'He looks as if he's gone to sleep enjoying himself.'

'He's dead,' she said. But Trevor was

right. In death Toby May looked more alive than he ever had in life.

'Sorry!' the boy mumbled.

It was the first condolence of many she'd receive during the coming weeks and, on reflection, Emmy decided, it was probably the most sincere.

CHAPTER TWO

It had been a slow news week for the *Clifton Clarion,* so Toby May's sudden death—'tragic death' amended the editor —proved to be something of a godsend. It was an excuse to dust off the history of the May family; to air the running grievance between the Clifton Preservation Society and the town planners; to pontificate about accidents waiting to happen in a death trap like the Adelphi; and to anticipate the convergence on Clifton Coombe of an assortment of celebrities, including the surviving Mays, for the funeral.

An extra pinch of spice came from an unexpected source. Harry Catchpole was delivering his weekly gardening column which he'd been writing with a broad-nibbed fountain pen for as long as anyone on the *Clarion* could remember.

He was totally uninterested in anything that couldn't be raked, weeded, sprayed, pruned, dead-headed, manured, watered, pinched out at the top or cut back hard and, when he gloomily intoned 'lightning strikes twice!', the sub who was wearily deciphering his copy assumed he was probably referring to some adverse climatic condition that would wreak havoc across the lovingly tended plots of Clifton Coombe for the second season in a row. (The sub, no gardener, he, had difficulty remembering to be kind to the potted Busy Lizzie his girlfriend had given him to cheer up his bed-sitter.)

'Happened before!' Harry Catchpole sucked hard on a troublesome hollow tooth. 'Oooh! Thirty-odd years ago. Chap fell.'

The sub pricked up his ears. 'What chap? Where?'

'Like I said. Happened before. At the Adelphi.'

And indeed, they discovered from the *Clarion* files, Harry was right. A chap had fallen to his death at the Adelphi over thirty years before. It hadn't been much of a story even in its day (misadventure had been the coroner's verdict), but it added a touch of morbid glamour to the feature on the old theatre.

'Merciful release?' suggested Horace

Lacey who presided over births, deaths and marriages.

'Good God, no!' said Emmy. 'I just want an entry, plain and simple.'

'Much mourned?'

'Hardly. Most people thought Toby should be put away and I suppose you could say he is now. How about: "He died as he wished to live"?'

'It's rather frivolous, don't you think?' Mr Lacey's disapproval seeped through the tone of the sepulchral gravity he adopted when speaking to the recently bereaved.

'Well, that's how he died, didn't he? Frivolously!'

'If you insist, Miss May.' He sounded quite frosty. It was on the tip of his tongue to say something about a seemly show of grief when he realized the telephone call had been abruptly terminated.

'Very odd!' He turned to a young reporter who was battling with a word processor, a dearth of original thought and a hangover, not necessarily in that order. 'Not at all like Emmy May. Pillar of the community and all that. She sounded positively cheerful.'

'Perhaps she is. Poor bugger! Toby May. Couldn't have been much of a life for him. Couldn't have been much of a life for her, come to that.' The effort of stringing two coherent sentences together proved too much for him. He winced as his throbbing head reminded him of a misspent night before.

'You want to watch it, my lad,' said Mr Lacy primly. He was due for retirement and regarded the younger element on the staff with almost as much suspicion as he viewed the input of new technology on the paper. Then, returning to his first thought, he repeated, 'But it is *odd.*'

As it turned out he was voicing the general consensus about Emmeline May's uncharacteristic behaviour. When word got around of Toby's death she'd received the many expressions of sympathy with her customary politeness but with absolutely no apparent sign that she was in need of consolation over the loss that had been visited on her.

Representatives (or, to be more precise, those who'd drawn the short straw) from the many charitable and voluntary organizations to which she'd given her time and money freely, were quickest off the mark wearing doleful faces and articulating a correct litany of condolence, given that Toby's place in Clifton Coombe society had been an awkward one to characterize. The chairman of the local amateur operatic group, of which she was a leading behind-the-scenes member, suggested a memorial concert, but was slightly put out when she insisted that Cole Porter and Irving Berlin would be more appropriate than Handel and Mozart. The president of the Clifton Preservation Society hoped this tragic event meant they could count on her support for a sympathetic restoration of the Adelphi, and the planning officer on the borough council was sure that in her great grief she would appreciate the necessity for pulling the thing down.

Without exception they all retreated, baffled by a response they could only describe as light-hearted. It wasn't like Emmy at all. Emmy had always been the stable May, apart, of course, from that adolescent lapse which only a few recalled anyway.

She wasn't like those flighty sisters of hers, Penelope and Cecilia and Valerie, who in their teens had achieved a brief celebrity in the pop charts as 'The Mayflowers' (a much-mocked sobriquet dreamt up by the agent who had spotted them and packaged them). Or Reggie who had studied at RADA and then cut a dashing figure in the British cinema over thirty years for which he'd been knighted in the previous year's New Year honours. Or old Gilbert May and his wife Madge who had toured the halls as a speciality song, dance and acrobatic act before inheriting the Adelphi from Madge's father.

As Gilbert used to say with some justification but not much originality: 'You can take the boy out of the circus, but you can't take the circus out of the boy.'

Even poor Toby—well, the way he died, for instance!—had been tainted with that exhibitionist urge that had driven the Mays.

But not Emmy. How Emmy had missed out was a mystery, a throwback perhaps to old Gilbert's past about which he had been, for him, excessively secret.

But now, here she was, acting most peculiarly. 'Almost as if death were some sort of gala,' said the Reverend Arthur Selby who, on asking what hymns should be sung at Toby's funeral service, was shocked to be told by Emmy, 'Onward Christian Soldiers' and 'That's Entertainment'.

'I don't imagine the mourners would think "That's Entertainment" quite—well, suitable,' he suggested gently. Although he was mindful that, as a notoriously progressive vicar who had once argued for the performance of a blasting rock requiem in the church, he was hardly in a position to protest against a jolly send-off for Toby.

'Probably,' she'd agreed, but before he could sigh with relief she added, 'but Toby would. And that's what matters, isn't it?'

Only Flo Gosling seemed completely at ease with Emmy's equable acceptance of her brother's death. 'Sod the rest of the them!' she said, raising a glass of cheap Lambrusco.

Flo was twenty years younger than Emmy, who had never seen her when she didn't look as if she'd been hit by a hurricane, with her wild red hair, trailing skirts and string bag stuffed with petitions and leaflets. Her one concession to conventional femininity was a refusal to wear short skirts or jeans because her calves were too thick. Never having seen them, Emmy had to take her word for that.

They made an ill-matched couple. 'I'm your skeleton in the cupboard,' Flo had once observed, with some truth: Emmy's financial support of the *Wave*, the militant feminist news sheet that Flo edited, was her secret, her one slender but satisfying revolt against convention.

Yet they both knew they were fooling themselves, Flo perhaps more than Emmy who had long seen her life as a series of charades, of keeping up a variety of appearances that had little to do with the small core of herself she was convinced existed and would spring into being when the time was right.

A revolt was hardly a revolt if the

object of the exercise refused to acknowledge that it was being revolted against. Clifton Coombe—at least, the old, established, male-orientated Clifton Coombe that mattered—seemed singularly unaware that its complacency was under threat from the radical demands of women's rights.

Occasionally, maudlin from too great an intake of cheap wine, Flo admitted she didn't know why she bothered: why she didn't pack up, go to London or Birmingham or Manchester and really get stuck into the crusade, channel her energies into tackling problems so immense and varied that there wouldn't be time for internal debate about doing the right thing.

'Then why don't you?' Emmy challenged her.

Flo hadn't answered, but she hadn't needed to. Emmy knew why. Flo was bound to Clifton Coombe as surely as Emmy was. In that they were alike. In Emmy's case, all the time Toby was alive, it was through necessity. Flo's motives were subtler, perhaps more deep-seated. Her presence in the town—unkempt, disordered, subversive—was a constant thorn in the flesh of the tenaciously respectable parents who abhorred everything she did and believed in.

'They don't even acknowledge me in

the street any more,' she'd laughed. But the laugh had carried no conviction. 'Am I a masochist or a sadist?' A bit of both, thought Emmy, but didn't say it. Flo was still paying her parents back for rejecting her as a no-good vagrant years ago.

Meanwhile, the *Wave* in its little way helped—a single parent having trouble with the DSS here, a runaway teenage girl there, a case of sexual harassment in the workplace.

'Sod them!' Flo repeated, her cheeks flushed with Lambrusco, indignation and a particularly violent shade of pink blusher. 'All those nice, proper citizens who don't give a damn about anything but their investments, their custom-built pine kitchens and keeping the peasants in their place.'

'Good people,' Emmy corrected her. 'They mean well. They *do* well.'

'Well, you *would* say that, wouldn't you? You're half one of them. What did they ever *do* for Toby? Except whinge on because he liked to take off and do his own thing now and then. Now it's all long faces and great loss and Father in heaven receive our beloved Toby who brought us such joy! You did your grieving and caring while he was alive, Emmy, old girl, when it mattered. Now it's your turn.'

'I hadn't thought of it like that,' Emmy

lied. She was good at lying. She'd always been good at lying.

With a snort of derision Flo pivoted round on her swivel chair looking for all the world like a particularly ungainly bird preparing to take flight. 'Oh yes, you had, old girl. Admit it!'

Emmy smiled, that small confusing smile which suggested she was privy to a joke too private to be shared. 'I admit nothing on the grounds that it might incriminate me.'

'Why don't you marry old thingy who's always hanging around? No, God, don't. That way lies disaster. I bet he's a drag in bed and I bet you don't even know,' she added, probing.

'Oliver? What an idea!' said Emmy, neither denying nor admitting that the relationship with the family solicitor Oliver Ballantyne was anything other than properly professional.

'Don't come the old acid with me,' Flo prodded her. Her speech was beginning to slur and she looked glumly at the empty bottle of wine.

Emmy laid a restraining hand on Flo's restless one. It usually came to this; not often, but now and then when Flo was drinking. It was a pity Flo couldn't accept that she really should get away from Clifton Coombe; from the daily hurt of knowing the lifestyle she flaunted was simply aimed like some poison dart at two bewildered, elderly people who lived in a nice detached house on the rim of the Downs and couldn't understand how they'd managed to produce such a child as Flo. So narrow a goal demeaned the woman and diminished the value of her work.

'That's enough, Flo.'

'No, it isn't.' Flo shook her hand free forcefully and then, quite suddenly, slumped back in her chair apparently exhausted. When she spoke again she sounded empty.

'The trouble with you is you've suffered from too much virtue and not enough sin all these years.' Living as she did on the rough side of town with a succession of casual but sexually insatiable boyfriends, who sponged on her earnings from part-time jobs at Tesco and a small legacy left her by a sympathetic grandmother, Flo never ceased to be baffled by what she regarded as Emmy's bloody-minded celibacy.

It all depends what you mean by sin, thought Emmy. After all this time the chill of memory never failed to send a shudder through her body. But she answered Flo brightly enough, giving a little to guard a lot. 'I wouldn't say that. I've a thirty-four-year-old-daughter who still blames me for not marrying her father. That was pretty sinful in the fifties I can tell you.' She sounded thoughtful as if trying to recall what it actually was like to be pregnant and unrepentant in that repressive decade before the liberating sixties.

'You know something?'

'Else?' Emmy sighed. 'I'd rather not, Flo. Not just now.'

'I know.' A wry smile softened the contours of a mouth more accustomed to expressions of grim determination or righteous indignation. 'You've wasted too much time with me already. Go on, say it! There are the funeral arrangements and the inquest and a hundred and one other things to be attended to. Not forgetting the *family.*' The emphasis was marked and not kindly.

'Flo, don't talk like that,' Emmy snapped. 'You're never a waste of time —except, sometimes I think, your own.' Then, quickly, before she had to elaborate. 'But, you're right. There's an awful lot to do.' An awful lot to do! Like regenerating her life.

'They know, of course. The family?'

'Oh yes. They know.' And she wondered why the rituals of death should have to impose such burdens on the living. Or maybe the burdens would turn out to be blessings, heavily disguised. She had no doubt that her comical God was working on that one even as the family composed its collective face for the forthcoming public scrutiny Toby May had so inconveniently inflicted on it.

CHAPTER THREE

A flicker of a smile lit up Emmy's expression as she picked her way down the rickety stairs of the tall, crumbling house which had been parcelled into far too many cramped offices for impecunious organizations like *Wave* that could just about manage the rent. On the landing she ran into a tiny little woman with a dark russety face like an overripe Cox's Orange Pippin puffing her way up.

'God Almighty, these stairs will be the death of me!' she wheezed, levering herself carefully on to an upturned dustbin that had been left behind by a previous tenant. She rummaged in her worn leather handbag and produced a fistful of typewritten notes triumphantly. 'This'll fix 'em. Read it.' She shoved the pages into Emmy's hand.

'You don't have to flog up here with

your piece, Alice. I'm sure Flo could get one of the girls to collect it,' said Emmy.

Alice Gravely considered the suggestion and discarded it. 'All the time I'm capable,' she said grandly, daring anyone to insinuate that at eighty-five she was incapable. 'My mother was still riding a bicycle when she was ninety. Mind you,' she added puckishly, 'that's what did for her. Run down by a bus. They came from all over England to see her off. The ones that were still alive. Worked with your namesake—Emmeline Pankhurst—in the movement. Did you know that?'

'You told me, Alice.'

'Go on, read it!' She pointed hump-backed arthritic fingers toward the pages in Emmy's hand.

Emmy glanced through the typescript imagining those fingers painfully picking out the words on the keys of the old Olympia portable. But the words themselves belied the frailty of the writer, arguing in strong, succinct, if alarmist, language against the hypocrisy of successive male-dominated governments in paying lip service to equal job opportunities for women while doing damn all about it. (Margaret Thatcher she dismissed as a quasi-man and no friend to women).

The fact that the issue (while no less, indeed more, valid) was currently clouded by recession and rising unemployment cut no ice with the author. It was all the same dastardly male plot that had enslaved women for centuries.

Mrs Gravely had a poor opinion of men in general and the architects of social, economic and political policy in particular—'bird brains with penises'. She was of an unforgiving nature. And while most of her derision was reserved for the famous (Winston Churchill was top of her hit list for his conduct as Home Secretary during the suffragette campaigns eighty years ago), she still bore a grudge against Mr Gravely for marching her down the aisle before she had enough sense to know better. If her husband had a Christian name she never used it, as if throughout their married life they had never been formally introduced. He'd escaped gratefully into the Navy at the outbreak of the Second World War and died at a pub in Portsmouth during an air raid. Mrs Gravely's only regret was that they'd never had a child. 'If it was a girl I'd have taught her what's what and if it was a boy I'd have taught him what wasn't.'

She lived in fiercely private poverty on her pension and a very little bit put aside in a damp, two-roomed high-rise flat on an estate outside the town. Whenever it was suggested that the council or the social services might do more for her she'd reply truculently 'I get by', and that was an end to that. And, in her way, she did. Get by.

Still breathing heavily from the effort of mounting the stairs she looked up at Emmy, squinting through pebble-lens spectacles. 'I'm glad to see you're not letting it get to you.'

Emmy handed back her article on equal pay and job opportunities. 'It's good. It's always good. Letting what get to me?' she asked, knowing full well.

'Toby, of course.' Mrs Gravely had always had a soft spot for Toby, perhaps because he was incapable of the sort of arrogant maleness she despised.

'I can't feel sad,' said Emmy. 'I mean, sad, yes, that he's gone. And I know when I go through his things I'll cry. It usually comes later, they say. But I'm not sad *for* him. If you could have seen him up there on that day, it was like—like a fulfilment.'

'Quite right. Sad for the living.' She eased herself up from the upturned dustbin. 'So—what are you going to do now? Sell the house? Move away? I suppose some man will present himself and all those Mays will tell you to get married. There's nothing like marriage for solving other people's problems.'

37

'What an odd thing to say. You don't even approve of marriage.' Alice Gravely may have had excessively strong views but at least they'd always been consistent.

'I didn't say I didn't. I said there's nothing like it for making other people feel secure and comfortable. Take your case. I imagine they'll all be coming to the funeral.'

Emmy nodded. 'Naturally.'

'Nothing natural about it. If they could get out of it without losing face I expect they would. And what do you think they're all wondering, my girl?' Toby was Toby, but Emmy had always been 'my girl' to Mrs Gravely. 'They're wondering: what's going to happen to Emmy now?'

Emmy could feel her mouth gaping open as the old woman articulated the preposterous question. 'Good God!' she said finally. 'What's going to happen? I'm not yet in my dotage. I'm perfectly fit and healthy and in full command of my faculties. I've never asked them for a penny or inconvenienced them in any way—except when Val came down and looked after Toby when I had flu once.' And what a disaster that had been, she was forced to admit.

'You're missing the point, my girl. It's not money. It's conscience. All the time you cared for Toby you had a life. Now you haven't. And they're probably scared stiff that you might take it into your head that you'd like to share theirs. Not that they don't love you dearly...'

'What makes you think I want to live with any of them?' Emmy heaved a sigh of exasperation. This wasn't the time to cope with Alice's wilder flights of exaggeration.

'*They* don't know that. Even if you told them they wouldn't believe it. But a nice, convenient marriage—now that would restore the status quo very well. No disruption. Emmy tucked up safely. Someone else's responsibility and nothing for them to worry about.'

'That's absurd. They're not like that.' Were they? She hadn't seriously thought about it, because the situation had never arisen.

Alice Gravely chuckled. It was a weird, unreal sound which seemed to ripple right through her body from her sturdy, scuffed shoes. 'So—they're all coming. The Mays.' The idea tickled her no end. 'That'll be one for the book. First time the family's been together since your dad died?' It was a question, not a statement. There was a streak of wickedness in Alice Gravely, not unlike old Mrs Richmond's persistence in looking on the black side of Toby May's scatty behaviour at Sunny Hill on the day he died.

'I'm not sure. Yes, probably,' said Emmy. 'It'll be...' What would it be?

'Interesting,' Alice volunteered. 'They never did get along, did they?'

Emmy smiled. 'Families!' she said, as if that explained everything, which in a way it did.

'Funny about your dad, though. Never quite the same after that thing at the Adelphi. I mean—'

'I know what you mean,' Emmy said briskly. 'It was a long time ago.' Her voice took on a steely tone which even Alice Gravely couldn't miss.

With a gesture of infinite tenderness she caressed Emmy's cheek with her twisted hand. 'When you're my age, everything's a long time ago,' she said gently.

Emmy noticed she was wearing knitted woollen mittens. And underneath her winter coat she was muffled up to the neck in a shapeless jersey and cardigan. Old people felt the cold so desperately. She realized it was the first time she had really looked at Alice Gravely, not just as a gutsy old girl she happened to run into now and then at Flo's, but as a person, complete and whole. It was the first time she'd noticed the clutter of clothes, the frayed cuffs and collars, the lisle stockings that were a size too large and wrinkled round her ankles; the first time she'd paid attention to the stooped posture, the breathlessness, the perpetual look of apprehension in the eyes that was the only sign she gave of being alone and old and vulnerable and at the mercy of others; the first time she'd fully appreciated Alice's need for those defiant gestures of pride that sometimes seemed so irritating.

It was as if she'd been not blind but partially sighted and now she was seeing clearly. It wasn't a pleasant experience. All these years she'd spent so much time caring for Toby, sitting on committees to devise ways of helping the needy without actually involving herself with the recipients of the charity, taking her turn at the nursing home, the local hospice and Oxfam without concerning herself emotionally with any single individual. That's the way it should be, the experts said. The moment you start getting emotionally involved, losing your objectivity, you become incapable of seeing the larger picture.

It had been a full and necessary life, she consoled herself, and it hadn't seemed wrong that there was room in it for only one deep personal commitment—to Toby. A commitment she'd promised to her father and to herself.

But now she was relieved of that commitment and she was seriously looking at Alice Gravely and at Flo Gosling upstairs. And at how many others who might be waiting in the wings to fill the gap caused by Toby's death? After the looking, wasn't something more concrete demanded?

'You know,' she said tentatively. 'I'm sure we could get you moved into a warmer, more convenient flat. On the ground floor somewhere.' Alice had always seemed so self-sufficient that any suggestion of help might have appeared an impertinence. She was held in a certain awe by her tougher, less educated neighbours who regarded her as a fount of all useful knowledge (such as how to squeeze an extra mite out of social security or screw a former employer into coughing up more redundancy pay) and kept a watching brief over her well-being. But times were changing, age was no longer respected for its own sake and old ladies on their own were fair game for kids who were running wild and the hoodlums who were invading the estate.

Alice, as Emmy expected, was affronted. 'I told you. I get by,' she snapped. 'You want to save your sympathy for those young girls who help Flo. Living in squalor, not being able to make ends meet and probably not much prospect of a job when they leave university, that is if they manage to finish the course. They're the future, my girl.

And God help us all!' she grumbled.

She eyed the flight of stairs ahead of her. 'Right. Full steam ahead! I can't waste my time gabbing with you. See you at the funeral,' she flung over her shoulder with the touch of spunky insolence that dared you ever to feel sorry for her.

For some reason Emmy couldn't bear to see her go. 'Come to tea. I'll collect you,' she called after her. 'Today.'

'I'm busy,' came the reply.

'Tomorrow,' shouted Emmy.

'Whatever you like.' (Not 'I', 'you', Emmy noted.) 'You know where I live.'

'I'll come about three.'

'Suit yourself.'

Emmy heard the door open to Flo's tiny office. 'I thought I heard you.'

'That Emmy May. Strange girl. They always used to call her the other one when she was little.' Alice Gravely raised voice floated down the stairs in anticipation that Emmy would hear it. Then the door shut.

For a moment Emmy stood unsurely on the landing. There was so much to do and in the middle of it on an impulse she'd committed herself to collect Mrs Gravely from way outside town, bring her home, provide her with tea and conversation and take her back. Commitment. Well, maybe it was a start.

She revved up the old hatchback and drove steadily through the town back home. She barely noticed where she was going for she knew the way so well. It was as if the little car were on automatic pilot.

Clifton Coombe was seedier than it had been in the pre-war days when it had been a favoured resort nestling in a cleft of the South Downs skirting the sea. But it still prided itself on preserving a faded dignity among its more raffish neighbours along the south coast which catered to a rowdier class of residents and holiday-makers. The pride was not totally justified. The town had the same problems as Brighton or Portsmouth, but on a smaller, more contained, scale. At least the notoriously 'bad area' was confined near the seafront and it was still possible to spend your whole life in Clifton Coombe in blissful—or wilful—ignorance of its seamier underside. A careful planning department had ensured that the industrial sites and ribbon development were located well beyond the limits of the town proper.

As Emmy approached the large, comfortingly ugly Victorian house on the hill overlooking the town that she'd shared with Toby it suddenly seemed no longer like home. Her mind was swimming with questions. Odd that it should be old Alice Gravely who had put them there. Questions about her future, the family.

She'd always taken the family for granted. That they cared about her she'd never doubted and didn't now. But she'd never really thought about their relationship with her. When she'd told them about Toby they'd reacted as she'd expected. Reggie, remote, rather vague. Val, flustered as usual. Penny, a little grand and suitably solemn. Cissie, tearful. And her own daughter, Fanny ('For God's sake, mother, not *Fanny;* Frances!'), businesslike, matter-of-fact. Dates were dutifully checked to make sure that they'd all have 'time windows'—Fanny's ridiculous expression—reserved for the funeral.

Without exception, though, they'd given the impression that they were sad about Toby, if faintly relieved, and very, very concerned about how Emmy was taking it. Did she need any help? The question didn't seem to have arisen when she might have been grateful for some help. And she wondered if Alice could possibly be right: that their concern was less about how she was coping with the immediate situation than about how directly they might be involved in securing her future.

Sell the house! Get married! To whom seemed beside the point.

She tried to visualize herself quite objectively as a marriageable—or even fanciable—prospect. Middle-aged but admittedly younger looking than her years. Unfashionably long, thick chestnut-coloured hair, liberally streaked with grey, which she always had difficulty keeping in some sort of order. Still trim-figured, although with the English-woman's tendency toward the pear-shaped that could easily be disguised when she bothered to take the trouble, which wasn't often. Over the years she had been more and more inclined to dress for comfort rather than style.

Her face, unlike those of her sisters, had never been her fortune. It was a good face, though, strong-featured with a determined jawline and sturdy cheekbones. But it was her arresting grey-green eyes that people remembered. Chameleon eyes that could change expression dramatically: frank or mysterious, cool or compassionate, involved or contemplative. Various rejected suitors had described them as sexy for want of a better word. But that was a long time ago, she reflected.

In the broad, semi-circular drive she noticed a new BMW parked outside the front door.

Oliver!

The BMW had that settled look cars

assume when they've been standing waiting rather a long time.

Oh God! She'd forgotten Oliver had made an appointment for eleven. It was now eleven-thirty. He strolled over, smiling, as if his time weren't really quite valuable. Thirty minutes with a client would surely be worth a hundred, depending, of course, on the fiscal standing of the client.

She studied him as he approached her. His hair was mostly grey now but he still had all of it. He wore his impeccably tailored business suit with a certain elegance while at the same time suggesting that he looked even better in casual clothes. He was a fanatical keep-fit addict, jogging once a day, tennis once a week and golf whenever he could steal time from the office. And the smile never changed. It was the same smile the May girls had fallen in love with, the smile that egged them on a little and then brushed them off just as appealingly.

What a rogue he was, thought Emmy. What an old rogue he is.

'What kept you?' He was still smiling, but it was a smile with half an hour's wated time behind it.

She didn't apologize. 'I was thinking —about the family.'

'What about the family?'

47

'I suppose—what they're thinking right now.'

He frowned. 'You're a puzzle, Emmy.'

'So I believe.'

CHAPTER FOUR

Sir Reginald May looked out over the immaculately manicured lawns that gently sloped towards the lake and then shaded into woodland. Beyond that there was an interrupted view of expensive Cotswold countryside.

He'd like to have claimed the hand of Capability Brown. But, failing that, he had been assured by the Mayfair estate agent who had sold him the finely proportioned early Georgian house that the landscaping had almost certainly been undertaken by one of old Capability's pupils.

A gardener was busy on the topiary which stood guard around an elaborate thatched gazebo, a much later Victorian addition whose charm was its very lack of harmony with the classical style of the house and grounds.

It was a sight that normally gave him great pleasure, a reassuring sense of well-being in himself, in his achievements and, most of all, in his possessions. But today he viewed the scene absent-mindedly as if it were no more than a backdrop for one of the fifty or more films in which he had starred. He'd had this unsettling feeling ever since his sister Emmy had telephoned with the news about Toby, and he was vaguely ashamed that his immediate reaction had been irritation that the funeral and subsequent family business would delay a long-planned holiday with friends in Jamaica.

He stroked his neatly clipped moustache, a trademark so beloved by his fans that he had received shoals of sorrowing letters when for one film he shaved it off. It was greying now and his hairline was receding. But age had, if anything, improved his looks, giving him a craggy, world-weary sexuality that compensated for a thickening around the waistline and a disinclination to undertake the strenuous stunts for which he'd been famous. His mellifluous voice had lost none of its seductive vigour. The bulk of his fan-mail was still from young girls in their teens, and some of it was quite outrageously suggestive. Since his knighthood the tone had, he noticed, been rather more restrained, almost respectful, for which he was grateful. While flattered, he was rather tired of being regarded as something of a dinosaur among movie idols, instead of the distinguished actor he knew himself to be.

'You're a selfish bastard, Reggie.'

He sighed. Unerringly she had pinpointed the guilt that he was trying to persuade himself wasn't deserved.

'What makes you so incredibly wise, Isabel?' It was meant to sound sardonic, but came out more as a grudging acknowledgement of her prescient understanding of his thought processes.

'Maybe living with you for thirty years. If you can call it living. Being tolerated. That's about the size of it, wouldn't you say?'

He turned away from the satisfying view and raised his hands in a gesture of abject but totally insincere surrender. He could barely recall the time when they'd been truly happy together, before their marriage had degenerated into a union of habit and then mere convenience. She'd enjoyed being Mrs and then Lady May, wife of the celebrated and sought-after actor, with all the perks of that status. He in turn appreciated the sense of balance she gave to his life and career, the public image of an invulnerable relationship which protected him from the messy scandals that dogged some of his peers in the profession and which, if he were honest, could as easily be ascribed to him.

She was right. She invariably was. They tolerated each other. But that didn't lessen his feeling of irritation that once again she'd found him out.

'Stop it, Isabel. Just this once. Stop it. Why suddenly am I a selfish bastard, *this time?* What heinous crime am I committing without even knowing it?' Well, he did know it. But he wasn't going to confess that just yet.

As he faced her he momentarily experienced that catch in the throat and the dizzy disbelief he'd felt when he'd first seen her as an over-anxious and heart-breakingly beautiful *ingénue* at Worthing Rep. She'd been rehearsing the role of one of the girls in *French without Tears* and it was clear that her acting would never improve beyond that mediocrity which is more boring than a thoroughly dreadful performance. The producer was relying on her astonishing looks to see her through and for a few brief years they did.

She'd been recruited for the Rank charm school and had been featured on the cover of *Picturegoer* in a Santa Claus hat, furry boots and a bathing suit for a pre-Christmas issue. She'd been seen a lot at film premières on the arm of some other Rank hopeful and made personal appearances at cinemas where the audiences had difficulty figuring out who she was but warmed to her sunny personality and blonde beauty. She even won the occasional bit part in the kind of factory-made film in which a pretty girl who couldn't act would be no particular handicap and might distract attention from the shortcomings of the plot.

When there was no further use in the British film industry for charm school graduates without the diploma of useful credits she escaped gratefully into matrimony and a far less wearing life as the glamorous appendage of a rapidly rising young actor.

For a second Reggie's eyes rested on her face, all rancour forgotten in his pleasure at the sight. She was still a stunning woman, even if the ash blonde of her hair was no longer natural and the slender lines of her figure were more angular than curvaceous. More than that, she generated an easy awareness of her own sensuality, which even now he found provocative. It seemed that, in her middle fifties, she had not only defied the years but defeated them. Yet, when the second had passed, the old antagonism returned. He could look at her coldly, impassively, without love or lust, admiring what he saw but not remotely attracted to it. He often wondered how she managed to conceal the outward evidence of the years of bitterness, of fractious squabbling. Was there perhaps somewhere in the attic a portrait that revealed the wear and tear of all those years? It was, he supposed (he knew), his fault. The wandering eye, his father Gilbert had warned him, would be his undoing.

He wondered as he had wondered often before whether he should have taken Isabel more into his confidence. Maybe it would have been better between them if he had. But that would be like betraying a trust. Whatever people might say about the Mays they were loyal, if not always loving, to each other. Long, long ago there had been an unspoken agreement that there were events in the family you didn't discuss with outsiders. How many May marriages and relationships had foundered on that rock of family solidarity?

He noticed that her expression had softened as if she sensed there might be a chance of some kind of *rapprochement*. And maybe this was the moment. After all, Toby was dead, along with Gilbert and Madge. There was no one left to protect. Except themselves, the surviving Mays. It was all too late, too late.

As he silently debated and discarded the option, she watched the play of emotions on his face. She grimaced with a kind of amused disgust. They were the same emotions the camera loved to capture. Millions of cinema and television viewers had as much access to them as she did.

'You're so bloody transparent, Reggie.' She didn't mean to start it up again but she couldn't help herself. 'Fantasy and life. It's all the same to you, isn't it? What you see is what you get. There's nothing else.'

'I don't understand what you're talking about.' And, in truth, he didn't. He couldn't be other than he was. Acting was his life. A good life. A rich life, in every sense of the word. She hadn't been reluctant to share in *that*, he thought, trumping her ace complaint that not only was acting his life, but his life had become an act.

She circled the room slowly and deliberately, punctuating each step with a carefully aimed verbal dart. He found himself measuring and admiring her performance quite objectively, as if she were auditioning for a part, and thinking what a pity it was she had never been able to display that talent for dramatic effect on stage or screen.

'Not a tiny *private* tear for Toby? Not a faint *personal* concern for Emmy? Don't you think she might appreciate a little support right now? But how can you be expected to bother about trifles like that compared with the massive sacrifice you're making? One whole week lost with—what's her name?—Rosalie? Or have I mislaid a lover or two in your rich, full life? Samantha, perhaps! What a pretty pair you made tripping out of Langan's the other night. Or that girl in the new TV sitcom. Shelley something...'

'Don't forget Madonna and Princess Diana, Isabel,' he mocked her, impressed as always by how she managed to keep up with the affairs he thought he conducted so discreetly. Osmosis, perhaps. Or one of those very best friends with whom you don't need enemies.

Knowing he could offer no argument even if he'd felt inclined to, he tried to change the subject. The eternal subject.

'Since when have you been so holy about my family? Toby. Emmy.'

'Since you stopped being human about them.' She palmed her fingers into small fists, smoothing out the wrinkled skin. 'Emmy was always nice to me. Maybe because she's not like the rest of you. An all-singing-dancing-performing May.'

'You amaze me, Isabel. It still rankles, doesn't it? You didn't make it. For Christ's sake, ninety-nine per cent of our profession don't make it. But they get over it. And you haven't had such a bad life.'

'I never *wanted* to make it,' she rounded on him. 'Not really. That's what you've never been able to understand. I just had the misfortune to marry into a family where the done sodding thing was to be good at something or other in front of an audience. If I'd been really, really great at juggling live snakes or swallowing swords they'd have liked me better. I can still see your old dad patting me on the head and telling me what a pretty little thing I was and knowing he thought I was worthless. And your mother, smiling, smiling, always smiling, and quietly putting in the boot. "I expect you'll do very well, my dear. But, of course, it's not just training, experience, it's that little extra something. Marcus Gammie—the agent, you know—he has high hopes for the girls."' She did a very good imitation of his mother, Madge, thought Reggie, as he waited for the next explosion.

'The girls! Val and Penny and Cissie! The Mayflowers! How on earth could anyone have high hopes for a group called the Mayflowers.'

She stopped suddenly, realizing he was looking at her in that detached speculative manner which made her feel like a strange organism under a microscope. She became wretchedly conscious of herself, of how she must seem to him, twitchy and childish, obsessed with picking over the trivial grudges of the past.

'What have I become?' She chuckled nervously covering up the embarrassment of having asked that most private of questions out loud. She hoped he'd say something soothing, reassuring. After all, it was six of one and half a dozen of the other, wasn't it? But he didn't speak. He just continued to observe her in that dispassionate way.

'Which would you prefer! A lie or the truth, Isabel?' he said finally. The melodic resonance of the famous voice seemed to accentuate rather than defuse the insult. It rebounded on her ears like an obscenity.

She hated herself for exposing to him that little chink of vulnerability and, redressing the balance, chose her words and tone with calculated malice.

'Those girls of yours. They must be easily satisfied—as I recall.'

She knew the reference to his feeble performance in bed, increasingly so as the years gained on him, had hit home. She watched his body stiffen, the mouth tighten, the cool mockery in the eyes give way to an expression of wounded outrage.

He half-raised his hand as if to strike her, then let it fall to his side. If he were a murdering man his wife would already be gushing blood over the Aubusson rug. The thought had crossed his mind temptingly once or twice in the past. But he consoled himself with the conviction that he wasn't the murdering one in the family.

He contented himself with a witheringly vindictive: 'bitch!'

'Why is it I always feel I've strayed into the second act of *Who's Afraid of Virginia Woolf?* when I come home?'

Neither of them had heard the muffled voices outside and the purposeful tread of their daughter Deborah as she opened the door to the sitting room. But if they had it wouldn't have made any difference. It was, after all, only Deb. And Deb had known her parents better than they knew each other since the age of ten when first her mother, then her father, had sought her allegiance in their endless marital feud. The child had survived the continuing domestic tumult seemingly unscathed and with a tolerant amusement at the wayward behaviour of those responsible for it.

She looked from one to the other and took the temperature of their glowering silence. 'No answer was the stern reply. "Perhaps, Deb, it's because we *are* perpetually in the second act of *Who's Afraid of Vriginia Woolf?*",' she volunteered.

Still no answer. Just a palpable aura of unredressed grievance.

'Of course, if I'm not wanted, I can always walk twice round the house and come back in banging a drum and singing "Jerusalem".'

The joke, lame though it was, elicited a faint smile from Isabel, and a heartier response from Reggie, whose relationship with his daughter was one of good-natured tolerance of her vaguely eccentric character.

Isabel, on the other hand, had never quite been able to comprehend how or why she and Reggie—by any standards, a handsome couple—had produced such a quaint offspring. She used the word 'quaint' purposely to forestall the more accurate description: homely.

She was a pale, bookish-looking girl who had inherited her mother's magnificent bones. But this was not immediately apparent as her hair hung like thick net curtains, flopping all over her unmade-up face.

Her sallow skin belied the fact that she spent a good deal of time outdoors communing with nature and running, with surprising efficiency, a mobile library for rural villages. On Friday and Saturday evenings she served behind the bar at the Horse and Groom and was a big hit with the regulars. So much for all that expensive education at Roedean, her mother moaned with monotonous regularity.

Above all, she was a fervent crusader

59

who was quite prepared to take on any authority whose actions or lack of them appalled her, from the local council over the siting of a pedestrian crossing to the Ministry of Defence over just about everything. She was currently 'walking the footpaths' to stop them being commandeered by farmers or quietly incorporated into housing developments. She lived nearby in a run down and probably insanitary cottage that she was able to rent for a pittance because it skirted the M4 and had somehow been overlooked for demolition. There was no principle involved: she just liked 'pigging it', as she put it. She relished the comforts of home sufficiently to return twice a week to wash her laundry, take several hot baths and monitor the state of play between the parents she regarded fondly as splendid relics of a bygone age.

Everything about her daughter baffled Isabel, especially her disinclination to get married or at least securely committed at the age of twenty-five (not, surprisingly, for lack of offers) and her indiscriminate rapport with the human race, however humble or noble. 'A good egg, that girl!' the Duke of Edinburgh had once complimented a flattered but amazed Isabel when they'd happened to exchange words at some regal function where Deborah, to her mother's nervous embarrassment, had held forth on the plight of badgers.

'We were discussing your Aunt Emmy,' said Reggie, which seemed appropriate if not strictly accurate. Emmy had somehow got lost in the debris of another argument altogether.

'Why Emmy? You never discuss the family—not if you can help it.' Deborah dumped a duffel bag full of dirty washing on the Aubusson.

Isabel lifted a delicate eyebrow. 'Do you have to bring that thing into the sitting room?' It was a rhetorical question, barely a grumble. 'Of course, you haven't heard. I can't think why you don't get a telephone installed in that awful hovel, so that we can keep in touch.'

The girl ignored the complaint, knowing full well that keeping in touch, with or without telephone, was not one of her parents' top priorities.

'What haven't I heard?' But she seemed to have anticipated the news. 'It's Toby, isn't it?'

Reggie nodded. 'He's dead.'

Deborah squatted awkwardly on the duffel bag and fished a packet of Embassy out of her string bag, studied it and then stuffed it back in as if making one of her many non-smoking resolutions. 'How did I know that?' she asked wonderingly of herself. 'Maybe because I had a dream last night about the old theatre and when I woke up...'

'Apparently,' said Isabel smartly, who considered other people's dreams a crushing bore, 'apparently he took a dive from the upper circle—dressed up like he does—did—sometimes.'

It came out oddly, comically, as if flying to the floor in an old theatre brought a party air to the tragedy of sudden death.

That, at least, was how it affected Deborah, who let out a hoot of laughter and decided on second thoughts not to give up smoking. 'Good for Toby! What a way to go!'

'You sound just like Emmy,' complained Reggie, ostentatiously waving the air polluted by his daughter's cigarette smoke. 'That's what she said. Maybe not quite that. But that was the gist of it. He'd never looked so happy! As if that makes suicide any less appalling.'

'I suppose,' said Deborah, dragging hard on her cigarette, 'he decided he'd had enough of being simple-minded and patronized and not in control of his life, when deep down he must have known how gifted he was. I can understand that.'

'You,' said Isabel witheringly, 'can understand anything and anyone who doesn't conform to acceptable standards of behaviour.'

'Like you and dad, I suppose.' But her heart wasn't in the business of riling her parents. Not this time.

'Of course, when she gets over the shock, it will be sad for Emmy. Toby was her life.' Without ever realizing it Reggie had slipped into the vernacular and tone of the caring slum priest he'd once played to great acclaim.

'That's an arrogant assumption,' his daughter retorted. 'How do you know what her life was? You haven't seen her for yonks—or Toby, come to that.' She paused. Then, grudgingly, as if it were being dragged out of her, 'I have.'

'When?' Isabel snapped.

'Oh, few weeks ago.'

'Why?' her mother persisted, regretting the question immediately as she saw her daughter's face assume that closed-in, none-of-your-business look they knew so well.

'I felt the need,' Deborah said deliberately, putting a full stop to the subject.

Reggie and Isabel looked at her helplessly. There were times when their daughter was unreachable and it was too late for either to attempt to bridge that gaping void between them.

'Why don't you invite her to stay here

for a bit?' The girl was not insensitive to her parents' feelings and she felt obliged to break the silence. At least it would keep them arguing happily for a while, although she couldn't imagine what Emmy's response might be.

'Who?' Isabel shook her head, still slightly dazed and not quite sure why the fact that Deborah should have felt the need—what need?—to see her aunt rather than her mother should be so upsetting.

'Emmy, of course. You like Emmy. You said so. Of all of them, you liked Emmy.'

'I know I did. I do. Well, maybe, maybe it's a thought Reggie. I mean, it would be a kind gesture.' Isabel decided she could easily convince herself that having Emmy around might be therapeutic as well as demonstrably Christian.

Reggie eyed her uneasily. If she were hoping to enlist an ally in his sister... 'It's early days,' he said hastily. 'First, she'll have to sell that barn of a house. And then, who knows? Oliver seemed quite keen. Widower.' He sounded almost cheerful, as if he'd suddenly hit on some agreeable solution to a problem he hadn't known he had. 'I always said Emmy would make someone a wonderful wife. Can't think why she didn't marry before. What with Fanny and everything.'

'You know perfectly well why she hasn't. Her father. Then Toby. Maybe she didn't want to get married. Some people don't.' Isabel flicked a knowing glance at her daughter. 'It's no picnic.'

'You two. You talk as if Emmy were a liability.' Deborah stubbed out her fag end in a very expensive onyx ashtray from Aspreys that was never used for that purpose.

'A responsibility,' Reggie corrected her without much conviction.

'A liability! Think of it from her point of view. For the first time she can be her own person. Maybe she's got a million ideas about what to do, who to be.'

'Who to be? I fail to see...she's Emmy! That's who she *is.*'

'People change,' said Deborah. 'This is her chance. Think about that. I suppose I'd better get a hat for the funeral.'

'If you've made up your mind to come, you'd better come with us. I don't want you turning up on that dreadful motorbike.'

'You'll be pleased to know I've chucked Freddie for a Mini. Guy at the Horse and Groom gave me a good deal on a repossession. Poor chap couldn't keep up the payments. That's your Tory government for you.' Isabel winced yet again: pets and ponies had names, not motorbikes.

Deborah picked up her duffel bag. 'I wouldn't miss it for the world. All those Mays!' She leaned forward conspiratorially. 'All those family secrets! I'd better get this lot into the washing machine if your lovely Mrs Mopp will allow me.'

'Mrs MacLaine is an exemplary house-keeper and I'll thank you, miss, not to antagonize her,' said Isabel pointedly, being a little afraid of the exemplary Mrs MacLaine herself.

'Point taken, guv'nor.' Deborah tugged an unruly forelock with exaggerated defer-ence.

'You know, I think Deb has a slight cast in her eye,' said Isabel when her daughter had left the room. 'I'm sure she never had it as a child.' She sounded, Reggie thought, as if she were leading up to something quite else and probably unpleasant.

'Norma Shearer had a cast in her eye.' When at a loss, he could always be relied upon to fill the gap with some useless titbit of movie trivia.

Isabel smiled, that occasionally acute smile that so disconcerted her husband now and then. 'Maybe that's why she sees through us so clearly. Like Emmy. Sitting back and taking notice. That's half the trouble, isn't it, Reggie? With Emmy,

I mean. She knows. God knows what, because you've never told me. But maybe now she won't be so keen to keep quiet about it.'

CHAPTER FIVE

'Do we have to go through this now, Ollie?'

Only Emmy ever called him Ollie. It was her way, he knew, of cutting him down to size, not allowing his status in the town to intimidate her. He didn't much care for it. But he was resigned to it, as he'd resigned himself to much about Emmy that both exasperated and intrigued him. Of all the May girls, she had always been the most fascinating, perhaps he could never be sure what she actually felt about him. The others had been quite blatant, flirtatious to the point of embarrassment. But Emmy was an enigma, which made him feel uncomfortable.

Oliver Ballantyne liked to be liked. He'd based his professional reputation on it. And he particularly wanted to be liked by Emmy: loved would be better. Not that he loved her. Being likeable, he had trouble with love, always had, even towards his wife. But now that she was dead he'd decided some time ago that Emmy and he suited each other. If only she weren't so damned mysterious. He was a neat man who courted neat solutions and he could foresee a neat future for both of them.

He was aware that those who knew them were convinced they were either having a discreet affair or contemplating one. He fostered that speculation by not actually denying it. He was accustomed to being admired and it irked him that Emmy, of all people, should deny him what he'd come to regard as his right. He knew it was a flaw in his nature because his wife in one of her rare outbursts of honesty had told him so. 'Everything has to revolve around you,' she'd said. He couldn't recall what had brought it about, probably the decision to send their son Toby away to boarding-school which she'd opposed and he'd insisted upon. Of course, he'd been right. Toby had joined the Foreign Office and was now serving his apprenticeship at a British consulate in some God-forsaken African state. They hardly ever met or corresponded. But the boy had done well. Although sometimes, he wished they'd been closer.

He shuffled the papers he'd taken out of his briefcase. 'You'll have to deal with it sooner or later, Emmy.'

She looked, he thought, amazingly serene for someone who had just lost a demanding but dear relative. But then you never could tell about Emmy. What thoughts were hatching behind those seemingly frank, slightly feline grey-green eyes? What feelings were being suppressed? It was a pleasant, invariably kind face, handsome even. Her father had once surprised him by describing his youngest daughter as Machiavellian, but he was, after all, American and probably didn't know the precise meaning of the word. Emmy, Machiavellian! Absurd!

The grey-green eyes smiled back at him.

'No. I'm sorry, my dear, it was thoughtless of me. I suppose I just wanted to see how you were.' He put his hand on hers and she let it lie there like any old thing without returning its warmth. She noticed his neatly manicured nails, much more carefully contoured than hers, which were ridged and jagged where they should be smooth.

'I know how you must be feeling, how we all feel.' His voice, matching the sentiments he expressed, had the silky smoothness of fine gloss paint. He cursed himself for sounding so phoney, for his inability to reach down inside himself to find genuine words to convey genuine emotion. Had all the years of cautious evaluations, careful deliberations and graceful social lies stripped him of the capacity to say what he honestly meant?

The grey eyes seemed to be understanding all this, but her response was cool. 'I don't know how you all feel, Ollie,' she said patiently. 'And I'm pretty certain you don't know how I feel. I wish people wouldn't expect me to blub on their shoulder. I'm sure they'd feel better if I did. Then after they'd consoled me they could comfortably gossip about how foolish I'd been in allowing Toby to wander around the town, being a danger to himself and everyone else. Can't you get it through your head, Ollie, that I *can't* grieve for Toby because he chose his own death and it was a happy death. It wasn't a happy life.'

For the first time she seemed to lower her guard. There was a note of agitation in her voice. He didn't know how to react.

'You did all you could for Toby,' he said lamely.

'I owed him that.' She sounded distant, the ambiguous comment meant more for herself than for him.

He took a deep breath. Surely now they could say it. At least to each other. And if Emmy didn't like it, so be it.

'I wish you'd admit what we all know,'

70

he said rashly, realizing instantly that he had overstepped the mark.

'All?' She rounded on him angrily.

'Me. The family. Face it, Emmy,' he persisted. 'Toby killed a man. He didn't know what he was doing. He wasn't responsible. Maybe it was a kind of game to him. Almost like a rehearsal for what he did to himself, more than thirty years later.'

He felt himself floundering under her withering glare of disbelief, but he couldn't stop now. It was the hurdle that had to be overcome if there were to be any hope of a future for them.

'I know you don't accept it. But it's the brutal truth. He *killed* a man. You've shielded him from that all these years. The family, I, have protected him from the consequences of what he did. He could have spent those years in a mental institution for the criminally insane. But that didn't happen because we all swore it was an accident. Give us credit for that. Give yourself credit for it.'

She clapped her hands over her ears in an uncharacteristically extravagant gesture more suited to the theatrical Mays. 'That's enough! We promised we'd never speak of that. Toby didn't kill anyone. Anyone!' She enunciated the denial loudly and carefully as if speaking to a stranger in a language not his own.

Oliver saw there were tears in her eyes and that she appeared to be striving to control them. It was a rare sight. Tears came easily to her sisters. It was part of their stock in trade. But not to Emmy.

Genuinely moved, he leaned toward her. 'Emmy, you're deluding yourself,' he said softly. 'You always have. And I respect your loyalty to Toby. But there's no longer any need for it. Toby's dead. It would be so much better for you to let it all out. Cry. Don't bottle it up inside. Cry!'

Finally, he felt, he was finding the right words. But for the wrong grievance, he suddenly realized. For she was wiping away the tears briskly as if the curtain had come down on a convincing performance before a responsive audience. She regarded him with a tenderness mixed with amused pity. 'Poor Ollie! If you only knew. You're really a very nice man. It's not your fault that you're just a little stupid.'

Her tone suggested that she was teasing him. But he couldn't help feeling affronted nevertheless. No one, after all, had ever called him stupid and meant it. He should by now be used to Emmy's unnerving changes of mood, he told himself. Voicing the secret they'd shared for so long seemed to have cleared the air between them, because she then said, quite calmly, 'So, what's the story?'

Her sudden lapses into outdated street slang, picked up God knew where, seemed no less quaint for being so patently calculated to unsettle the listener.

They were back to business and he felt himself on more secure ground. This, after all, was his territory. 'Story?' he echoed, knowing perfectly well what she meant, but following his customary practice of putting the client to the disadvantage of having to elucidate the problem while he pondered its solution. It was a practice he'd carried over into the general barter of social intercourse since his career had flourished and he now no longer realized he was doing it.

'What's the business you wanted to discuss with me? Toby didn't make a will, you know. Well, you would know. But he didn't have anything to leave, apart from his bits and pieces.'

'It wasn't Toby I was thinking about. It was you. What are you going to do now? You realize, I suppose, that you'll be quite a rich woman. Well, rich is relative, these days. Certainly very comfortable.'

She nodded without much interest. 'Toby's trust fund. I'm sure you and your colleagues invested it very prudently over the years. Nothing too speculative.

No nasty shocks when the big bang—or was it bust?—took everyone by surprise on the Stock Exchange a few years ago.'

He frowned. 'You're not taking this seriously, Emmy.' In his book this was a cardinal sin. Money was a serious matter. Emmy now had a lot of it; to speak of it in such a cavalier fashion was not only unseemly but ungrateful. 'You should,' he reminded her, 'be pleased to have been spared those "nasty shocks", as you put it.'

'I know, Ollie,' she said with a hint of repentance she found difficult to sustain. It was so easy to mock his sense of the fitness of things where money was concerned. 'And I *am* truly grateful. I don't know what Toby and I would have done without your guidance.' She piled it on, enjoying the spectacle of him, at first mollified, then preening just a little under her glowing testimonial.

'As you're aware Gilbert left a tidy sum to be set up as as trust fund for Toby and administered by me and you. On Toby's death the capital—the residue of Gilbert's estate—is yours, to do with as you see fit.' He recited the terms of Gilbert's will by rote as a duty, although Emmy knew them as well as he did. It was, she supposed, part of a solicitor's training to take nothing as read until it had been repeated six times over, the general public—the clients—being on the whole nincompoops when they weren't rogues.

'You've told me that several times, Ollie,' she reminded him.

He wished she would stop the 'Ollie' now that they were speaking on a businesslike basis. 'It doesn't hurt—' he began.

He was interrupted by a voice that announced its presence with the pushy disregard of a souped-up banger speeding down the fast lane on a motorway.

'Didn't know you had company.' It didn't sound like an apology, nor was it meant to be. 'The wasp man's come and gone.'

Oliver Ballantyne's lips curled into an expression of extreme distaste.

Terry Roberts was one of Emmy's waifs and strays. She gathered them around her like a DSS Pied Piper. It was, Oliver supposed, all very admirable, but he saw it as another impediment to a closer relationship between him and Emmy.

Then it occurred to him to wonder who the wasp man might be and feared the worst. It sounded very Emmy.

The arrival of the wasp man seemed to cheer her no end. 'Did he manage to locate it?' she asked.

The young man grinned, thrusting his hands hard down into the pockets of his grimy jeans. 'A whopper! Beautiful. Just like a bloody cathedral. You could have exhibited it at the Tate. He brought it out of the loft to show me.'

'It's a shame in a way,' said Emmy. 'All that labour.'

'He said a few might try to come back after they've done the day's shopping, but the stuff he sprayed in would stop them. Anyway, they'll probably find another hole in the roof or under the eaves next year. Amazing little buggers!'

'What on earth are you talking about?' Oliver addressed himself to Emmy, trying to ignore the offending Terry.

'For heaven's sake, Ollie! Where do you live all your life? Or does your obliging handyman keep you in ignorance of inconveniences like wasps? They find a weak spot in the bricks and mortar, fly in, build a nest and lay their eggs. It's their home. We're plagued with them. I expect you are too. Old house. I'd check. You can usually tell where they're swarming if you look closely.'

He stared at her, amazed. She showed a good deal more animation discussing the life cycle of wasps than her own future. Perhaps she realized how odd it must seem to him for she added by way of explanation, 'Well, you have to attend to these things whatever else is

76

happening. Wasps don't drop everything because Toby's dead.'

Her remark, which made perfect sense to her, elicited a slow hand-clap from Terry Roberts. 'Right on, Emmy. I thought I'd clean up a bit. Place looks as if it needs it.'

She nodded. 'You can leave Toby's room.'

'Want some help?'

'No. I have to sort out his—his personals myself.'

He shrugged. 'Suit yourself. Room's a right tip, though. I just thought you might like someone else...you know...'

For all his seeming self-confidence, he was as much at a loss when it came to Emmy's reaction to her brother's death as everyone else. He was a tall, very skinny young man whose hands and feet seemed several sizes too big for him. A large protruding Adam's apple propped up a rather small face which had the drawn look of a malnourished childhood. It was a face that could appear mean and insolent, but the surprisingly lustrous blue eyes lavishly fringed with girlish eyelashes warmed with affection when they were directed at Emmy. As old Gilbert May would have said, he looked as if he wouldn't make old bones.

She returned his affectionate glance.

'That's very nice of you, Terry. But I think I'd rather. There are some things better left to me.'

'You'll have to get rid of him,' said Oliver firmly when Terry had left the room to do his clearing up a bit.

'Why?'

'I don't mean to interfere, Emmy. And by the way, you shouldn't let him call you Emmy. And you know I never approved of you giving him room and board in the house as well as a salary.'

'He was very good with Toby. He humoured him. He understood him.'

'So...?'

'So what do you propose I do? Throw him out? He's nineteen. He has no family. He's unemployed.'

'He could go on a youth training scheme.'

'He's been on a youth training scheme and it didn't get him a job. He works hard. He cleans, gardens and he's not a bad cook either.'

'That's not the point, Emmy. There are plenty of women who would be happy to come in a few times a week.'

She chuckled, reading his mind. 'And that would make it correct and respectable. What are you worried about, Ollie? Me and a nineteen-year-old boy alone in this big old house?' She had never let on to

78

anyone, least of all to Oliver, that she had first made Terry's acquaintance when he had tried and failed to nick her handbag in the high street.

He shrugged. 'Something like that.'

'And you wouldn't like to meet him in an alley on a dark night.' She snorted derisively. 'You're so old-fashioned, Ollie. You don't think you are, but that's the size of it.'

'It's not unheard of for defenceless women—'

'...of a certain age...'

'...to be, well, victimized, by a young man,' he said heatedly. 'Besides it's all hypothetical now. You'll obviously sell the house. It's far too large for one person, expensive to run and a white elephant.'

'Sell Rushey Green!' (Her parents had named the house after the London suburb where they'd first met on the same bill at the local music hall.) 'Sell Rushey Green!' she reiterated as if he'd suggested tearing down Buckingham Palace and setting up the royal family at the Palladium.

'I know it has a good deal of sentimental value for you. But I'm sure the family would agree with me that you'd be far better off in a modern, purpose-built complex. For the time being anyway. Until you've really sorted yourself out. Talk to Reggie about it when he comes down for the funeral.'

'I suppose you've spoken to him already.'

'Just briefly,' he admitted.

'And Val and Penny and Cissie and maybe Frances, too,' she said angrily.

'Of course not. Just Reggie. He's concerned about you. It's only natural.'

'You could have fooled me,' she said. 'He sounded quite relieved when I told him about Toby, until he heard that the funeral would interfere with a holiday he was planning.'

'Why are you so bitter about them, Emmy?'

She sighed deeply. Is that how she sounded, bitter? 'I'm not. It's just they've never been a part of me and Toby. Me particularly. And I don't think it's any of their business what I do with my life.'

She seemed quite suddenly so alone and vulnerable and he felt what was for him an overwhelming wave of sympathy for this woman who had always somehow eluded him. 'I suppose you're right, Emmy. You've managed so far. I just want to help. You must know that.'

Contrite, she squeezed his hand. Why did she always feel the need to belittle and challenge him? Except that it wasn't the man but his values that seemed so alien to her. Was it possible anyway to divorce the two?

'What sort of money are we talking about?' She changed the subject. 'From the trust fund.'

'Naturally the capital has appreciated considerably over nearly thirty years, especially as you didn't even use the full extent of the income it generated.'

'Ollie!' she said again. 'How much?'

Her directness shocked him, coming from someone who evinced so little interest in money, he supposed, because she'd never been short of it. 'Upwards of half a million, probably more, when all the sums have been done,' he replied, equally directly.

She pursed her lips as if making a mental calculation. 'I could do a lot with that.'

'And then the sale of the house would add substantially to that.'

'I thought you said it was a white elephant.'

'Only to you. To someone interested in making it over as a nursing home or a small hotel it would be a very tempting proposition. Planning permission shouldn't be difficult. It's ideally located in the country, but near the town and the sea. On the other hand it might be more profitable for a developer to take it over. This recession won't go on for ever and anyone with some ready capital could hold off until the economy starts to recover.'

'Poor old Rushey Green!' she said wistfully. 'Such sadness. You know what I dread, Ollie? The inquest. More than the funeral. All that probing and picking over the remains and dragging up the past.'

'It won't be like that, Emmy. It'll be a formality. Death by misadventure.'

'Misadventure. Just like the other one.'

'There's no need to dwell on that, Emmy.'

But she didn't seem to hear him.

'Harvey Persky,' she said as if to remind herself. 'That was his name. Harvey Persky.'

'I'd forgotten,' he said uncomfortably.

'No you hadn't. No one forgets a name like Harvey Persky.'

CHAPTER SIX
18 DECEMBER 1957

'Harvey Persky, ma'am. And you must be Miss Emmy.'

Smarmy, she'd thought, without looking up from her programme, although she could recite every word of it, having helped her father design and write it. All those elaborate and exaggerated biographies of individual members of the May family and a pantomime history of Dick Whittington interspersed with advertisements for lively coffee bars and dainty tea shops and Clifton Coombe's premier gentleman's outfitters and Player's cigarettes and Tangee Lena-lure Lipstick in Four Ravishing Pinks.

'Emmy!' her mother had prompted her and she'd looked up at the short, dark, edgy man who had made his way across the crowded circle bar to where they were sitting, where they always sat on opening nights, to 'get the feel of the audience' for Gilbert who was attending to a hundred and one unforeseen crises backstage. Only tonight he wasn't backstage. He was escorting Harvey Persky across the bar area, accepting the compliments from theatre regulars almost absent-mindedly, as if it didn't matter what the audience reaction was to the most lavish and commercially crucial event of the Adelphi year, the Christmas pantomime.

That was Emmy's major first impression of her meeting with Harvey Persky. Why wasn't her father backstage? Admittedly, he'd given up performing himself, except for a jaunty appearance in the chorus at the line-up before the final curtain. Nearing fifty, he'd decided that the circus high-wire stunt with which he'd thrilled his audiences in previous years was too risky after a momentary loss of balance and, subsequently, nerve in rehearsal. In any case times were changing. The youngsters wanted pop songs and TV celebrities: a lot of them didn't believe in fairies any more and quite a few knew another definition of fairies which spoilt it for the others. Gilbert May was always one to keep up with the times.

All the same, thought Emmy, despite her father's minimal participation on stage this year, it wasn't like him to desert his habitual post on opening night.

He'd seemed more nervous, too. Not the nervousness of wondering how the show was going and whether the box office take for the 1957-58 season would be up on the year before and what kind of muck-up the much-loved but notoriously unstable comic playing the Dame would make of a complicated slapstick routine involving a broom, a frying pan, a string of sausages and a trained dog who didn't like him. It was more a kind of apprehension, a waiting for something that might not be pleasant.

Even as a child Emmy, of all of them, had sensed what lay deep inside Gilbert, heavily disguised by his constant air of *bonhomie*. Now she was older, she was even more observant of her father's little give-away signs the others didn't notice. She wondered if even her mother could see the agitation behind Gilbert's jocularity as he introduced his wife and daughter to Harvey Persky.

'Harvey Persky, ma'am. And you must be Miss Emmy.'

No one, she thought, is *that* courtly any more, even an American. Then she'd turned her attention to the man. He was slight and wiry, barely her height, she guessed, and his body even when it was still, pulsed with energy. He was also quite ugly, his features splayed out across his face as if they'd been flattened in a fight, which they probably had, and quite old by a teenager's standards, about her father's age. And then she found herself looking into his eyes and not being able to look away. They were the eyes of a confidence trickster. There were plenty of those in her father's profession, but none had the mesmeric quality of Harvey Persky. When you looked into those eyes you forgot that he was unprepossessing, shabbily dressed in a too gaudy, purplish suit that had seen better days.

You forgot the ungovernable Brooklyn accent that chewed up the English language like a ravenous dog attacking a bone. All you felt was the power of persuasion that could melt a woman or threaten a man or bring a recalcitrant animal to heel. Although then she couldn't have put that feeling into words. All she knew was that the burning sensation his attention generated in her made her uneasy for herself and, more especially, for Gilbert.

'Emmy's the bookish one,' said her mother tritely, covering up Emmy's silence while helplessly signalling to Gilbert: 'Who is this man?'

'I knew your old man back in the States.' Unlike the rest of them Harvey Persky seemed very much at ease as if he thrived on being the assertive force in a fraught situation of his own making.

'That was a long time ago. Wasn't it, Gilbert?' Madge May was beginning to sound desperate. She was a bright, pretty, efficient woman who abhorred scenes and moods and unaccountable happenings. Born into a relatively affluent and relentlessly jolly show business family she had learned to live with the darker side of her husband largely by ignoring it, except—as now—when it threatened her own sense of well-being. After all, it *was* opening night.

'Wasn't it, Gilbert?' she repeated with some acerbity.

'You could say that,' he replied. His voice sounded feeble and underneath the stage make-up he'd applied in readiness for the closing number he looked pale, as if he'd seen a ghost.

But Harvey Persky was no ghost. He

slapped Gilbert smartly on the back, two old mates meeting up after all these years. 'Did he tell you we were in the circus together back in Kansas. Jesus! It must be what? Thirty years ago?'

'No, he didn't tell us you were in the circus together.' Emmy heard herself speaking up very clearly, enunciating each syllable precisely. At the sound of her voice, high and rather prim, Gilbert snapped out of his brown study.

'Can you imagine, meeting Harv after all this time. Just by chance. He happened to be passing the Adelphi as I was getting the boys to fix that poster for the show. You know how they never site it right to catch the passing trade...'

'Well, you caught me, old buddy.' The two men laughed and punched each other lightly on the elbows as if it were the best thing that had happened to them all year.

'And what brings you to Clifton Coombe, *Mr Persky?*' Relieved that the tension had relaxed, Madge had decided to make this unlikely 'old buddy' feel welcome in the hope that it might hasten his departure. It was a contrary stratagem that she found invariably worked.

'That's right ma'am. Persky. Folks never got around to changing it when they came to the States. I do a little of this and a little of that. Came to Europe after the war managing a dancing troupe. That's what I did after I left the circus. No future there. I used to put together variety and burlesque acts. Beg pardon, ma'am. I guess you never had burlesque over here.'

'Nudes!' sniffed Emmy, determined not to be impressed by the name.

'Emmy!'

'No, ma'am, I guess she's right in a way. Burlesque was near the knuckle stuff. But I soon got out of that.'

'No future?' yawned Emmy.

'Everything was movies or radio. Variety was dying except in the sticks. So I guess I had a kind of hard time for a while, during the depression. Then suddenly during the war there was a demand for entertainers for the troops and I went back into agenting and managing.' He seemed intent on pouring out his life story as quickly as possible, as if to convince his listeners that he was straight and direct and didn't have a thing to hide.

Liar, thought Emmy, for no good reason.

'And that's what you do now, Mr Persky? Agenting and managing?'

'Harvey or Harv, please, ma'am.'

'And that's what you do now, Harvey?'

'Sure thing. That's how I heard about...' he paused, then 'Gilbert here.'

'I thought you said you passed the Adelphi by chance, *Mr* Persky.' Emmy looked up at him, not fearing those eyes now that she felt she could outsmart them.

He returned her stare with a mocking expression that seemed to challenge her.

'How old did you say you were?'

'I didn't.' She lowered her eyes. Then grudgingly, 'Seventeen.'

'Seventeen going on twenty-nine,' he said reflectively. She knew what he meant. She'd always been old for her years—or so she'd been told.

He turned to Gilbert. 'She's one sharp cookie, all right. I guess you caught me out in a little lie there—just a white one. I wasn't sure whether Gilbert would remember me so I thought I'd surprise him.'

The excuse seemed to satisfy her parents. At least, they didn't question it.

'Is there a Mrs Persky?' said Madge hastily.

'Well, now, ma'am, that's a kind of a sad story.'

But they didn't get to hear it, because the intermission bell rang and Gilbert was inviting Harvey backstage after the show and urging Madge to find him a seat near her and Emmy for the second half.

'You mean you don't *have* a seat, Mr Persky?'

'Well, Emmy—you don't mind me calling you Emmy, do you?' She opened her mouth then closed it. She didn't care what he called her, so long as it wasn't 'sharp cookie' or 'cute one'. 'You see I could only get a ticket in what you call the "gods". It'll be real nice to see the show in style.'

'Why?' her mother hissed behind his back as they moved back into the theatre.

Gilbert shrugged. 'Because!' Then he thought better of it. 'Do me a favour, Madge. Be nice.'

Emmy, watching, had seldom seen her father so anxious. There was a note of pleading in his voice, but her mother didn't catch it. Harvey Persky was merely an inconvenience she could do without.

'I'm always nice,' she replied through gritted teeth.

When Emmy thought about it years later she remembered they'd all been there the night that Harvey Persky came into their lives. All the relevant parties, as Oliver Ballantyne would say in his legal manner.

On stage Val was playing Dick, a Whittington with two cats, Penny and Cissie, who did a tap dance and closed the first act singing 'Spread a Little Happiness' in harmony with their sister.

90

They hadn't wanted to call off their tour of the provinces on a bill with Dickie Valentine no less, but neither could they resist their father's appeal to filial loyalty. The Mayflowers topping the cast in the Adelphi pantomime would be an added box office draw.

Reggie had come home for Christmas from a season in rep sporting a new girlfriend on his arm, a ravishing young actress named Isabel Dawn whom his sisters privately considered an empty-headed nit. There had been some soul-searching on Madge's part as to whether it would set her daughters a bad example if Reggie and Isabel were allowed to share a room in the family home. But then, as Reggie explained, they were practically engaged. He didn't add that they'd been living together anyway for the past six months. Their parents' prudishness was a constant source of amusement to their older offspring, who couldn't understand how they'd survived all those years in show business without learning the facts of life.

Young Oliver Ballantyne, who was thought to be courting one if not all the May girls, was occupying a box with his father Crawford, whose firm of solicitors and actuaries was the most prestigious in Clifton Coombe.

Even Toby was there, allowed to 'help'

prop man Alf in the wings, provided he didn't get under his feet. Toby worshipped Alf almost as much as he idolized his father. Alf understood about Toby, how he wasn't too quick on the uptake and took a while picking up practical things, how he cowered from strangers and was reluctant to speak when he was spoken to.

And Brad. She'd almost overlooked Brad. But then it was easy to overlook Brad. That was half his trouble. Gilbert said he was talented enough, but people had a problem placing him. If you couldn't be placed, you'd never be a star. Which showed how wrong Gilbert could be.

Brad Hastings was a fresh-faced, well set up Canadian who had come to Europe on a scholarship and then, to his parents' distress, had given up his studies, changed his name from Arthur Eddy and decided to try his luck as an actor. It was Reggie who had introduced him to Gilbert with the dismissive comment that 'he's a nice enough chap but a bit thick and he looks good in tights.'

On the night of Harvey Persky he was looking spectacular in tights, playing a dashing nobleman who woos a humble flower-seller on the streets of London: a romance that didn't have much to do with the story of Dick Whittington but padded out a spare section in the second act conveniently. In the event their duet stopped the show: a medley of 'Love Is a Many Splendored Thing', 'Love Me Tender' and 'Too Young To Go Steady', a song whose inapproprietness to the period of the pantomime was far outweighed by the rapturous response it received from the teenagers in the audience. Brad, whose sights were set on Shakespeare, had been a last-minute replacement for a tenor who was too fond of a nip during costume changes.

If he hadn't been so preoccupied Gilbert May would probably have spotted that, whatever Brad Hastings lacked, he was a big hit with the girls.

Flushed and beaming he took his bows with the rest of the cast at the end of the show. The Mayflowers even insisted he join them at their solo curtain call.

From the wings in his clown costume and heavy make-up Gilbert May listened to the applause and felt, as he always did, a swell of pride that this was his baby and it had been born kicking, healthy and full of life. They were in for a good season, he reckoned. The old May touch. It never failed.

For a few giddy moments he could forget Harvey Persky, forget that moment when this stranger in a purple suit had breezed into his tiny office above the dressing rooms, hand outstretched as if he'd been expected. He really hadn't recognized him. He was used to agents, salesmen, hustlers of all kinds barging in at any time and he never made them feel unwelcome. He'd developed a knack of seeing them off the premises while at the same time making them feel they were the one person he'd been hoping to see. It was one of the reasons why Gilbert May was so respected in the business.

'And you never know,' he advised his daughters sagely, 'that pain in the ass might be the next C.B Cochran.' They took heed because when their father resorted to vulgarisms he meant what he was saying.

The fact that he was juggling with the dozens of problems that bedevil an opening night had made no difference: he could still find a minute or two for the man in the purple suit.

'You don't remember me, old buddy. You've got that same look on your puss that you always had when you weren't sure.'

The voice should have alerted Gilbert. Certainly not English. American. Brooklyn. But he met a lot of Americans through running the Adelphi, especially now when it was becoming a two-way traffic for entertainers across the Atlantic again after the war.

'I'm afraid I don't, Mr...?' He beamed, grasping the hand that was offered.

'Persky, pal, *Harvey Persky*. From the old days. Back in Kansas.' He glanced appreciatively around the office and out of the high octagonal window that looked down on to the bustling stage and beyond into the empty auditorium. 'Very nice. You've done very nicely for yourself. But then I always knew you would. You were always real smart. A kid with your kind of guts! You were a natural. A natural. That's what you were. You don't mind?' He took a cigar out of his breast pocket, bit off the end, spat it out and moistened the mouth of the cigar with his lips.

The colour had drained out of Gilbert's face and is if in a trance he leant across his desk, a lighted match in his hand.

'Your hand's shaking—Gilbert. That's right, isn't it? Gilbert May. I like it. Classy!' He gripped Gilbert's hand and puffed on the cigar as the flame ignited the tobacco.

'What do you want?'

'Now is that any way to greet an old friend? And me all tickled pink when I saw your photograph in the trades. I thought: I know that face. Older, sure. But I'd recognize that kid I knew in the circus anywhere.'

'What do you want?' Gilbert's voice was firmer now.

'What kind of a question is that? Friendship. A chance to get to know each other again.'

'We were never that friendly.'

'Well let's just say we had a kind of bond between us.' He continued puffing easily on the cigar.

'If it's money...'

'Who said anything about money?'

'I assumed—'

'Assumed! Ain't we the English gentleman? That's what I like about you, Gilbert. You're adaptable. You've a swell set-up here. Swell family, too, I guess. Me! I never had no family. I'd really like to meet the folks. You wouldn't deny an old buddy that now, would you? I can be real discreet, if you know what I mean and I figure you do.'

'I don't—'

'Sure you do, Gilbert. Think about it. I guess you're pretty busy now, so I'll leave you to get on with it. What do you call it? Pantomime! We don't have that in the States. It'll be a real pleasure to see one. Tonight, Gilbert, tonight. And then—who knows? Like I said: think about it, Gilbert.'

96

The smell of cheap cigar smoke and the echo of Harvey Persky's voice reiterating the name 'Gilbert' lingered long after he'd sauntered out of the tiny room.

Gilbert sat silently at his cluttered desk until he was called away to soothe the ruffled feelings of the wardrobe mistress who was engaged in a running battle with the theatrical costumiers, and to sort out a contretemps between the set designer and the electrician. By the time he'd achieved a sort of truce he felt more in control of himself. This, after all, was his territory. His domain. Harvey Persky was no threat to that. Harvey Persky was no threat at all.

After all they had worked side by side as roustabouts and jacks of all trades in the circus. They had shared cigarettes and moonshine liquor and, on one memorable occasion, the randy wife of the lion tamer. Probably it was just as Harvey said. He'd seen the photograph and was looking up an old friend. And, although he'd denied it, they had been friends of a sort. The least he could do was put a good face on it, act hospitable. Tomorrow Harvey Persky would be on his way. Tomorrow he could begin to forget Harvey Persky ever existed. Maybe if he was hard up, the odd fiver to see him through. So long, Harvey!

The applause persisted, growing louder,

through five curtain calls.

'You've got a winner here, Gilbert,' a voice whispered in his ear. He hadn't been aware that Persky had sidled up behind him in the wings.

'How did you get back here?' muttered Gilbert before he was dragged on stage to acknowledge another round of applause. He glanced back into the wings where Harvey Persky was clapping as furiously as everyone else, a proprietorial grin on his face.

CHAPTER SEVEN

She walked around the garden for a bit after Oliver had left. It was, she thought ruefully, a fairly sorry sight. Like the house. She hadn't seriously noticed before. After a while shabby upholstery, faded carpets, snagged curtains, unkempt lawns and flowerbeds became just part of the domestic scenery. It wasn't that she couldn't afford to put Rushey Green in good order. The trust fund had seen to that. The kind of neglect that would immediately strike the outsider had become for her comfortable familiarity.

But now she was seeing it all through

Oliver's eyes. No wonder he suggested that the best solution would be to sell the place. Dear, neat Oliver! How offensive he must have found the unruliness of Rushey Green and how hard it must have been for him to conceal that feeling from her.

She shivered slightly, pulling her cardigan around her. The holiday-makers in Clifton Coombe were still trying to persuade themselves that it was summer. But autumn was already crisping up the air and the first flowering cherries in the overgrown arbour were beginning to shed their leaves. Too early.

'Maybe only God can make a tree, but I wish He'd clean up His mess afterwards,' she muttered. Then, raising her eyes, 'Sorry, God.'

Sorry, God, for not concentrating. Sooner or later she'd have to get down to it, to sorting out the bric-à-brac of Toby's life before they lowered him into the grave. She dreaded it. Coping with the floods of memories his treasures and trophies would reveal and knowing that alone, among his precious things, she would feel the full impact of his death and with it would come the tears, the grief, the guilt.

It was so much easier to deal with the paraphernalia of death than with the reality. The precise funeral arrangements. The quality of the coffin. Whether there should be flowers or donations to Mencap. Arranging a caterer for the gathering after the ceremony. And should it be a large gathering or just a close family and friends gathering?

Then there were the condolence letters and the messages of sympathy. Flo and the art students from the college, who regularly used to visit Toby and admire his strange paintings, would probably help with those. Oh yes, there were plenty of willing helpers. But no one could really help you face that private reckoning when all the evidence is assembled and you are forced to become your own advocate, judge and jury.

She kicked furiously at a wayward mahonia, almost losing her balance, then laughed at her own childishness. C'mon Emmy girl, straighten up and fly right! Straighten up and fly right! What on earth made her think of that? It had been a song. A gung-ho wartime song. She must have heard her father, home on leave from one of his ENSA tours of army bases, sing it when she was barely more than a toddler. Yet she could remember it so vividly, the tune—exactly. She hummed it softly to herself, finding it oddly comforting.

'Emmy!'

She looked toward the house. Not the *Clarion* reporter yet! She'd reluctantly promised the paper an interview, fixing it for an evening hour when she could conjure up a good excuse to get rid of him or her quickly. She didn't mind the thought of talking about Toby and herself and the other Mays. She knew exactly how to deflect awkward questions: Gilbert had taught her that. It was just that she didn't see much point in it. The paper would print what it wanted to print anyway and most of it would come from cuttings. Pity, though! She'd like to have looked nicer, changed into a frock, applied a speck of make-up, run a comb through her hair. But then, who would care? 'If you don't care for yourself, no one else will,' Gilbert used to say. He was good at little homilies like that, she thought. The old fraud!

'Emmy! Fanny! Telephone.'

Fanny! Frances! It's not her usual day, was her first thought. Unless she was off on a job her daughter always telephoned with meticulous regularity on Sunday evenings between the old film on TV in the afternoon and the news and weather forecast. She'd somehow convinced herself that her mother liked to put her feet up in the afternoon on Sundays before preparing a meal for herself and Toby. She had certain fixed ideas about the conduct of Emmy's life whether they were true or not, just as she had fixed ideas about almost everything from the state of the country's economy to the necessity for taking in adequate fibre in the daily diet.

In anyone else Emmy would have admired, even envied, such certainty. In her own daughter it baffled her. How she had grown into the young woman she was was a constant amazement. If someone had been able to convince her that Frances wasn't her child she'd probably have believed them. Yet, God knows, she could recall every moment of the pregnancy and birth, the fight she'd put up to ensure that Frances was actually born at all. At best a discreet adoption, at worst an illegal abortion: the options had been offered. Gilbert had connections. The promise of no recriminations and then Emmy could get on with living as if nothing had happened. But no argument or pressure could persuade her. She'd wanted that child. It was the only time in her life that she had not allowed herself to be swayed by other people's advice or wise judgement. Perhaps that's where the seed of Frances's self-assurance had been sown. In the womb. She'd drained all the resolve out of Emmy, leaving her mother with nothing but a wobbly tolerance of people, however weird or bizarre or downright bloody-minded their attitudes might be.

Their relationship wasn't an easy one.

Loving, but not easy. They appreciated the problems each posed for the other while in no way understanding them. The nearest they could come to a definition of each other, and then only when they were inclined to levity on the subject, was that Frances was a young fogey and Emmy a middle-aged hippie. It had become a family joke. A slick, tidy half-truth that packaged them up into convenient little boxes 'Frances' and 'Emmy'.

She sighed. C'mon Emmy girl, straighten up and fly right!

'Mother, I wish you'd tell that *boy* not to call me Fanny.'

Frances was using her businesslike, don't-mess-with-me voice, a sure sign that she was ringing from the office at the independent television company where she produced a fortnightly current affairs documentary, *Eye of the Storm*. It was a controversial programme, highly acclaimed at BAFTA award time and roundly abused by targeted officials all the time, which liked to think that it dared to go where more timid TV programmes feared to tread. It was a stressful claim which was becoming increasingly difficult to sustain as the market in taboo subjects diminished. And Frances was a highly stressed human being.

It was all very well being a wonder girl

who'd worked her way up meteorically from researcher to producer, but it was in the nature of the job that you were only as wonderful as your last series. 'And what with every potty soap opera awash with dying gays, corrupt politicians, battered wives and abused children nowadays, there's not much left for a serious programme like ours,' she grumbled only half in jest to Emmy on one of the rare occasions when she had taken her mother into her confidence.

When Frances complained about being called Fanny, it was, Emmy realized, the pressure that was talking.

'I'll tell Terry, Fa...Frances. Sorry. Habit.'

'No, I'm sorry,' Frances apologized. 'It's just that I get called enough names around this office without being likened to somebody's *derrière*.' She sounded slightly mollified, but not much.

'I suppose you're right.' Emmy knew it was always better to let her offload her irritations before attempting a calming conversation.

She heard a faint chuckle at the other end of the line. 'Humouring me again! Poor old mum. It's a life's work, isn't it?'

'And not so much of the old,' they said in unison.

'I just—just wanted to know if you were all right, holding up. Other people can be hell at a time like this. They mean awfully well, of course, but... Well, you know if there's anything I can do, I'd be only too happy—' She stopped mid-sentence and Emmy heard that brusque change of tone in her voice as she told someone called Bill she wasn't taking any more shit from someone called Vernon and they'd better both put up or shut up. Emmy wondered what heinous crime Vernon had committed.

'Sorry, sorry,' Frances came back to her.

'Sorry for Bill and Vernon,' murmured Emmy.

'Sorry nothing. There's no room on the team for slackers.' She laughed nervously, seeming to realize that she was sounding like some ghoulish headmistress handing out black marks after school prayers. 'I'm not always such a pill,' she said contritely.

'I know you're not, Fanny.' Hard luck about the *derrière* but her daughter would always be Fanny to Emmy. 'Now what did you want to say to me?'

'Just—if there's anything I can do. Of course I'll be down for the funeral. I was fond of Toby. You know that.'

She didn't actually, but she let it pass. Frances had always treated her uncle

105

with that suffocating consideration which sometimes disguises embarrassment in the face of disability. If she felt real concern for him (and it was quite possible that she did), it was on the same intellectual level that she viewed the victims of neglect or hardship or congenital disease on her TV programme.

'Can you manage to stay over? I'd like that, Fanny.' She surprised herself, realizing that she meant it sincerely.

Frances caught the unexpected note of loneliness. 'I'll try. No, I'll *make* time. Somehow. Mother...' she paused as if trying to assemble a difficult arrangement of thoughts, '...there is something else.'

Emmy braced herself. Her daughter hardly ever sounded so tentative, so unsure of the response. 'I guessed there might be,' she said. 'Except on Sundays you don't usually waste a phone call on idle conversation.' As soon as she'd said it she wished she could take it back. It was a mean remark, uncalled for. Why did she want to make it so hard for Frances to unload her information? Perhaps to protect herself in advance from the impact. Perhaps it was just as simple as that: the best method of defence being attack.

If Frances registered the criticism she didn't bother to acknowledge it. 'I saw Brad.' It came out bluntly. The only way, really. In itself it wasn't much of a bombshell; her mother had always known that Frances met Brad Hastings regularly. Indeed he'd also visited Emmy and Toby now and then over the years since he'd been whisked away from Clifton Coombe to Hollywood by a movie talent scout.

But from the way Fanny had announced the fact Emmy knew there was more to it than that.

'And?' she prompted her.

'He has AIDS.' Frances paused. 'Sorry if that seems so bald. But the only way to say it is to say it.' She was having difficulty covering up the genuine anguish she obviously felt. Even so, she sounded close to tears.

Emmy started to speak, then drew back. She had to think of the right words, but they wouldn't come. Just pictures of Brad—young Arthur Eddy—when he'd first been signed by Gilbert for a season at the Adelphi, full of health and vitality and a simple, innocent faith in a glowing future; Brad, so unselfconscious about his looks that he didn't even realize the effect he had on half the female population of the town under fifty and quite a few who were older; Brad, gently encouraging Toby to try—whack a ball, climb a tree, paint a landscape the way he saw it—with that infinite, tender patience that always

107

seemed too good for the hard life he'd chosen.

And, most of all, Brad escaping from all the attention to her room in Rushey Green where they shared their hopes and dreams and fumbling desires. 'I feel comfortable with you, Emmy. You don't expect me to put on a show. Everyone else here does.' The Mays, she'd reminded him, were show people. 'All except you, Emmy, all except you.' Then, like a baby who can fall asleep in a blink of an eye, he'd stretched out on her narrow bed and dozed off.

'Mother, did you hear me?'

She shook her head violently, trying to exorcise the memories of that cheerful, fit, handsome boy. To put in their place—what? Images of frail, wasting men who had nothing more to do with their lives but wait to die.

'How far?' she managed to ask.

'It's in the early stages. But I guess he knew he had the virus for a while; just hoping against hope, I suppose.'

'Poor Brad. Hoping against hope. But then he never was a very rational man.' ('There *are* no silver linings or rainbows or sunny sides of the street in this business,' Gilbert had warned him when he accepted the Hollywood offer. He'd been glad to see him go, all the same. 'He'll either end up as Gregory Peck or as a punk on Skid Row,' he'd predicted. And Emmy had been left to nurse her guilt that she could have made it different.)

'How can you be so cruel, mother? I thought I was tough. But you...!' All Frances's pent-up feeling seemed to explode. 'You don't give a damn about Brad. I don't think you even give a damn about Toby's dying. He just said he wanted to come to see you, to come to Toby's funeral. Brad. That's all I had to tell you.'

'Fanny...'

But her daughter had slammed down the receiver.

I've goofed again, thought Emmy. If only I could wallow like other people in compassion instead of bottling it up inside.

Or was she just making excuses? Was there perhaps some kind of electrical fault in her emotional mechanism? She'd have to get back to Frances. But not now. Later. When she was better prepared.

After cutting off her mother, Frances May swivelled round in her executive chair and looked out of the vast reinforced window at the complementary tower block of offices across the Euston Road. There was probably a view worth looking at somewhere down there but no one was much bothered to find it. Functional.

That summed up the office. 'And that,' she murmured to herself, 'sums up me.' Except when it came to Brad. She felt the tears pricking her eyes and told her secretary to hold all calls.

'What about the viewing? The footage on the rape feature?' the girl reminded her petulantly. She'd suffered the sharp end of Frances May's tongue often enough over some real or imagined oversight and she wasn't going to be accused again of not telling her boss about a vital meeting.

'I'll get to it,' said Frances, fearing she might not.

She couldn't remember anything or anyone ever before interrupting her working schedule. Everything could be neatly slotted into the routine, a fast five minutes of commiseration or condolence, a quick trip to a hospital bedside or down to Rushey Green: all carefully inserted into the occasional time window that presented itself between location shoots or high-level briefings or headaching sessions in the studio. Private life was a large impersonal flat in Kensington, a late supper usually with an associate or some executive who needed buttering up and the occasional lover who never lasted longer than a week—that's as long as it took her to realize that, however attractive the partner, she couldn't stand him cluttering up the bathroom, mooching around the kitchen and messing through her video collection.

But whenever in the black, small hours of the morning she wished she were different, she'd console herself with the thought that there was always Brad. Anyone who had Brad Hastings for a father couldn't be a total disaster.

Not that Emmy had ever admitted it in so many words. Or any of the others, come to that. It was just accepted; unspoken but accepted. It would explain why Brad had left so hurriedly for America when Emmy had turned down his proposal of marriage. That's what they'd told her when she was old enough to come to terms with the fact that she was illegitimate. Even when she was growing up in Clifton Coombe she'd known that Brad was her father, guarding the knowledge like a secret treasure from the other girls who drooled over his poster, which advertised some new must-see kiss-kiss-bang-bang movie.

She hadn't wanted to share with them the excitement of his postcards and letters and birthday presents and the visits to some grand London hotel with Emmy when he came to Britain. They were hers, all hers.

It hadn't been a bad growing up. Whatever people might whisper about Emmy and the Mays behind their backs they were sufficiently in awe of them not to say it out loud. You couldn't really cold-shoulder a family that so resolutely refused to acknowledge it was being cold-shouldered. And besides, times were changing. It was the sixties. The pill had liberated the sexual urges of young women everywhere and while pregnancy was still generally associated with wedlock it was no longer an absolute requisite. After all, if Vanessa Redgrave could do it! That had been Frances's smart reply when a bunch of girls at Clifton High had taunted her in a half-hearted way, more because of her academic excellence than because she was illegitimate which, secretly, rather intrigued them. It made her parentage a lot more interesting than their own stuffily unchallengeable pedigree.

She never could fathom Emmy's imperturbable refusal to admit that Brad was her father. (When she was older it had amused her: 'I'm an immaculate conception,' she had joked with Aunt Val.) 'He is, isn't he?' she'd badgered Emmy after one especially wonderful visit to London when he'd showered her with gifts, taken her to the theatre where she'd basked in his reflected glory and insisted Emmy and she should share one of the Savoy's most expensive suites overlooking the river.

'Does it matter that much?' Emmy

had said. She had always been an unorthodox mother and it seemed beyond her comprehension that Frances might actually be concerned about the identity of her father.

'Yes,' her daughter had replied promptly, although in her heart she knew it didn't really matter. *She* knew. That was what mattered.

'Then—then you must believe it.'

It was the nearest Emmy had got to an admission. Why else, after all, should he be so attentive, so anxious to keep in touch despite the commitments of his career?

And why else, much later when his popularity had waned, had he chosen to return to England, to settle in a comfortable cottage on the riverside at Kew and open a bookshop in nearby Richmond? Why else, if not to be close to her? Why else had he never married, although his name was linked with many famous beauties, if it weren't that he was still in love with the girl who had got away—Emmy? So Frances had rationalized throughout her life. When she'd felt able to question Brad his wordless paternal embrace had confirmed her belief.

He'd been so proud of her success. And she'd been so certain of him that she'd never really registered his lifestyle, the young men who helped out in his bookshop, the business manager who so conveniently shared the cottage in Kew. When she thought about it now she was amazed that she of all people could have been so unobservant, so unquestioning, so dense. How could she not have noticed the pallor, the loss of weight, the sapped energy? She still saw him as that dazzling creature, a hundred times life size on the big cinema screen.

It was just by chance, when they'd been lunching at one of those cosy restaurants in Kew he always seemed to patronize before the food critics caught on to it, that he told her. She'd been preparing a feature on AIDS and was discussing it with him. He was picking at his food, which worried her in passing but not seriously.

'You'll fade away,' she'd joked.

'Possibly,' he'd replied and saw that he wasn't joking.

She'd felt a sudden alarm. 'Brad?'

He'd leaned over and touched her hand, withdrawing it quickly, perhaps uncertain about her reaction. People, he'd discovered, responded differently. Even a woman of the world, and she was certainly that, might not be able to conceal an initial revulsion although she'd cover it up immediately. But the damage would be done, the first instinct noted.

'You've come to the right person, I'm afraid, Fran.' He never called her Fanny.

'About your documentary. I have AIDS.'

He faced her squarely and she hadn't flinched. In that moment the objective exercise of putting together a programme about a little-understood and frightening disease became real and personal.

Neither of them spoke. They didn't talk about it in detail until later: how far advanced he was, what treatment he was receiving. But a new, different bond between them had been established in just that fleeting moment. He was no longer a hero, an idol, a creature from some other glamorous planet. He was the man she loved most in the world, in pain.

She closed her eyes tightly, remembering that moment. When she opened them, the tower block across the road seemed to bear down on her, blocking out sky and sun and fresh air.

'Mamie!' she barked through the intercom, 'tell them I'm on my way.'

CHAPTER EIGHT

Emmy was still brooding over France's telephone call when Terry announced the contingent from the *Clarion*. She hadn't bargained for a photographer as well and decided to drape an expensive Liberty silk scarf in shades of green, a gift from Reggie, round the severe neckline of a Marks and Spencer frock. Vanity! she sighed, then removed it.

'Give 'em an inch and they'll take a yard,' Terry muttered. 'You don't have to, you know. I'll tell them you're not up to it.'

The reporter, a pretty, hyperactive girl who betrayed her nervousness by smiling too hugely, seemed aware that the paper was pushing its luck in getting an interview at all with Emmeline May at a time like this.

Her roly-poly, middled-aged companion, festooned with the paraphernalia of his trade, dumped his gear unceremoniously on the nearest chair, oblivious that he might not be welcome. He was a part-timer who had been called into service when the paper's regular photographer had been sent off to cover a multiple pile-up on the A27 just north of the town. A perenially gloomy man, who took deaths and disasters in his stride without regard for anybody's finer feelings, he belied the impression of robust good humour that his pot-bellied girth and ruddy, teddy-bear face promised. He treated the girl with a weary veteran's scorn for a novice who not only didn't know the score but hadn't even

116

got the hang of the game.

'It's all right Terry,' Emmy emphasized, shooting a warning look in his direction. 'Perhaps you could rustle up some tea, coffee?' She glanced questioningly at her visitors. The girl nodded brightly to both. The photographer looked as if he'd prefer something stronger. 'Tea *and* coffee, Terry,' said Emmy, shooing him hurriedly to the door.

She felt safer with him out of the way, more in control. You never knew with Terry when he might fly off the handle and he had no love for the *Clarion*. The paper had once identified him, with some justice but too little regard for the law, as one of Clifton Coombe's problem teenagers in an article advocating stern measures to reduce the juvenile crime rate. 'It wasn't as if I'd even been doing anything,' Terry had grumbled. 'Well—*caught* doing anything,' he'd conceded, noticing Emmy's sceptical eye when he'd told her about this gross violation of his rights as a private citizen.

'I really appreciate your seeing me...us...' the girl corrected herself. She sounded apprehensive, a touch too ingratiating. It was only the second time she'd been sent on an assignment other than Women's Institute meetings and golden wedding anniversaries. The first time had been tailing a junior minister at the

Department of Transport as he toured the contentious route of a proposed bypass and incurring his displeasure when she'd ingenuously enquired whether he would fancy living beside six lanes of concrete. The interview had been abruptly terminated. The junior minister, a staunch ally of the more motorways for Britain lobby, was understandably sensitive about living in a protected area of outstanding natural beauty. Thereafter it had been back to WI meetings and golden oldie anniversaries. Until now.

She cleared her throat. 'I mean at...'

'At a time like this,' Emmy finished the overworked sentiment for her. She felt sorry for the girl. She reminded her of her sister, Cissie, the younger twin of Penny by ten minutes, who had never managed to be quite in step or in tune with Val and Penny but put up a game show anyway. The girl had the same uncertain eagerness to please, the same rather sad bravado of someone who is trying to convince herself of her own worth. Just like Cissie. At least, the Cissie Emmy knew.

What a job to be lumbered with! thought Emmy. 'Cut on down to Rushey Green and get a few quotes from Emmeline May about her brother, but make sure you find out who's coming to the funeral—Sir Reginal May, the sisters, any celebrities.

Get something on the father and mother and the old Adelphi, too. And don't forget to look up the cutting on that other nutter who took the plunge at the Adelphi.'

Emmy could imagine the briefing. Maybe not as polite as that: old Emmy May and that crazy brother of hers.

'A character!'

Emmy realized that the girl had been chattering on while she mused.

'Your brother was a great character in the town,' the girl repeated. 'A much loved character...' she prompted, a note of desperation in her voice for she was sure this was going to be another no-no interview, another nail in her coffin at the *Clarion*.

Emmy clasped her hands together and paid attention. It really wasn't fair to leave the girl floundering like this. After all, she'd agreed to the meeting. And she looked so forlorn, with that awful photographer in his sloppy slub slacks and suede jacket that didn't meet across the middle not bothering to disguise his contempt for her inexperience.

Maybe I'll give her a very good interview, an interview to astonish her superiors at the *Clarion*. The mildly subversive thought cheered her up a little. It would take her mind off the news about Brad and Frances's angry criticism. She smiled, although it was barely more than a lifting of the corners of the mouth. Who, she thought, am I fooling? Brad, poor, brave Brad!

The girl mistook the smile and smiled gratefully back.

'What's your name?' said Emmy.

The girl blushed, feeling stupid. 'I'm sorry. Didn't I introduce myself?'

'They just said a reporter. Straight from school?' Emmy cursed her insensitivity. It sounded so patronizing. It *was* patronizing. How dare she imply that youth precluded talent.

'Not quite,' said the girl crisply, clearly affronted.

That's better, Emmy approved. Don't grovel. Don't ever grovel. What could she give the girl that would be special? Not the truth. Never the truth. A little bit of Toby, perhaps, that very few people knew about: something that would alter Clifton Coombe's perception of him as the daft May with a screw loose.

'I'm Marian Fancey,' said the girl, rectifying the oversight, 'and this...' The photographer was gazing vacantly out of the window at the unkempt garden, plainly bored. 'Norman Jessop,' he yawned. 'Nice house, Miss May.' He seemed about to add that it was a pity it was so run-down but decided not to. 'Always liked it. When we were lads, my mates and I used to come scrumping in the orchard. Your dad caught us once or twice but he never seemed to mind, just ticked us off and warned us not to get caught again.' He scratched his chin, still looked fixedly out of the window. 'That puzzled us. We'd have got a clip round the ear if it had been our parents. But he didn't say anything about not doing it, just don't let me catch you doing it. Odd!'

Emmy smiled. The photographer was right. Gilbert had been tolerant to the point of carelessness. He and her own tearaway, Terry Roberts, would have understood each other perfectly.

'That was typical of my father. He was never a disciplinarian.' She was struck by the absurdity of summing up that complex man in bite-sized judgements. Well, what harm would it do now? Hadn't they all fostered this selective image of Gilbert May one way or another?

'Will you keep on the house, Miss May?' Marian Fancey felt it was high time to retrieve the initiative. It was all right for Norman Jessop to rabbit on about his schooldays. All he had to do was take a few snaps. She had to get the quotes and then agonize over the words.

'Why not? It's her home,' the dreaded Norman continued, unabashed by the withering look that was being beamed in his direction. He made it sound as if Emmy were being hurried into an old folks' home and needed an ally in asserting her independence.

No thank you very much, thought Emmy, I can do without your approval. She turned to the girl. 'I haven't really given it too much thought yet. It's a big house and it will seem...' she was going to say 'lonely' '...strange without my brother. We've lived here all our lives.'

She looked round the stuffed, high-ceilinged sitting room; at the dingy, decorated cornices and the central rose plump with muddy, plaster petals and predatory leaves; at the jewel-coloured tiling of the fire surround reaching up to the ornate mantelpiece.

All those fleshy, fake flowers painted, etched, chiselled, moulded, embossed on wallpaper and woven into fabric. There had been a time when, like many young people of her generation, she had loathed Victorian décor. Now she found it rather comforting: it provided an ambience that seemed to encourage secrets, tucking them away in all those hidden nooks and crannies along with the cobwebs and exhausted wood lice and accumulations of dust.

'It must have been a great place for

parties. You don't mind?' The girl switched on her tape-recorder.

Emmy nodded. Why not? 'Oh yes, we had great times here.'

Almost without any prompting from Marian Fancey, she found herself recalling some of those times, when the house had always seemed to be open house, ablaze with light and laughter. The Steinway that now stood forlornly in the corner was never silent as Jack and Cicely and Binnie and Bobby and Jessie and once even Noel kept up a singsong patter of their own subversive lyrics to old tunes.

She had never quite understood how the manager of a provincial theatre, of which there were many in England at the time, could have been so closely acquainted with the great entertainers in the West End stage. But Gilbert, and to a lesser extent her mother, had always had that knack. They had only to meet someone once to be forever friends on drop-in-when-you're-in-the-vicinity terms. And they did drop in. For late suppers, picnics, Boxing Day festivities, first-night parties. Not just the famous, but anyone who caught Gilbert's fancy. They had all welcomed the goggle-eyed May children into this private show business society as of right. Even Toby. But not Emmy, who had sat taking it all in, always the observer, never the performer. She hadn't minded, though, that they had regarded her as 'painfully shy', an object of some pity. She, after all, had known better. There were other ways of being yourself than cutting loose in front of an audience.

That's the way it had been. Until Harvey Persky. Harvey Persky changed everything.

She hadn't mentioned his name, at least she didn't think she had. But the girl, Marian Fancey, did. She said it without guile, just quoting from the cuttings.

'It must have been a shock when that man died at the Adelphi.' She hesitated, suddenly aware of how closely Toby's death had re-enacted the previous one.

'Of course. It was a shock.' Emmy spoke deliberately, concerned but not overly so, as if talking about a remote tragedy whose only relevance to herself and her family was that it happened in the theatre Gilbert managed. It wasn't the girl's fault.

'I suppose you're thinking it's strange that my brother should choose to die the same way.' Better to say it, dispose of it, rather than let the reporter tiptoe round the subject, not quite suggesting it out loud but implying it all the same.

'Choose?' Norman Jessop had roused himself from his torpor. He wasn't as thick as he seemed, I'll give him that, thought Emmy. 'So it *was* suicide.'

'A slip of the tongue,' Emmy corrected herself, glancing meaningfully at the tape-recorder purring gently in the background. 'I simply meant strange that he should die that way.'

'It was a splendid death,' said Marian Fancey in a low voice. She had forgotten her gaffe in bringing it up at all and her plump, unblemished face wore a rapt expression, the job in hand momentarily forgotten. 'Almost—operatic.'

Emmy looked at her with renewed respect. She understood. Maybe it was given to the young to appreciate a grand gesture better than their elders, to whom death is a cold, bleak prospect, too close for comfort.

'You're very perceptive, Miss Fancey. It *was* almost operatic. Not many people understand that.'

The photographer, Jessop, was clearly not one of them. He could think of more congenial ways of ending it all, if he thought about it at all: an overdose of sleeping pills or drinking your way through a lifetime's supply of Johnnie Walker. But he wasn't a man for hypotheses. He'd been patient enough.

'I thought we might get some shots in the garden. Not so gloomy as indoors. I mean, lightwise. Nice room, but dark.'

'Is that really necessary? Photographs?'

queried Emmy, wishing she had kept on the Liberty scarf.

'It would help the piece,' said Marian Fancey with some urgency, seeing her feature relegated to two bottom columns on the left-hand page of the women's section for want of an eye-catching picture.

Emmy shrugged.

'Schizophrenic, was he? Your brother?' Norman Jessop was not calculatedly callous, but he worked on the principle that if someone agreed to see the press they should be prepared to take whatever was thrown at them. And, more accurately perhaps than his young colleague, he'd judged that Emmeline May was quite capable of handling the situation. She didn't seem distressed, almost the reverse. He'd seen it before. It was sympathy that destroyed them.

Emmy responded quite calmly. 'No.'

It no longer bothered her that people speculated about the precise nature of Toby's mental state. But neither was she prepared to elaborate on the subject. Since he was a kiddie he had been tested, examined, prodded and probed by experts. He'll never have to be scrutinized again, Emmy had decided when she assumed responsibility for him.

The psycho-analyst to whom their doctor had first referred Toby when he was still a small boy had been encouraging but not specific. He was a considerate man who did his best in a field still woefully experimental. But the traumas of war had thrown up more deserving cases for his skills—former POWs, shattered veterans of too many campaigns, bomb-shocked civilians, the victims of horrendous injuries—than a little boy from a caring, comfortable home with what seemed no more alarming than a learning disorder.

There was nothing frighteningly wrong with the lad. Toby, he told them, was suffering from a form of mental malfunction which made it difficult for him to relate to everyday life in the way children usually did. It was quite possible that he would outgrow it in time. In some areas he would be slow and backward and require patience. In others he could be outstandingly gifted. And so it had proved. In the vivid, private world of the imagination Toby had outshone them all. But he had never become normal.

'Whatever *normal* might be,' Emmy would round angrily on her sisters and brother who thoughtlessly dropped the odd 'dummy' or 'daft' in Toby's hearing.

'It was a *joke,* for Christ's sake, Emmy! Toby doesn't mind. Look at him. Where's your sense of humour? You're such a grouch.' It was Val, usually Val, who called Emmy to account for fussing over Toby. Maybe she was right, Emmy had thought more than once. Maybe I am overprotective of him. But he was her legacy. Val, pushy, extrovert Val, would never understand what that meant.

Increasingly over the years, with a couple of gins inside her and often more, her mother would blame herself for Toby. On and on. 'It must have been my fault, Emmy. And being born in the war. Maybe I had you all too quickly. Except for Reggie.' Her eyes would light up momentarily when she mentioned Reggie. The golden boy!

She'd lean over heavily toward Emmy, a little tipsy now, and it saddened her daughter to see the way the drink had puffed out her once delicately formed features. 'It's not that I don't love you all, Emmy old girl. It's just...it's just...the first is the first. You'll never know that Emmy.'

'I've a daughter, ma,' Emmy had reminded her. Towards the end of her life her mother was always forgetting, losing track of who was married, divorced and how many children they all had.

'So you have.' Madge had raised her glass, tipping half its contents on to her lap. 'But Emmy. Toby! He wasn't my fault, was he?'

'Of course he wasn't, ma.' She'd rescued

the glass from her mother's wavering hand. 'And Toby's fine anyway.'

'You're just saying that. I know. Just like your father before he died. And all the rest of you. It's my fault. My burden.' Then she would become weepie and Emmy would help her to bed. The next morning she'd be bright as a button, spending hours choosing a dress to wear, applying the layers of eye-shadow, mascara, blusher and lipstick and torturing her bleached blonde hair into a crazy caricature of some extravagant *coiffure* she'd seen on a model in *Vogue*. A travesty of the sparkling little soubrette with whom her father had fallen in love.

'Would the garden be all right?'

She realized Normal Jessop had repeated the question at least twice. He must, she thought, think I'm as barmy as he's convinced Toby was. She was suddenly struck by how foolish it all was. What on earth did they want a picture of her for? Just to decorate some unnecessary piece about the Mays for the local paper. They'd get all their pictures at the funeral. She couldn't think now why she'd agreed to see them.

No. She'd show them something they'd never seen before, Clifton Coombe had never seen before, something of Toby, she decided then and there.

'I don't think a photograph of me would be appropriate,' she said commandingly. 'I'm sorry.' But she wasn't sorry.

Norman Jessop threw up his hands. 'Well, that's that then, isn't it!'

'Not quite. Come with me.'

Without looking to see if they were following, she led them through the wilderness of the garden to the old wooden hut nestling beside the wildlife pond. It was larger and more ornate than a shed. When they were little it had been their doll's house, a hidey-hole from the grown-ups, where they'd played their games of make-believe. Later it had been Toby's secret place, his workshop, his studio, the light filtering through the window that covered one side of the slanting roof. As she unlocked the door, she heard Marian Fancey gasp.

'My God!' exclaimed the photographer.

When they stepped inside the blaze of colour seemed at first too rich, too blinding, to be absorbed. As their eyes became accustomed to it, they realized the walls were covered with crude but brilliantly executed murals painted in bold, primary colours.

Emmy pointed to the mural facing the door. It was a jungle scene, but the jungle was Clifton Coombe, with the Adelphi, the war memorial, the clock tower, the white cliffs sloping to the sea clearly identifiable. Plodding, climbing, stalking, flying through the familiar landmarks there was a variety of creatures, half real, half imaginary.

Their faces were recognizably human: the faces of individual members of the May family.

'Toby's family portrait.' Emmy looked at it with the awe and pride she always felt when Toby showed her the fruits of his uncanny talent.

'But—but they're all *animals,*' the girl whispered. 'At least—they are, aren't they?'

'That's how Toby saw us. My father Gilbert as a tiger. My mother Madge as the gazelle. The three chimpanzees are my sisters, Valerie, Penelope and Cecilia. The bear is my brother Reggie. And me...' She chuckled. 'I'm the elephant. I can't think why. Maybe the elephant that never forgets.'

'And that?'

In the corner of the mural lurked a watchful crocodile with an unfamiliar face. It looked almost benign, except for the bared teeth.

'That's nobody.'

But it wasn't. It was Harvey Persky.

'I've seen pictures of your family and the likeness—the facial likeness—is extraordinary. But it's so odd. Animals! Didn't your family think it was odd?'

131

'Why?' said Emmy to be contrary, for the mural had been thought very odd indeed. 'None of us is quite what we seem. In a funny kind of way it's quite apt, although I don't think my sisters fancied being depicted as chimpanzees.'

'They don't all live in Africa. Bears and tigers!' exclaimed Norman Jessop pedantically.

'It's not an African jungle or an Asian jungle. It's my brother's jungle.'

'I don't suppose you'd let me take a few shots of this? In colour. For the supplement. As well as some black and whites for the paper.' His professional interest, she was glad to see, had been satisfactorily aroused.

'Why not? It's a lot more fascinating than a frumpy, middle-aged woman looking embarrassed in the garden, wouldn't you say?'

She hoped that Toby would forgive her, then remembered he was beyond caring who saw his work. Yet how jealously he had guarded his paintings from prying eyes during his lifetime! He would show them, and then reluctantly, only to those with whom he felt comfortable, unthreatened, as if they were deformed children who needed to be protected from the insensitive gaze of the outside world. Even some of the chosen few couldn't appreciate the scale of his vision and the raw skill with which he expressed it.

Val for one. 'It's so, so comic, if it weren't so gruesome,' she'd shivered. Val, whose notion of high art was a ten by eight glossy preferably snapped by David Bailey.

As she watched Norman Jessop clicking away, trying to find the right lens and focus the light, she felt pleasantly fulfilled. This would surely give Clifton Coombe something to think about. Toby the fool or Toby the genius!

She imagined Val's reaction when Toby's family portrait was made public and was even more cheered. Bitch, she silently chided herself, but without remorse.

CHAPTER NINE

In the top-floor flat of Drake House in Dolphin Square Valerie May awoke uneasily to a noisy dawn chorus of pigeons clumping around in hob-nailed boots on the roof. She was conscious of some stirrings of life in the gardens below around which the huge complex of self-contained residential units clustered like a redbrick fortress on the Thames at Pimlico.

She would have preferred a flat with an outside river view but was in no position to make demands or even requests, despite her twenty-year tenancy. She was behind with the rent; not a lot, but enough to be slightly embarrassed if she should run into the general manager of the trust that administered the block of flats in this uniquely non-profit-making housing association in the centre of London.

Jobs for a fifty-five-year-old actress of no outstanding talent were thin on the ground and she had long since given up the time-consuming exercise of pursuing her elusive ex-husband, Gunther Hesselmann, for the alimony he was supposed to pay but seldom did. In any case their two children were not only off hand but practically out of sight so she figured 'the Hun' felt he was no longer under any obligation to them or to her.

For several minutes she stared at the ceiling then risked raising her throbbing head from the pillow. It wasn't so bad once you were upright. It had been quite a night, ending up at the Hard Rock cafe where she knew she'd made a fool of herself but didn't much care. She could imagine her brother Reggie's reaction: what on earth is a woman your age doing in a hamburger joint for kids? He had always been slightly disconcerted that she should insist on using the family surname professionally, especially since the knighthood. The only consolation was that it wasn't a particularly uncommon name.

'What the hell!' she groaned, sliding her legs to the floor and kneading the base of her spine with the palms of her hands. Her back was killing her. Her back and her head. She noticed that she had shed her nightgown—not a pretty sight—and reached out for a robe to cover herself.

'What the hell!' she groaned again.

'Whats'at?'

The figure beside her stirred then slumped back into the pillows. His long, slim legs stuck out from under the duvet, the feet curling round the bottom of the mattress. Curls of chestnut hair lay sweetly on the back of his neck. He was, she noticed, rather spotty and he looked a little unclean behind the ears.

He'll have to go, she sighed. Starving actor or no starving actor.

'C'mon, Kev. Wake-up time.'

'I'm not going anywhere.' He pulled the duvet back over his shoulder and prepared to go back to sleep. And he could do it, too, she thought. How lovely to be so young that you could tell yourself to go to sleep and do it, just like that.

'But *I* am,' she said, 'going somewhere.'

He managed to rouse himself sufficiently

to turn round and look up at her, blinking those incredible blue eyes with their double fringe of lashes to which no man should be entitled. She was aware that she looked like the back of a bus but he should be used to it by now. In fact he actually seemed to like it, maybe it made him feel even more vigorous and untouched by the ravages of time. 'I have this thing about older women,' he had told her when they first met while filming a TV sitcom, as if it were a wonderfully original concept. How often she'd heard that, although she had to admit it still gave her a small shot of adrenalin, a small assurance that she wasn't yet totally over the hill.

'That's right, I remember,' he yawned. 'Sister Penny. What do you think the chances are? Any tea?'

'Coming up.' She levered herself off the bed, not bothering to disguise the ache in her back that slowed her movements. She caught his fleeting expression of distaste. Maybe it was finally getting to him: the reality behind his fantasy of an older woman. Well, it was high time he grew up. 'I hear you can get arthritis, lumbago, sciatica in your teens. Think about that,' she said spitefully.

Now who needs to grow up, she thought. 'Sorry,' she said, stroking his smooth chest pensively, then more urgently.

He blushed, like a sheltered young girl not quite sure how to handle a suggestive proposition.

'I'll get it,' he said, leaping out of bed. 'Tea.'

It wasn't getting older that she minded, it was ageing, she reflected.

'Fine.'

She watched him padding, naked, to the kitchen, so sure of his body, knowing with absolute certainty that it would effortlessly do what he commanded it to do.

'Breakfast?'

'Just muesli,' she said. It was a token effort, just a wee discipline in the interests of a healthy diet. The days when she could follow a thick night with sunny-side eggs and fried bread for breakfast were a distant memory.

He came back with a mug of tea. He put on her old bathrobe, which looked better on him that it ever did on her, she decided. He wasn't usually so modest. Or so solicitous. She couldn't remember that he'd got breakfast before in the weeks since he'd moved in with her.

'There was something I was meaning to tell you last night, but it sort of slipped my mind.' He sat down on the dressing-table stool opposite her, his arms and legs seeming to shoot out in all directions. That was the thing about young men. They took up so much room. It really might be nice to have the place to herself again. Until the next time, at least.

She chuckled. She had a lovely, throaty chuckle which she'd learned early on was one of her charms and she practised it as diligently as a concert violinist tuning up her instrument. 'I don't think either of us could be held responsible for anything that did or didn't happen last night.'

She winced as soon as it was out. Coquetry had never been her strong suit and at her age it was positively ludicrous. But he seemed concerned with his own thoughts. He rolled his mug around between the palms of his hand. A few drops of tea spilled on to the rug.

'Watch it!' she warned, headmistressy, redressing the balance.

'Sorry.' He sighed heavily. 'It's not a good day.'

'It never is. What is it you were meaning to ask me?' She chose her words carefully. What with her head and her back and the prospect of meeting her sister Penelope she didn't think she could cope with anything else taxing. A loan? Well, he'd be out of luck there, but he'd never asked her for money. An introduction to someone she might know in the business? God, not Reggie, she hoped. He'd be out of luck there, too. In any case he hadn't said 'ask' but 'tell'.

He cleared his throat, the way you did before embarking on the big speech. Then he took a running jump at it. 'I've had this offer to join a theatre company up north. I met this guy I knew at drama school yesterday, just by chance, in the pub. It's a small group, starting up. They've managed to get some funding from the local council and a pittance from the Arts Council. But with the local support, and there's a community hall they can use...' His voice tailed away as if it had run out of steam.

'Lucky them!' she prompted. 'And they want you to join the group?'

He nodded. 'You've been great, Vee, just great. Really helped me out when I was in a spot. But I think—I think it's time I was pushing off.'

'Oh!'

Although she'd been half expecting it she still felt faintly aggrieved. This wasn't the way the scene was supposed to play. She was the one who should do the pushing off. Except that hadn't been the pattern lately. If only they weren't so damned deferential when they called it a day. It made her feel almost as old as her years. She would, of course, be frightfully gracious. Nothing etched itself on the face so much as rancour. Anger was OK. It cleansed the blood.

'I'm very glad for you, Kev. Seriously. You deserve a break and, who knows, this could be it. From little acorns...!' She smiled her lovely *Dear Octopus* mother smile. 'Anyway, you know when you come back south you'll always be welcome.' Pull the other one! 'And if things don't work out you can always stay here for a bit.' Fat chance!

Pure Dodie Smith, she prided herself.

He looked relieved. 'You're brilliant, Vee. Real brill.'

She sighed. He'd never make it. Even his slang was outdated. But oh, those eyes! Give them a great big close-up on television and he might be the next Jason Donovan. Just like Eddy Arthur who became Brad Hastings. None of them had ever rated his chance and look what had happened to him. She frowned. What *had* happened to him?

'So, when will you be leaving for the frozen north?'

'I thought maybe you'd want me out straight away. But Friday would be fine, if that's convenient?' Their relationship had changed completely. He sounded like a supplicant applying for a bank loan.

'Stay as long as it suits,' she said airily. 'I won't be here anyway. I have to go to my brother's funeral.'

He looked instantly stricken. She was quite touched. 'You didn't say.'

'Didn't I? I suppose I forgot. He'd seemed dead for an awfully long time.' What a dreadful thing to say, she thought, but it was true up to a point. She'd never been able to relate to Toby, not like Emmy. And she had tried. But perhaps, like dogs and horses, he'd sensed her unease and withdrawn into his shell when she attempted a friendly approach.

'Poor Vee,' he whispered sadly, not knowing what else to say.

'Oh, for heaven's sake, Kev, everybody dies.' She made it sound unfeeling because she had too much on her mind to even begin to explain how she actually felt. Regret, guilt, a suspicion that all the reasons she'd given herself for not being around when she might have been useful to her father, Emmy, Toby, were just an excuse for opting out.

He looked crestfallen at her rebuff. It wasn't fair, she thought. He was entitled to feel sorry for her.

'What I meant, Kev, is—is that we'd been expecting it.' It was a lie, of course. Who could have expected that Toby would decide to take a dive from the balcony of the Adelphi? But it was the sort of comforting lie that made people feel easier, like 'a blessed release.'

'A blessed release?' he said obligingly.

She smothered a smile. 'Exactly.' She didn't know how she'd put up with him even for a few weeks. Well, she did. But you couldn't spend all your life in bed.

Having relieved himself of two anxieties —Toby's funeral and telling Vee that he was leaving—he became positively jovial, singing the score of *Follies* (he rather fancied himself as a singer) while he shaved, showered, dressed and cooked a fry-up for his breakfast. 'Good times, bum times,' he crooned.

Good times! Bum times! What the hell would he know about either at his age?

I really must get off this age thing, she thought, and switched on the television as much to drown out his pervasive good humour as to catch up on the morning news. She could hear it rabbiting away in the corner as she carefully inspected her wardrobe and decided what would be the most appropriate—no, persuasive—outfit to wear for lunch with her sister. At the Connaught, no less! Well, Penny was rich enough. She chose the Chanel suit she'd picked up at a bargain price in a Knightsbridge sale. It was two years old but, thankfully, still unmistakably Chanel. Penny would approve of that. Highly suitable for the Connaught. Not garish, not dowdy. Quietly confident with a touch of glitz at the neck and waist.

She surveyed herself in the mirror with some satisfaction. Properly girdled, her figure was still trim. She was glad she had persevered with the longer, carefully careless hairstyle which gave her face an illusion of youthfulness. Only when you peered closely could you discern the crows' feet and sag of flesh around the jawline. Cosmetic surgery would fix that, but it would have to wait until the nice little earner her agent was always promising her would turn up.

It wasn't enough, though. What had happened to the dazzling career that had seemed so certain when she and her sisters and been top of the pops in the fifties, when *Melody Maker* had tipped her for stardom: 'Valerie May, the lead singer of the Mayflowers, may not have the greatest voice in the charts, but her looks and pizzazz deserve a wider showcase. Given the right grooming she could even rival Audrey Hepburn on the big screen.' But Audrey Hepburn had remained unrivalled. Bad luck, bad timing, bad judgement, whatever it was, she'd somehow just drifted. The Associated British Picture Corporation option hadn't been picked up; they'd been concentrating on Sylvia Syms. The Hollywood biblical epic had been a flop at a time when American studios were falling out of love with imported British starlets. The big TV series, for which she'd refused a role in *Coronation Street,* had turned out to be a failed sprinter not the long-distance runner that had been predicted. Thereafter she'd been the third or fourth choice for anything worth having, but a hardy perennial in low-budge B movies, mindless TV quiz shows and daytime soaps whose plots were as shaky as the scenery.

If she were feeling really vindictive she could always blame it on her impulsive marriage to the famously infamous Gunther Hesselmann and promptly having two children at a crucial time in her career.

But she was not really a vindictive woman. She had always known that Gunther operated just this side of being an out-and-out crook with his shady deals and import-export-God-knew-what business. And she'd known too that sooner or later he would stray over to the other side and that would be the end of Gunther and their marriage. She admitted freely that she had been seduced by his charm and his knack of making her feel she was the one and only woman in the world. (In that he'd reminded her of Harvey Persky, which was a disastrous basis for a marriage).

Common sense, of course, should have

warned her that the kind of man with that particular gift was also the kind of man who would spread it around generously: there were, she had discovered, quite a few one and only women in Gunther's world. But common sense came later after he had pawned her jewellery, taken out a second mortgage on their nice little house off the Brompton Road and ransacked their joint bank account. Ah well! *C'est la vie!* Her life anyway.

'You look nice,' said Kev, aiming to please now that he had no special need to be pleasing. 'She sounds—' he searched for the word—'formidable.'

She inclined her head in the mirror like royalty, accepting his compliment. 'Penny? I suppose she is. A little. You'd never think she was a twin. She's quite unlike Cissie.'

'Do they look alike?'

She couldn't be sure whether he was genuinely interested in her sisters or just making polite conversation, because that, after all, was all they had left in the short time they still had together.

'They used to. Look alike. When they were little. But I suppose circumstances, the life you lead, the people you associate with, affect the way you look as you get older. If they weren't related I doubt whether they'd have the slightest thing in common. I suppose,' she ruminated, 'that goes for all of us.'

'Still—family!'

'Oh yes. Family. Makes all the difference. I can't think why. But it does.'

She decided it was time to get off this particular merry-go-round. How could he possibly know or understand or even care about the Mays? He was already visualizing those rave reviews he would get for his Henry V or Jimmy Porter or Jack Worthing at his theatre up north.

'Where is this company you're joining?' She sniffed. 'Your bacon's burning.'

She watched him dealing with the kitchen crisis with the deftness of someone who had spent a good deal of time sharing bed-sitters with other impecunious actors.

He started tucking into his fry-up straight from the frying pan with relish.

'There are plates. There's no law,' she said.

'Sorry. Leeds. You asked where the company was based. Leeds.' His hand strayed to a plate in the rack but as he'd already half-eaten his breakfast he decided not to bother.

'That's really north.'

'Jake said it's going to be a really nice mix,' he said through a full mouth.

'Jake?'

'The guy I was telling you about.'

'Oh!'

'Coward, Shaw, the entire canon of Brecht.'

'The *entire* canon! Goodness! That *will* pull in the punters.'

He looked at her sideways, not quite sure whether she was being sincere or sarcastic.

The television was still rumbling away in the corner. It was the commercial break. She heard her own voice seductively extolling the merits of a new ultra-bright, ultra-strong, ultra-kind washing powder while six cartoon gnomes spun round the washing machine working miracles of cleaning power.

'It's magic!' purred the off-screen Valerie.

'It's crap!' said Kev.

'It's a pay cheque. There'll come a time when you've finished canonizing Brecht and you'll find the odd commercial comes in very handy.'

'If you say so. What is it?'

She'd leaned forward listening to another voice that was attached to a long, lanky young man with a duffel coat and jeans, his floppy fair hair straggling over his forehead. He looked, as always, perished.

'Robert Hesselmann is the leader of the group of protesters petitioning the Secretary of State for Defence for action,' the commentator was explaining over the voice she recognized.

Eyes blazing, the lanky young man was haranguing a crowd of angry tenants outside a block of flats. 'The MOD deliberately allowed these redundant properties to be sold in the full knowledge that they were poorly constructed and potentially unsafe. Now they refuse to accept any responsibility for them.'

'But surely—' an unseen reporter attempting to play devil's advocate was cut off smartly.

'And furthermore there should be a public enquiry into MOD policy towards all the properties built for service personnel which are now empty due to defence spending cutbacks, while there are hundreds of homeless families in the towns all along the south coast.'

'You know him?' said Kev.

She smiled ruefully. 'I should. He's my son.'

She peered more closely at the screen. An equally scruffy young woman at his elbow was nodding in furious agreement. 'But I didn't know he was so thick with Deb.'

'Deb?'

'My brother Reggie's daughter.' She imagined her brother's discomfiture at the sight of his expensively educated daughter in the company of her reprobate son.

'You're a funny family.' Kev shook his head. His own were stiflingly conventional. 'What does he do apart from good causes?'

'He's a lecturer in social history or some such tedious subject at Sussex University.'

'Do you see him often?'

'Now and then. I don't think he approves of me.'

'Earnest sort of bloke.'

'Oh yes. Both my children are earnest. My daughter Gloria's off studying the habits of the apes in Africa somewhere. All the earnest on my side of the family rubbed off on them. I can't say I blame them.'

She switched off the television. Enough was enough. Maybe she'd get a chance to see Robbie when she went down for Toby's funeral. He might even be there if he were seeing Deb. Her niece would certainly turn up, if only as moral support for Emmy.

'I'd better be going. I want to look in on Marcus before I see Penny.'

'Why don't you get yourself a decent agent, Vee. You're too good for him. He's played out.'

'He's a wise old bird, Kev. And, besides, it's been a long time.

'You're too nice.'

'Not nice. Lazy.'

She gathered her handbag—the good leather one—and the matching gloves and debated a brolly as the sky looked threatening and she was trying to cut down on taxis.

'I'll wash up and double-lock when I go out,' he promised. He kissed her gently on the cheek. 'Good luck!'

Christ, she thought, I don't know if I can stand all this unnatural tenderness until Friday. But she took his hand and gazed meaningfully into his eyes.

'Years from now when you talk about this—and you will—be kind!'

His eyes were moist with tears. 'Vee, how could you possibly...?'

She opened the flat door and closed it firmly behind her, a gleeful smile playing on her lips.

Tea and Sympathy. Act three. But he'd never know. It was much too fifties.

CHAPTER TEN

She was ten minutes late for her appointment at the Connaught. She'd tripped on a loose paving stone in Lupus Street on her way to Pimlico underground station, laddered her tights and had to rush into an Asian self-service for a spare pair. The Pakistani lady had been solicitous

150

but couldn't quite understand that 'barely black' and 'sunburst bronze' weren't much of a selection, seeing as her own legs were covered by a graceful sari. Valerie made do with the 'barely black.'

The tube trains were at sixes and sevens because of a bomb scare at Piccadilly. And when she did finally get to Oxford Circus Marcus Gammie was otherwise engaged for half an hour in his crummy top-floor agency. She suspected he might be sleeping off a previous night's binge or indulging in the hair of the dog.

When he did see her he was the same old Marcus, amazingly like he'd been when he had promoted the Mayflowers. Even thirty years ago his skin had been blotchy, his hair thinning and his eyes bloodshot. But, as then, he was lavishly encouraging. In Marcus's book there were always good times just around the corner.

'I just know it, Val, if you can get Penny and Cissie to agree to this TV show, it'll make all the difference. Exposure! Make them remember you. And it'll be a very nice bargaining counter in getting you the mother role in the new Judi Dench comedy series.'

'Judi Dench is as old as I am,' she protested.

'Not Judi *Dench's* mother.' He waved his hand in front of his face. 'Never mind. It's a good part.'

'What are my chances?'

He hunched his shoulders and puckered his lips in an iffy gesture. 'Like I said, the exposure will probably do the trick. A lot of people have forgotten the Mayflowers and they're the viewers a Judi Dench series will most appeal to. Cheer up, Val. Just talk nice to Penny.'

'What if she says no? She didn't sound enthusiastic on the phone. Cissie's no problem. She'll fall in with anything Pen says, provided it doesn't take her away from her menagerie for too long.'

'If she says no, well, we'll just have to work at it that much harder.' He beamed cheerfully as if enjoying the prospect of a challenge.

She beamed back. You really couldn't lay the awful truth on Marcus at his time of life. If he hadn't accepted by now that show business was a tough, ruthless profession with a woefully short memory he never would.

Of course Kev had been right. Marcus wasn't an agent for the 1990s. But she could no more shed him than she could discard the 1959 *Evening News* Most Promising Film Newcomer award that she had won after going it alone when the Mayflowers split up.

'By the way, I was sorry to hear about

Toby,' said Marcus. 'How's Emmy holding up?'

She looked at him, surprised, and caught herself wondering how he could have known about her brother and sister. Then she remembered how much a part of the May family he had been in those hopeful days when he was predicting great futures for all of them and touting the Mayflowers around the disc jockeys, record and TV companies.

'I always felt sad about Toby,' he ruminated. 'So much talent locked up there inside. The way he used to ape your father.'

'He still did, up until the day he died.'

'I know.' He nodded. 'Emmy told me. Don't look so amazed. I hear from her quite regularly. Sometimes I went down to visit. Not recently, though. It's the gout. Never know when it's going to flare up. I'll try to make the funeral, though.'

'I'm staggered.' It wasn't an exaggeration. 'All these years you've been in touch with Emmy and you've never told me. Neither did she, come to that.'

'You never asked. Besides, what's to tell? So, how is she?'

For some unaccountable reason she felt oddly rattled as if by keeping in contact on the quiet they were betraying her. 'I suppose you'd know better than I would, seeing as how you're so thick with her.'

He sighed, then rummaged in the drawer of his desk and brought out a bottle of Scotch and a couple of glasses. 'Stop being such a prima donna, Val.' He gestured toward the Scotch and, after debating the matter, she shook her head.

'Better not. And it won't do your gout much good, either.'

He ignored the caution, pouring himself a large tot. 'Won't do your complexion much good, but I don't suppose that stops you. Good party last night?' he asked slyly.

How the hell did he know what she did with her nights?

'I get to hear these things,' he said, as if in answer to her unspoken question. 'Sad! Sisters! You should be closer. Particularly now.'

'We never were close, Marcus.'

'I remember. She was always the odd one out. But she was brilliant with Toby. She never put him down, never made him feel—lacking. You know? I asked her once if Toby would sell me that family portrait he did of you, but he wouldn't, didn't really like me seeing it.'

She looked at him in horror. 'Not the *animal* thing! It gives me the shivers. I must try to persuade Emmy to burn it now.'

'That would be criminal. Maybe not on the scale of Graham Sutherland's portrait of Churchill, but a terrible waste. It may not have been the most flattering picture, but, believe me, it was a work of rare art. I know about these things.'

'Well, I wish you'd forget them, Marcus. I—we—don't want you meddling now that Toby's dead.'

He lifted his hands in mock horror. 'Would I meddle?'

'Always.' She stood up and chucked him playfully under his flabby chin. 'You're a terrible old reprobate.'

'But you love me. Now go and be charming to Penny. Give her my best.' He waved her away. 'I won't get up. You can see yourself out. I've got work to do, people to see.'

But she knew he hadn't.

He was a crafty devil, she thought, keeping in touch with Emmy all these years. It was strange what a hold Emmy seemed to have on everyone who came in contact with her, seemingly without even trying.

She walked to the Connaught, skirting the heavy Regent Street traffic and down the back doubles to Carlos Place off Grosvenor Square. Rich, she breathed. You could almost smell money.

'You're late,' said Penelope sharply. 'I

haven't got all day even if you have.'

Her sister was seated on a banquette in the grill room. She looked as immaculate as ever. At her side an attentive waiter hovered lovingly over the favoured Mrs Penelope Eardley and inclined his head to Valerie in deference to the company she kept. Like her surroundings, Penelope exuded an air of comfortable well-being.

'I hope you're paying.' Valerie couldn't resist the small dig at her sister's affluent lifestyle, while mentally promising to behave herself thereafter. Penelope didn't take kindly to sarcasm or irony.

'Does that mean you're broke again?' She lifted a disapproving eyebrow.

'It was a *joke*, Pen. You know, ha ha type. But since you ask, I'm not exactly flush. That's why this TV show could be so useful.' She hated sounding penitent but she knew Penelope would be swayed by nothing less than total capitulation to her own superior good sense.

The waiter coughed discreetly. 'Would you care to order, madam?'

'We'd better,' agreed Penelope. 'Val?'

Valerie appeared to be listening to a different tune. 'You see it's a great showcase and...'

'Later!'

There was no ignoring that warning tone. It seemed to slice through the hushed

156

babble with the resonance of a dinner gong. Penelope was used to being heard and paid attention to. And she was not inclined to discuss family matters in front of waiters.

They disposed of the menu quickly. A frugal omelette and green salad for Penelope. A robust duck pâté and roast beef for Valerie, who reasoned that it wasn't every day she ate lunch on Harry Eardley's expense account and, whatever the outcome of her meeting with Penelope, at least she could take away the memory of a good meal.

'And to drink? I'm having mineral water.'

Valerie smiled. 'A nice bottle of claret, I think,' she said, consideringly.

The wine-waiter beamed. 'I can recommend...'

'A *half*-bottle,' said Penelope, frowning slightly but not so much that it might crease the porcelain perfection of her make-up over which the beautician at Elizabeth Arden had laboured with such dedication.

'I promise I won't stagger out of here like a woman under the influence,' Valerie whispered loudly, cursing herself for forgetting her vow to behave.

Penelope looked at her complacently. 'I know you're just riling me because you don't like to have to ask for something. It's always nettled you, hasn't it? At first you were always the dominant one and we did as we were told. Now you're not in a position to be domineering about anything and you don't like it. I don't mind.' She waved her hand over the cutlery. 'Get it out of your system if it makes you feel better.'

Valerie stared at her sister, feeling patronized and not a little surprised. It was easy to categorize Penelope: wife of a wealthy financier, impeccably groomed, exquisitely well mannered and totally empty-headed about everything except the trivia of life. But her sudden shafts of insight were unnerving. They chipped away at Valerie's perception of a woman who had struck it lucky in spotting Harry Eardley's potential and had long since lost touch with the concerns of the plebs.

'I can't think why you don't chuck it all in,' Penelope continued. 'You must have a bit put by. I could help a little. There's lots of things you could do...'

'Like?'

'You could maybe live with Emmy for a while. She'd like that, especially now.' She spoke with the supreme confidence of someone used to ordering other people's lives. It didn't seem to occur to her to question her certainty about what Emmy might or might not like—especially now.

Valerie pulled a face. 'What—and give up show business?'

They both laughed, a little shame-faced. It had been Harvey Persky's joke. The one about the mucker-out in the animal cages at the circus who, bemoaning the long hours and the dirt and the hard labour, responded to a suggestion that he get another job with the immortal exclamation: 'What—and give up show business!'

The Mays had adopted it as their own: a response for all contingencies.

'You're going,' prompted Valerie, reminded of Toby's death.

'Of course. Harry, too. He likes funerals. He says they bring families together.'

'Probably his back-to-back upbringing in the north.'

Penelope flicked a sprig of watercress to the side of her plate. 'Probably,' she said. 'So—what's this wonderful show you were going on about?'

Valerie leaned forward, conscious that she had to make it sound good and wondering how best to appeal to Penelope's self-esteem. 'It's called, provisionally, "Where Are They Now?"' Immediately she realized she was off on the wrong foot. Nobody should have to ask where Mrs Penelope Eardley was now. Tucking into an expensive lunch at the Connaught!

'Ghastly!'

'Just listen, Pen. It's a two-hour special on people who...' she thought quickly '...who were shaped in the fifties.'

'I suppose this was Marcus's idea. I can't think why—'

'...I don't get a decent agent. I know. Someone else said that to me today.'

'Sounds like someone sensible.'

Valerie scratched her chin pensively. 'I don't think you'd think so.'

'Oh God, not one of your young men. Well, he sounds sensible anyway. Marcus is such an old fool. He only keeps that agency going because he has nothing else to do with his days.'

'Could be. But can we leave Marcus out of it? It was proposed by a light entertainment producer.'

'BBC?' asked Penelope. A glimmer of interest.

'LWT.'

'Oh!'

'They do really good stuff, Pen. Weekend viewing, peak time.'

'Didn't they do that not long ago. The fifties?'

'That just scratched the surface. This will be better. More celebrities. Not studio bound and not just entertainers. Writers, artists, designers, playwrights.'

'Really?'

She knew this was her ace in the hole. Penelope fancied herself as a patron of the arts.

'You seem awfully well primed. You're not usually so positive.'

Valerie was silent for a moment. She wasn't at all well primed. She was making it up as she went along, anything to persuade Penelope.

'And where do we fit in?'

'What do you mean, where do we fit in? We were one of the top singing groups. There'll be clips of us in the old days and then interviews with us now. You could talk about all your charities—'

'And Cissie could talk about her dogs and cats, and you, Val, you could talk about your glorious career as an actress.'

'You don't have to be bitchy just because you're paying for lunch.'

'Sorry. But I'm not sure about Harry. He's not keen on publicity.'

'I suppose hob-nobbing with the Waleses and the Kents at charity dos isn't publicity.'

'That's different. How's your beef?'

'Suddenly tough.' She put down her fork. In the face of Penelope's put-down she had lost her appetite for a free lunch.

'I'll have to speak to Harry,' Penelope insisted.

'Oh, c'mon, Pen, when was the last time you consulted Harry about anything? You know he couldn't care less. In fact he's rather chuffed that his wife was an entertainer.' She avoided her sister's stony stare. 'All right, so you want time to think about it and speak to Cissie.'

'That's another thing. Cissie. Maybe she won't be keen to do it.'

'You know perfectly well she'll go along with anything you decide. What are twins for? The point is we have to let them know in two weeks, maximum. And don't think there aren't plenty of fifties stars who'd be glad to fill in if we dropped out.'

'Is that supposed to bother me? I think I'll have a smidge of Brie. What about you?'

'I think I'll slit my throat if you turn this down. If I lose the chance because of you.' She realized that she was almost serious. It did mean that much.

Her sister was studying her keenly. She leaned across the expanse of white tablecloth and patted Valerie's hand. It was a gesture that implied sympathy without actually acknowledging it. 'I'll let you know on Friday at the funeral.' She sounded less abrasive now.

'Pen, it's not really the money. I can always make a living. If only with voiceovers, stuff like that. It's the exposure

I need.' She echoed Marcus Gammie, but outside his office the remark sounded foolish if not downright nonsensical. In Penelope's world exposures were for photographs in the *Tatler*. 'You know what it's like in this profession. If they don't see you every other day on the box they forget you exist. And there's this really juicy part coming up in a series. With Judi Dench.'

'Judi Dench!' repeated Penelope, impressed.

'If I—we—get some coverage in the TV show it might swing it for me. It *will* swing it for me.'

Penelope shook her head sadly. 'It's no life, Val.'

If she didn't know her sister better Valerie would have sworn there was genuine compassion in her voice.

'It's the only life I have. And it's too late to change now.'

'That beastly Gunther! He ruined you.' Penelope blindly believed that a woman's destiny was always dictated by some man or other, oblivious to the fact that she was the last person to be dictated to by any man.

'Save the sympathy, Pen. Any ruining that's been done has been done by me. I had my choices. I just need a little help right now.'

Penelope decided to be gracious. 'Tell

163

Marcus to go ahead. I'm sure I can bring Harry round,' she added, keeping up the fiction that her husband's word was law.

'Great! Great!' her sister repeated as if to convince herself that it wasn't just a tacky enterprise she was proposing that might as easily sink her career as resuscitate it. 'It'll probably be fun, too,' she said hopefully.

'Just so long as they don't expect us to wear bouffant skirts and winkle-pickers.' Penelope lifted a languid hand for the bill. 'I'll speak to Cissie tonight. Meanwhile...' She paused.

Wait for it, thought Valerie. A favour for a favour.

'I think it might be nice for one of us to stay overnight with Emmy before the funeral. Rather than all turn up on the day. It wouldn't look good. You know what they're like in Clifton Coombe. Anything for a little gossip and they've had enough of that from the Mays to last a lifetime.'

'And I'm elected,' Valerie prompted her.

'Well I wouldn't put it quite like that. But you're not working just now. Are you?'

'Unless you call waiting for the phone to ring working,' Valerie admitted.

'Reggie's—well you can't rely on Reggie and Isabel. Cissie's so scatterbrained she'd probably lose her way. Harry's insisted we pick her up for the funeral to make sure she gets there. And Frances is up to her eyes, I imagine. Smart girl, that!'

'And what about you, Pen?'

'My dear. I've a million things to do. Can't possibly put them off. No, Val, you're the logical one.' And that was that. She stood up, looked around the restaurant and waved at an acquaintance, smiling sweetly. 'What does she think she looks like,' she murmured under her breath still smiling. 'You're looking rather good, Val. I remember that Chanel. 1989. Before Thatcher's downfall. It suits you. But you could lose a pound or two before this precious TV show.'

She led the way out of the grill room and into the lobby of the hotel. 'Do you know I can still get into the pale blue taffeta with sequins we wore for the Royal Variety Show,' she threw over her shoulder like a conciliatory bone to a dog.

Valerie picked it up with relish. 'I thought you were far too high and mighty these days for that sort of thing. You mean you actually still *have* that dress? I haven't got mine and I imagine Cissie's torn hers up for dish rags ages ago. Fancy that! Where do you keep it? In a glass case? Or packed up in tissue paper and lavender?' She bit down hard on her lip to suppress a giggle, but failed.

Penelope turned to face her sister. She was not amused. 'I don't see what's so funny.'

'You never do, Pen, you never do.'

'I'd just as soon not appear on this damned show, you know.'

Valerie took the hint. 'You're quite right, Pen. It's not funny at all,' she said, contrite. 'You did promise?'

'Oh, all right. And you promised, too. Emmy,' she reminded her.

'I didn't. But I will,' Valerie conceded.

As she pecked her sister on the cheek and waved her into her taxi, she realized with surprise that she would quite look forward to a spare day at Rushey Green, away from London and the phone that didn't ring and Kev packing up his belongings and looking guilty at leaving her.

More than that, she didn't want Emmy doing anything that might embarrass the family before the funeral. Emmy was a problem. In her quiet way, she was capable of anything.

CHAPTER ELEVEN

'That was your mother,' said Emmy, replacing the receiver with one hand holding out her glass for a refill with the other. 'I gathered you'd prefer me not to make your presence known.' It came out rather grandly and she realized that she was feeling the least bit tipsy. It had been a long and trying day.

'Gawd, no!' Robbie Hesselmann crossed his eyes in mock horror. He lifted the decanter of sherry. 'You sure?'

'Yes. I mean no, I'd better not. I like the feeling but I loathe the hangover.'

'Who doesn't?' He was an ungainly young man in his middle twenties a perpetually worried expression that sat well on his gauntly handsome face, all planes and angles, no padding. More than a few female students fantasized about his life and how much more rewarding it would be for him if they were a part of it, there to share his bed and board and suffering and fears and causes. If he'd been promiscuous this romantic image of a soul in torment in need of care and protection would not have arisen. He'd be just another randy goodfella on the make to be embraced, denied or fought off (a common enough occurrence). But the fact that he seemed so unreachable made him more attractive, even when it carried with it the inevitable suspicion that he was probably gay.

The simple truth was that he preferred to keep his academic and private lives separate. It helped his concentration for matters that really concerned him: the plight of the homeless, students forced to exist on the breadline, anything remotely appertaining to green issues and the cumbersome insensitivity of all kinds of bureaucracy. He was also not very highly sexed, a lack which he convinced himself was due to the off-putting example of his mother and her undiscriminating love life after she'd broken up with his father.

'I saw the protest on television this morning,' said Emmy resigning herself to an evening of sobriety. 'It looked very effective.'

'About as effective as a gnat biting an elephant.'

'Gnat bites can be very irritating. And nothing concentrates the mind of politicians so much as public perception of injustice. Particularly when there are votes in it.'

'You don't really believe the country is run by politicians, do you?' he snorted.

'I'm enough of an old-fashioned liberal to hope so.'

He shook his head and ran his fingers through his unruly hair, releasing a scattering of dandruff. 'You really are living in a dream world, Emmy. It's money that rules the world. Money and secret societies that are responsible to no one. We're all pawns in a vast Masonic society.'

'The Masons?'

'A figure of speech.'

'Well, that's that then. Have you tried a good dandruff shampoo?'

'What?' He brushed a light snowfall from the shoulder of his sweater. 'I've more important things to think about,' he said dismissively.

'You have indeed. So, when's this baby due?' She brought him back to the purpose of his visit.

Reluctantly he abandoned his diatribe against the establishment. He felt easier setting the world to rights than dealing with inconvenient personal matters. 'About seven months, I think. Yes. That's what Deb said. Seven months.'

'She hinted as much when I spoke to her last, but I'd no idea you were involved. Has she told her parents?'

'Reggie! Isabel! Can you imagine their reaction? Their daughter mixed up with Valerie's weirdo son!'

'I don't know. At least it would keep it in the family.' She looked at his stricken face and realized she was being crassly flippant. 'I think you might be surprised at their reaction. That's what I meant to say. They're used to Deb being—well, unorthodox, I suppose you could say.'

'She's not sure she wants to have it,' he said.

'She's leaving it a bit late. I don't think I'd take that too seriously. If she honestly hadn't wanted to have it she'd have had an abortion by now and not even told you. Are you sure she's not leaving it up to you to make a decision?'

'Like what?'

'Marriage, for instance.' What the hell was she doing pontificating about marriage when she'd decided against it herself? For a moment her mind wandered back, asking herself the question that had bothered her for so many years. Had she done the wrong thing?

'What do you think, Emmy?'

She realized he'd posed a question too and she hadn't heard it. 'About what?'

'Our getting married? I want to. She's not sure. Whatever you may think, I'm not vacillating and trying to duck out of my responsibilities. I'd like us to be together, with or without benefit of clergy. It would simplify things.'

'Babies never simplify things, they complicate them. And anyway simplifying *your* life is no basis for any till death us do part commitment.'

'Nobody believes that crap any more, Emmy. It's till one or the other decides they've had enough these days.'

'And hard luck on the poor little blighter they've brought into the world,' she said thoughtfully.

'That's not what *you* thought,' he reminded her. 'You were famous for doing the unconventional thing. A legend in the family.' He chanted the phrase with an operatic flourish.

'Perhaps I was wrong. I haven't been a very good mother.' Maybe it was the two glasses of sherry on a fairly empty stomach, but she felt surprisingly sad as if faced with a wasted life.

'Why did you come to *me*, Robbie?' she said, suddenly.

He shrugged. 'I don't know. I suppose because we always come to you. Me, Gloria before she went overseas, Deb, Martie, when being the cherished only son of the celebrated Eardleys got too much for him. We did, didn't we? You were our rebel without a cause, the May who wasn't like all the other Mays with their clannish worship of the great god show business.'

'Very poetic!' She felt ridiculously flattered and clandestine, like an undercover agent in covert activities for the good of the nation.

'I'm serious, Emmy.'

'You always are, Robbie. That's half your trouble. Why can't you take time off to enjoy what you've got once in a while? Do you love Deb?'

'I think so. No, don't look at me like that, I'm not trying to be evasive. It's just—love, what's love? It's not an exact science. You can't measure or quantify it. What I do know is that I love *being* with Deb. And it's not just sex. Sex hardly comes into it. We think the same things, like to do the same things, care about the same things. We...we fit. Do you understand what I'm talking about?'

She nodded. 'Peas in a pod.'

'Sort of. Sex just happened—as naturally as writing petitions to the MOD and lobbying against the dumping of nuclear waste.'

'That must have been exciting,' she murmured. 'A nourishing roll in the hay after all the petitioning and lobbying.'

He caught the amused look in her eyes and had the grace to laugh. 'I know how I seem to people. Like the guy in *Invasion of the Body Snatchers* running out on the highway yelling, "The pods are coming."

Well, the pods *are* coming and if we're not vigilant they'll get us. And most people are too apathetic to give a damn. That's not me, Emmy. And it's not Deb. We may not win but at least we'll bloody a few noses before we go under. If, when, we have this baby, it's not going to be a vegetable.'

She smiled. 'It'll be what it wants to be, Robbie. If you try to impose your values you'll be no different from your parents. You know,' she prodded, 'the ones you're both so keen to distance yourselves from.'

He brushed aside her little homily on the hazards of bringing up children. 'Will you speak to Deb? She listens to you.'

'If you want,' she said reluctantly. Advising anyone was the last thing she wanted to do just now. But a certain vanity that she recognized in herself compelled her not to refuse him. 'Maybe I'll persuade her to stay after the funeral. You, too, if you like. God knows there are loads of empty spare rooms. Only you must promise to help Terry with the chores. I know what a sloppy lot you academics are. And he gets very edgy when he thinks he's being put upon. Quite rightly,' she added as if to convince herself that Terry's tantrums were always justified, which she didn't believe. He could throw a fit more spectacularly than anyone she knew, with the possible exceptions of Penny and Val in their prime.

She yawned rather pointedly. It *had* been a long day. Much as she admired Mrs Gravely, the sprightly old lady could be wearing, she'd realized when they'd taken tea together—Mrs Gravely's expression—that afternoon.

Robbie unwound himself from the settee mumbling something about an early call tomorrow.

'I hope Deb's given up the motorbike now,' said Emmy. She'd worry about Brad later, she promised herself.

'She's got a Mini.'

'I suppose that's safer. By the way, have you told Val? I'd better know. She's coming down tomorrow. I think she thinks I need to have my hand held or something.'

'I'd rather you didn't. Tell her—about the baby. It'll be time enough when we get things settled, one way or another.' He didn't look too sure that anything would ever be settled.

'Cheer up, Robbie! The world's not such a bad place.'

He stood before her, shoulders hunched and his long, thin hands thrust deep into the pockets of the unseasonal parka he'd just struggled into. He looked, she thought, like a fine, mournful Labrador with an impeccable pedigree and an infinite capacity for sorrow.

'When you come, you and Deb, I'd like you to choose something of Toby's for a keepsake. One of his paintings, perhaps. I believe he did a charming watercolour of Deb when she was little—not at all his usual style. I'll look it out.'

He puckered his lips into a semblance of a smile and nodded several times. 'We'd like that.'

He bent down to kiss her on the cheek. She caught a whiff of lunchtime garlic and tobacco.

'You ought to give it up,' she chided him. 'I should have thought that would have been one of your causes. ASH.'

He frowned, not understanding.

'Action on Smoking and Health,' she elucidated.

'Oh—that!' This time he managed a proper smile. 'On some subjects, you'll be pleased to hear, I'm quite prepared for people to go to damnation any way they please.'

'Why do you think she really wants to come the day before the funeral?' he went on, changing the subject abruptly.

'Val?'

'Of course. You don't seriously think she feels obliged to give you moral support.'

'Help with the ham sandwiches perhaps?' She sighed. 'I don't know. I gather it was an idea cooked up by Penny and her over lunch. I'm sure it's very decently meant.'

He looked at her askance. 'I never know whether you quite believe what you say.'

'You *do* have a poor opinion of your mother, don't you?' She couldn't think why it surprised her. Sooner or later children always rated their parents low in the popularity poll. It had happened to her, but that had passed. First it had been the shock of discovery of deep imperfection in someone she'd regarded as perfect. Gilbert May. Then anger that he had revealed himself as tragically flawed. Then, gradually, pity, acceptance and finally understanding. She wondered if Frances had gone through all those stages over her and thought probably not. Frances seemed to have had her measure in the cradle. By never expecting too much from Emmy she had never been disappointed. Just—distant. Lately she'd begun to realize how badly she'd let Frances down and it made her sad not only for herself but for that great sorority of baffled mothers in a conflict with their offspring they couldn't comprehend.

She came to Valerie's defence with more warmth than she actually felt toward her sister. 'Val's impulsive, unthinking sometimes. But she means well. Whatever you may think she's always cared about you and Gloria. And it hasn't been easy, especially since Gunther left.'

He grinned. A rare, pleasing sight. 'You can save the sob story, Emmy. Let's just say we don't get on and leave it at that.'

'And she's funny,' Emmy persisted. 'It's a virtue, you know.' All the same she couldn't resist voicing the niggle that had been worrying her ever since Valerie had announced that she was coming down to Rushey Green ahead of the others. 'I think maybe she wants to make sure I don't do anything,' she paused, choosing her words 'let's say, untoward—that might embarrass the family.'

'And would you?'

A puckish expression of satisfaction spread over her face. 'I might,' she conceded. 'I just might. In fact I might have already.'

'Good for you.'

When he'd gone she put on a shawl—the night air was becoming increasingly chilly —and picked her way through the dark to Toby's workshop at the bottom of the garden.

The blaze of shocking colour as she opened the rickety wooden door was even more startling than it was in daylight. As she stepped inside it was like entering another world. The interior world of Toby's imagination. The tragedy was he

could never bring himself to talk about it.
Heaven knows, enough people had tried to
unlock the secrets of that frenziedly creative
mind. Analysts, therapists, teachers, her
mother and father—before they'd subsided
into themselves—and she herself.

Maybe Alice Gravely had been wiser
than all of them. 'If he'd let it all out he'd
probably have lost it. There'd have been
nothing left to paint. I'd rather leave one of
these funny old murals to posterity than all
the talk in the world. Talk's cheap. You've
only got to look at all those TV chat shows
and preening politicians to realize just how
cheap.'

Alice had never seen Toby's work
before. To Emmy's shaming recollection
she'd never even visited Rushey Green
before that afternoon. Toby, it seemed,
was making them all—family, friends,
acquaintances—reassess their relationship
with each other. As if he were conducting
a new interpretation of a rigidly familiar
theme from some podium in the sky.

When she had gone to collect Alice as
she'd promised, the old lady had been
sitting bolt upright on a kitchen chair
waiting for her. She was fast asleep,
dressed in readiness in her old Henry
Heath brimmed hat, which could be
battered into any shape she fancied, her
one good Harris tweed coat, worn leather

gloves and sturdy cuban-heeled brogues. A handbag of portmanteau proportions was propped up on the kitchen table beside her, one hand resting on its clasp as a defence against anyone who might want to steal it.

The woman in a flat along the concrete passage, which rimmed the outside of the sixth floor of the bleak, soulless block on the estate, let Emmy in when she received no reply. The lift had worked in fits and starts and during one fit she'd been sharing it with a hefty tattooed teenager with a shaved bullet head, several rings through one ear and muscles the size of Rambo's. She hadn't known whether to be relieved or concerned when he grinned at her.

'Don't live 'ere, d'yer?'

'No.'

'Visitin'?'

She nodded. 'Mrs Gravely.'

'She's a good 'un,' the boy had said, as the lift started functioning again, he'd courteously stood aside for her to leave when it reached the sixth floor.

'Paranoid!' she'd reprimanded herself. Still, mugging did happen all the time. Everyone said so. Whoever 'everyone' was: some wretched invention of a divided society that felt more secure with stereotypes than with individual human beings.

'Are you sure she's expecting you?'

179

the woman had asked, dabbing her hand ineffectually behind her at an inquisitive tot who could have been a boy or a girl and was tugging irritably at her skirt. 'She usually has a nap in the afternoon. We try to keep the kids quiet. She's a nice old lady. Smart—up here,' she tapped a finger on her forehead. 'Knows the law. I wouldn't be one of those smart assess behind the counter at the Social Security when she gets going.'

'I know,' chuckled Emmy. 'She's a very positive lady. I'm taking her out to tea.'

The woman looked dubious. She had a worn but feisty face and an over-ample figure. She was probably no more than twenty-five years of age. 'That'll be nice for her,' she said, without conviction. She peered closer. 'I know you, don't I?'

'Do you?'

'Don't you help out at the Sunny Hill? My sister's a cleaner up there.'

Emmy nodded impatiently, anxious to collect her charge.

'Thought so. Seen your picture in the freebie, too.' She slapped the fractious infant lightly who let out a howl of frustration. 'Stop it, Dirk!' she yelled. 'He can be a right little bugger when he feels like it. I have to keep him in. Not safe to play down there.' She indicated the square of scuffed grass and stunted trees

180

six floors down. 'Wasn't your brother the one who...' She stopped, embarrassed.

'Yes,' said Emmy. 'He—he had an accident at the Adelphi.'

'Terrible. I remember him. Me and my kids used to talk to him when he used to parade around the town all done up like Bruce Forsyth on the telly. Well, you know what I mean. In that gear.'

'You used to talk to him?' Emmy could hardly believe what she was hearing. Toby had never mentioned that he chatted to people in the town when he went on one of his walkabouts in Gilbert's old music hall costume. 'I never realized...he never said. He was always so secretive.'

The woman didn't appear to appreciate that she'd opened another little window on to Toby's very private life. 'Well, that happens, doesn't it? Sometimes it's easier to talk to strangers. He used to tell my other one, Marilyn, about his dad and the theatre and his sisters. He taught her how to twirl a stick.' She thumped her head. 'Cane! Like Fred Astaire. I had to tell her who Fred Astaire was. But she's never forgot how to do it, practises all the time with a bit of old twig or my broom handle. I haven't told her he's dead. She gets upset, not like this one.' She jerked her head at Dirk who was working up a fine sweat whizzing up and down the

181

narrow hall of her flat in imitation of a racing car. 'The more dead bodies on TV the better he likes it. Callous little sod.' But she beamed at the breathless child with maternal affection. Dirk was obviously a source of great pride to her. Perhaps because he *was* a callous little sod. In the harsh, unyielding world she inhabited he'd probably have a happier time than Marilyn who got so upset.

'I'm really sorry about your brother.' She sounded awkward putting a sympathetic sentiment into words.

'That's kind of you,' said Emmy. 'People are very kind,' she added as if it were expected of her.

'Not around here, they're not,' said Dirk's mother grimly. 'I'll get the key. Alice leaves one with me. Just in case, you know.'

'Visitor, Alice,' she called loudly as they entered Alice Gravely's flat.

'She's asleep,' she whispered to Emmy when they went into the kitchen. Then, loudly, 'Been having a little snooze, dear?'

Alice Gravely shook herself awake. 'I haven't been sleeping,' she said tetchily. 'I've just been resting my eyes.'

'I know, dear,' said her neighbour. 'Asleep! I told you,' she mouthed at Emmy.

'You have a nice afternoon.'

'Stupid woman,' grumbled Alice Gravely when she'd gone. 'But her heart's in the right place. Thinks she has to look after me. I can't think why.'

She was still grumbling as they took the lift down to the entrance to the block of flats.

'I've been thinking about your dad,' she said barely changing her tone of voice.

'Really.' Emmy couldn't think of anything else to say. Alice looked up at Emmy, who was guiding her through a maze of rubble on the outskirts of the estate. 'And don't come the old "really!" with me, miss. I've lived a lot longer and I know a lot more. He wasn't a happy man, was he? That's what Alf always said. Not that you could ever tell. But Alf was sure. I should have married Alf, not his brother,' she ruminated, temporarily forgetting that she didn't approve of marriage.

Emmy wondered how the prop man, Alf Gravely, at the Adelphi, who had been so fond of Toby, could have known so much about her father.

When they reached her car she noticed that in her absence someone had swiped the rubbers from the windscreen wipers. 'Damn!' she looked round helplessly and thought she heard a snicker from behind the adjacent brick wall, but decided not to pursue it. 'Let's hope it doesn't rain.'

'Tea and crumpets and cucumber sandwiches. Haven't had that in a long time,' said Alice Gravely complacently as she settled herself in the passenger seat.

And you won't get them today, thought Emmy, remembering Terry's lumpy rock cakes, her own salmon pâté doorstops and Mr Kipling's Bakewell slices that awaited them at Rushey Green.

CHAPTER TWELVE

'I know him. Knew his father too *and* his grandfather. Bunch of layabouts. Not an honest day's work between them.' Mrs Gravely picked up a rock cake and proceeded to inspect it fastidiously through her spectacles.

She had taken an instant dislike to Terry and didn't bother to disguise it, making sure he was within earshot when she pronounced her judgement on him and his forebears.

'Likewise,' he growled, making a protest rather than any perceivable sense.

'All *right*, Terry.' Emmy elbowed him firmly through the sitting-room door. 'She didn't mean it,' she hissed, outside. 'She's old.'

'So what? I'm young.' Although slightly mollified he still sounded aggrieved. 'Never seen the old bitch in my life. I hope she chokes on it.'

She probably will, thought Emmy. She knew Terry's rock cakes of old. She couldn't think why he persisted in knocking up great batches of them when they always went so disastrously wrong, rock being the operative description. But she hadn't the heart to tell him so. It showed willing and that was to be encouraged. His meringues were a poem, but he was choosy about the people for whom he deigned to bake them.

'Someone called when you were out. Didn't leave a name. Didn't sound familiar. Chap,' he said in a take-it-or-leave-it tone.

Emmy frowned. 'I suppose he'll ring back.' Oddly, there hadn't been that many calls since Toby's death. In Clifton Coombe people sent notes, sometimes flowers which they deemed appropriately life-enhancing, like daffodils in spring and roses in summer, the more sombre irises and lilies reserved for the funeral wreaths. Otherwise, in the very English fashion, they kept their distance, fearing that they might be intruding on someone's grief. Intrude, intrude, she silently pleaded. I'm no more a pariah now than I was last week.

'You look done in,' he said, not sympathetically but critically as if she'd brought it on herself. 'Why d'you want to waste time on that old cow?' He didn't expect an answer. 'Mind if my girl spends the night?' He didn't expect an answer to that either. It was just a courtesy reminder to Emmy that he had a private life which he fully intended to live, with or without her permission.

Terry's girl, Lorraine, was bold and brassy and several years older then he. She bossed him around unmercifully, had a surprising fetish about neatness (which suited Emmy admirably) and generally kept him in line when he threatened to break loose.

'Do what you like, Terry,' said Emmy. 'Just don't make things more difficult than they are just now. Please!'

She didn't wait for the apology that she knew would be forthcoming. Terry and she had an unspoken and perhaps not completely understood rapport which transcended any minor irritations. But she sensed a restlessness in him, an urge to be on the move. With Toby gone maybe he felt his usefulness eroded or maybe he was just fed up with being at a middle-aged woman's beck and call—in theory, anyway. She made a mental note to have a word with Lorraine about him tonight.

'I looked something out,' said Alice Gravely as she topped up her tea. There was nothing finicky about her appetite, Emmy noticed thankfully. She'd made short work of the salmon pâté sandwiches, sampled Mr Kipling's Bakewells and was munching on a rock cake. 'Not bad,' she conceded grudgingly. (Perhaps, for once, they weren't, thought Emmy.) She ate like a squirrel, grasping the cake with the fingers of both arthritic hands as she brought it to her mouth and nibbling without pause until it was finished. She'd reluctantly agreed to take off her coat but refused to remove her hat, which had assumed a rather rakish, lopsided angle. She looked much older, much more frail, more vulnerable than she had in Flo's office.

Seeing people out of context cast them in an entirely different light, thought Emmy. Alice no longer seemed the tough, opinionated crusader quite capable of taking on any authority that happened to offend her sense of right and wrong. There was an apprehensiveness in her eyes. Emmy had seen it time and again in the elderly ladies at Sunny Hill, although Alice would have been appalled to be compared with them, the ones who had given up. And when they were most frightened they were most irrational.

'I meant what I said yesterday. About getting a better flat,' said Emmy.

'I'm perfectly all right,' Alice snapped. 'There are too many meddlers in this world.'

'Meaning me?'

'If the cap fits.' She edged back in her chair, her hands in her lap, ankles neatly crossed. The matter of nicer flats was at an end. 'I wouldn't mind another cup of tea.' Emmy drained the pot into her teacup. 'You're a funny one, Emmy May. You always were. That's what Alf said. He was a rare one for understanding people. But he could never work you out, he said.'

'Half the time I can't work myself out,' admitted Emmy. 'I'd forgotten that your brother-in-law worked at the Adelphi until you reminded me. He was always so kind with Toby. No, not just kind. He gave him time. I think that's the most precious thing you can give anyone. Your time.' She thought she'd put it in a nutshell rather well until Alice Gravely contradicted her.

'Or the worst.'

'What do you mean?'

'Well, if you spend that time abusing or harming someone you can hardly call it precious, can you? That's your trouble. You don't organize your mind properly. You talk before you've thought.'

Emmy was shocked. 'You can't be referring to Alf?'

'Well, of *course* I'm not referring to Alf,' said Alice irritably, implying that Emmy was being annoyingly dense. 'But what about the other fellow? He spent a lot of time with you all and caused nothing but grief. At least according to Alf, and he didn't miss much. I got to thinking about it last night. When you're a light sleeper things pop into your mind that you haven't thought about for years.'

Emmy didn't need to be reminded who the other fellow was that Alice was talking about. She could only mean Harvey Persky. She wondered how much else Alf Gravely hadn't missed and how much of it he'd passed on to his sister-in-law.

'It's a long time ago,' she said sounding, she hoped, uncompromising. Harvey Persky was not a subject she felt like discussing with Alice, who always seemed to see a lot more beyond the surface than was comfortable.

Like now. The old woman was looking at her intensely as if bringing her keen intelligence to bear on unravelling an intriguing puzzle.

'I told you I'd looked something out.' Alice heaved up her handbag on to her lap and fiddled with the clasp.

'Let me help,' Emmy offered.

189

'I can manage.' She dabbed away Emmy's willing hand. After a struggle she unlatched the clasp and the copious leather holdall seemed to explode, depositing pension book, diaries, hankies, brochures, maps, sheaves of paper, ball-point pens, tissues, cotton-wool balls, aspirin, Rennies, Earex, Germolene and other assorted medication on to her lap.

'It's here somewhere,' she worried, fumbling through the debris.

'What are you looking for?' Emmy was beginning to be worried, too. Even allowing that everyone likes to take the spotlight now and then Alice was making a production of it.

'Here it is,' she said at last, triumphantly. In fact it had been tucked away neatly into a zipped pocket, the kind of receptacle for something you didn't want to lose, always provided you remembered you'd put it there in the first place. A sheet of cartridge paper carefully folded into four.

Before opening it out she laboriously stuffed her bits and pieces back into the handbag and secured the clasp.

'There,' she handed it to Emmy. 'What do you make of that?'

It was a pencil drawing, faded but the outlines still bold enough to be recognizable. Recognizable, too, as one of Toby's fantasy sketches. The drawing was immature, childlike in its directness. But there was no mistaking the latent talent.

It wasn't the talent, though, that Emmy found arresting this time. It was the subject of the sketch. It was, she assumed, a circus scene: the canvas big top and layered audience smudged in the background. But the foreground was sketched with thick, angry strokes. A trapeze was stretched tautly across the page and a figure in tights was diving from it into the abyss below; only on closer inspection he wasn't diving, he was falling and all the features of the face were contorted into one terrified scream. It was the face of Gilbert May, although it was doubtful whether Alice would have realized that. Poised above him securely on the wire was another figure, throwing back his head and laughing, his hands raised as if they had just pushed the other from the wire. It could have been anyone. But she knew it was Harvey Persky.

It was an unnerving sketch even if you couldn't put names to faces. When you could it was frightening.

'Where did you get this?' she whispered.

'Alf had it. When he died it was among his things. I just put it away, along with a nice little likeness Toby did of him working the lights at the Adelphi.'

She took the sketch out of Emmy's

hand. 'I suppose it must mean something.'

She choked on the words as she suddenly registered the reaction her offering had prompted. Emmy just sat there, numbed and pale, staring at the sketch, seeing in it far more than the surface illustration.

'Stupid! Stupid! I'm a stupid old fool,' the old lady muttered. Tears welled up in her eyes, misting the lenses of her spectacles. 'I didn't think, didn't know it would get you so upset. I just thought it was something clever of Toby's you might like. You wouldn't think I did it on purpose...it's none of my business...' Her voice trailed away.

Emmy didn't answer for a moment. When she roused herself from her contemplation of the gruesome scene Toby had envisaged she saw the distress in Alice Gravely's eyes and felt in some way responsible. How could Alice possibly have known what memories that drawing might conjure up? It was obvious that she hadn't identified Gilbert May and certainly not Harvey Persky in Toby's obscure caricature of a misjudged circus stunt. Perhaps she hadn't even lookd at it properly, merely thinking of it as Toby's along with the likeness of Alf.

She moved over to Alice, knelt on the floor beside her and put her arm around the thin, hunched shoulders.

'I'm really pleased you brought it, Alice, and I'd love to have it. I'm not upset. Promise. It's just—early days after Toby's death. It brought him back. But...' she searched for the right words to console the old woman, 'that's good. It was kind of you to bother. Now, what about a nice glass of sherry? Cheer us both up?'

Alice blew her nose into a spotless lace-bordered hankie. The lace was almost certainly hand-made and her initial was intricately woven in the corner. A relic of her youth, perhaps, carefully washed and preserved over the years, a reminder of times when craft was cherished and not even a humble hankie was considered disposable.

'It's pretty,' said Emmy, fingering the soft lawn fabric.

'My mother gave me two for my tenth birthday,' she said fondly, grateful to Emmy for changing a subject in which she was beginning to feel trapped. She was prepared to be contrite over an error of judgement but it didn't come easily to her. Tears, apologies were admissions of weakness and not showing weakness was the only pride left to her. 'It was during the war. The First World War,' she explained. 'Everything was short. The men were all away at the front or in munitions. There were four of us girls and we needed things you couldn't buy. So mother cut up her wedding dress into shimmies and blouses and these two little hankies for me. The lace and embroidery were all her own too. It was the loveliest present I ever had. Of course I don't use them every day, just—for special occasions.' She looked stern as if to discourage Emmy from thinking there was anything particularly special about being taken out to tea at Rushey Green.

'That was a wonderful thing to do, to cut up her wedding dress.'

Alice nodded. 'Oh it was. Unheard of. When my dad came home from the war—he'd been in the veterinary corps in France—he was furious. Scared the life out of us, he did. You see it was those big boots they had in the army. The littlest ones used to run and hide in the coal cupboard when they heard him coming. You couldn't blame them. There hadn't been a man about the house for years, just us and my mum and aunties. All suffragettes, but they turned patriotic during the war, Emmeline said it was our duty. I was the eldest girl.' She stopped fingering the handkerchief and looked up at Emmy. 'All gone. But me. Two of consumption and one of the flu after the Great War. That's what we called it. The Great War. It was, too. Worse than the last one. At least then we knew what we were fighting for. Not that I did. I was a pacifist.' She chuckled. 'Mr Gravely never forgave me for shaming him like that. He'd have walked over hot coals for Winston Churchill. Damn near did, too. It was an inferno, they said, that pub in Portsmouth they bombed. Where he died.' She seemed happy ruminating and Emmy realized that there couldn't be many people she could ruminate with, who had time to listen to an old woman's memories.

Then, abruptly, she stuffed the handkerchief in her cardigan pocket as if cross with it for encouraging her to reminisce.

'Didn't you say something about a glass of sherry,' she asked brusquely. 'I may be old but I'm not teetotal.'

'I suppose you must have been named after Emmeline Parkhurst,' she said, as she sipped her sherry.

'I've no idea,' Emmy replied, finding it hard to keep up with Alice's straying thoughts.

'Nice drop of sherry,' said Alice approvingly. Her eyes kept returning to Toby's sketch on the table between them. 'Odd. What must have gone on in that little lad's mind?' Emmy suspected she always regarded Toby as a little lad even when he'd reached adulthood. 'Not my kind of art. Give me a pretty Pre-Raphaelite any day. Very liberated, the Pre-Raphaelites,

195

you know. But I know something clever when I see it.'

'You're right,' said Emmy. 'Toby was a very gifted artist.'

Then Emmy had shown her Toby's hideaway and his murals and they'd talked about his unfathomable talent quite calmly and objectively until it was time for Alice to leave. 'Never miss *Eastenders*,' she said, pulling on her coat and adjusting her hat. She caught the flicker of a smile on Emmy's face. 'Don't laugh!' she reprimanded her. 'It's very instructive.' She couldn't be persuaded to watch *Eastenders* on Emmy's TV. 'I suppose it's all right for you to drive,' she said, suddenly alarmed.

'I don't think a small sherry will put me over the limit,' Emmy assured her.

'I suppose you'd know,' said Alice sounding as if she doubted it. She held out her hand politely. 'Thank you for having me,' she said like the little girl whose best birthday present had been two initialled handkerchiefs cut out of her mother's wedding dress.

Terry was nowhere in sight as they walked to Emmy's car. Probably sulking, she thought. The sky looked threatening and Emmy hoped the rain would hold off until she'd delivered Alice safely to that miserable little flat in the high-rise block. It was a bit late in the day to start worrying about her living there among the vandals and layabouts and the damp, grimy columns of concrete. She should have cared a lot sooner. Anyway, to Alice Gravely it was home. What right had anyone to convince her it was a prison, and a potentially dangerous one at that.

She was mentally reminding herself to get the windscreen fixed the next day when a rakish Mercedes sports car drove through the gates, circled the drive and pulled up behind her hatchback.

'Why didn't you let me know?' It was the first thing that leapt to mind and it was out before she could think of something more welcoming, or at least well-mannered, to say. But she hadn't expected him and she always felt flustered when she met him after a stretch of absence. Not that it had been that long, but what she'd learned about him in the interim from Frances made it seem an eternity.

'I did try,' said Brad Hastings, unwinding himself from the deep-slung driving seat. 'But your young man didn't seem to want to take a message.'

She smiled. My young man! Terry. Terry who at this very moment was probably screwing the imperious Lorraine in the bedroom he occupied over the garage.

'I must admit I didn't insist,' he

admitted. 'I wasn't sure you'd want me to come down before the funeral. Maybe not even come to the funeral...'

'Brad! Of course I wanted you to come to Toby's funeral. You and he were friends. And...oh God!' It was too much, too much. She waved her hand around in indeterminate directions as if trying to find something solid to hang on to.

He looked so drawn, thinner than when she'd last seen him and somehow ridiculously miscast as the owner of a nippy sports car.

'Brad I'm so pleased to see you,' she said breathlessly, knowing that she meant it sincerely although he had taken her unawares.

'I'm glad.' He took her hand, turned it palm upward and bent to kiss it as he always did: a meaningless, flamboyant gesture that made her feel vaguely uncomfortable. Then, abruptly, he pulled back.

'Brad. I know,' she said softly, touching his cheek.

'How much longer?' Alice Gravely had poked her head out of the passenger window of the hatchback. Routine was important and missing the opening credits and theme tune of *Eastenders* would put her out of sorts for the rest of the evening.

Emmy pulled a face at Brad. 'She has to be back for *Eastenders*. You'll stay?'

He shook his head and she didn't try to dissuade him. She mistrusted spontaneity in herself and needed time to think through her response to him and the desperate future he was facing. Besides, she was expecting her nephew Robbie that evening.

'I've booked in at the Metropole in Brighton. I'm visiting an old chum. You'll remember him—Barney Oates, from the Adelphi days.'

Emmy nodded, summoning up the image of a jaunty young black man with a spine-tingling baritone voice singing 'Ole Man River' in *Show Boat*.

'He's poorly. Not too much they can do for him, I'm afraid,' said Brad. He didn't elaborate.

'I'm sorry. I didn't know.' It was a stupid thing to say. She hadn't known since Barney Oates had left Clifton Coombe to join the cast of a West End revue that transferred to Broadway. She did remember that he was glad to leave. In those days Clifton Coombe flattered itself on its tolerance without feeling the need to put it seriously to the test by welcoming its token black wholeheartedly in the community.

'Yes, well, people don't on the whole. Barney's one of the disappeared.'

She knew he hadn't meant it as a criticism of her. After all, she hadn't seen or heard Barney Oates for years. But it came out sadly as a reproach.

'You'll come back tomorrow morning,' she urged him.

'Sure.' He smiled. Still the charmingly lopsided smile of a movie heart-throb as indelible and probably as durable as that of the Cheshire Cat.

They heard Alice grumbling to herself. 'I could walk quicker.'

He jerked his head in Alice's direction. 'Cantankerous old bird!'

'Sometimes.'

She was grateful that Alice was silent on the drive back to her flat. Emmy suspected that she was nodding off and wondered how much of *Eastenders* she actually saw each night to justify her faithful viewing.

She thought of Brad and Barney Oates and how nothing seemed to work out the way you anticipated. She remembered telling her sisters when she was twelve years old that if she weren't rich and married with four children by the time she was forty she'd slit her throat. She liked to shock, as compensation perhaps for not being able to get up and sing and dance, and her sisters were duly shocked. But she'd half meant it, too. That was a laugh: a great, big, whopping laugh.

'What are you cackling about?' Alice Gravely was eyeing her suspiciously.

'Nothing,' said Emmy. 'Nothing at all.' Just my life.

CHAPTER THIRTEEN
CHRISTMAS MORNING 1957

'It's lovely, Brad.'

She held the pretty mother-of-pearl pendant up to the light for them all to see and marvel over. Pretty! It wasn't at all, she thought irritably. She'd wear it only today to please him, to please the family.

It was a rule on Christmas Day at Rushey Green that no one was ever grouchy, no matter if presents did fall short of expectations, or the turkey was underdone and the pudding yielded no sixpences or the crackers were all tissue-paper and no charms or mottoes.

It had to be happy time—or else. You had to save your bile for Boxing Day. Christmas was one of the few days when you didn't have to worry about a show or a rehearsal at the Adelphi and all the family and friends could be happy together. Happy!

Reggie's girl Isabel had helped Madge

with the tree and, though there was still a shortage of lights and tinsel and trinkets in the shops, Gilbert always knew a man who knew a man who would produce cartons of them for the May decorations. Late the previous night, after the Christmas Eve show, Madge had rearranged all Isabel's handiwork on the tree. 'That girl's useless,' she'd told Gilbert, meaning useless for Reggie who was at least worthy of Janette Scott or Natalie Wood.

But that was last night. Today was Christmas Day. Happy, happy! She'd even kissed Isabel on the cheek that morning and told her she looked a younger Gertie Lawrence, which she didn't at all. But they all knew Madge's idol had been Gertrude Lawrence so it was a rare if insincere compliment in keeping with the spirit of the day.

'Brad, you shouldn't have,' said Emmy knowing what Gilbert paid him, just barely the Equity minimum, and how hard it was for him to keep up with the rent on his bed-sit over the pet shop in town. It was another way of saying thank you without quite saying thank you.

Gilbert had prepared the punch as he always did and even Toby was allowed a glass. He was happy, surrounded by the sketchpads and paintboxes and art books they all gave him at Christmas, and Reggie was especially in favour for presenting him with an easel and an assortment of oils with which to experiment.

'Where's Oliver?' said Val, mindful that she mustn't sound sulky and feeling it all the same. Oliver was her property. He always had been, whatever Penny and Cissie might think. And he wasn't here yet to share in the experience of being very, very happy.

'It's only eleven,' said Emmy, thinking she'd never seen anyone look as carelessly gorgeous as her sister who was draped over an armchair in the gauzy housecoat she'd deliberately worn in honour of Oliver, despite her mother's protestations that she should put on something more seemly. 'Poor Ollie, he's not even allowed to be two minutes late,' Emmy goaded her, cross that her sister looked the way she did.

'Don't let him catch you calling him Ollie,' Cissie reprimanded her primly. Cissie was a stickler for manners, which was probably why she couldn't throw herself as wholeheartedly into their singing act as the others. It went against the grain making goo-goo eyes and goo-goo sounds into a microphone. But she couldn't remember when it hadn't been taken for granted that she'd back up her sisters as the third member of the Mayflowers. She'd have been far more contented being a vet or a stable girl and she was vaguely ashamed that her father had started his career in a circus with dancing elephants and caged lions. But she wouldn't think about that today. Happy day!

A long-play Frank Sinatra was serenading swinging lovers on the record player in the background and Emmy noticed that Gilbert was slumped in his chair in the corner taking no part in anything. Not happy at all.

'Hi, everyone!'

It was a greeting and a command. They all looked up from what they were doing. You didn't ignore Harvey Persky.

Emmy observed the fleeting expression on their faces, not quite sure what her own betrayed. Her feelings about him had become confusingly mixed over the past week that he had been staying with them—taken up residence would have been more appropriate, for he had settled in as comfortably as if this were his home.

'Hi!' said Val, looking bright and flirtatious. In lieu of Oliver she wasn't choosy on whom she tested her charms. Even Harvey Persky would do. Particularly Harvey Persky, Emmy suspected.

Neither Cissie nor Penny returned his greeting but it was clear how they regarded him: Cissie disapproving, Penny mildly amused at his presumption—she liked his jokes even if he were common. Reggie and Isabel, preoccupied with each other, seemed rather embarrassed at his arrival as if he'd caught them out in some reprehensible act.

Brad waved in a good-natured if slightly perplexed manner. He couldn't understand why this Persky guy had been welcomed into the May home and certainly no one had attempted to enlighten him, but he reasoned it was none of his business and, coming from an authoritarian, uptight Scots-Canadian family, he rather enjoyed the unpredictability of the Mays. He resolutely set aside his serious objection to Harvey Persky: his obvious interest in Emmy, whom Brad had considered his girl.

'Did you enjoy the service?' Madge looked worried as if trying to sort out her own ambivalent feelings. If Gilbert wanted him around that was good enough for her, but it didn't make his presence any easier to accommodate. 'We should have gone.' She sounded even more worried. 'We don't usually miss the Christmas service.'

Harvey didn't seem the kind of man much given to religious observance. But just as he had insinuated himself into the May home so he was infiltrating the life of the predominantly Anglican Clifton Coombe society with ingratiating determination. In the past week he'd become sleeker, better groomed, the purple suit discarded in favour of tweeds and pin-stripes.

Gilbert stared stonily, silently, into the middle distance, somewhere above Harvey's head, not registering any emotion.

'You seem out of sorts, old chap.' Harvey, Emmy noticed, was adopting outmoded British expressions as enthusiastically as everything else; his Brooklyn accent made them sound doubly quaint.

Perhaps it was the ridiculous 'old chap' that did it. 'Who's out of sorts? Not me. It's Christmas, everybody.' Gilbert snapped out of his stupor as if suddenly remembering it was incumbent on him to be the life and soul of any party.

He jumped up like a jack-in-the-box, all uncoiled energy, dragged Madge to her feet and swung her to the centre of the room, leading her into a foxtrot with endlessly tricky variations of his own invention. She followed him as naturally and easily as she had done since they'd first teamed up as a professional act. 'You make me feel so young,' bellowed Gilbert in Madge's ear.

His mood was infectious. It always was. A heavy, threatening cloud seemed to have lifted.

'You make me feel so young,' Penny, Cissie and Val harmonized with Sinatra, underscoring the beat of the arrangement and adding a flourish or two of their own.

Then it was Reggie and Isabel's turn, rocking and rolling to the tune and shrieking with laughter as they avoided colliding with Gilbert and Madge.

'Emmy?' She looked up at Brad. He was offering her his hand. Only Brad would be so proper on an occasion like this. She wished she didn't find that so annoying. Why couldn't he be beastly to her, the way Oliver was often beastly to Val? Then, at least, he'd be a challenge.

'You know I don't dance, Brad.' Give me an argument, she thought, but she knew he wouldn't. He'd just look crestfallen and she'd feel guilty.

'That's crazy! Everyone can dance.' Almost before she'd realized what was happening Harvey had pushed Brad aside and lifted her off her feet.

'Put me down!' she hissed, pounding his shoulders with her fists. But the others were laughing and she felt stupid protesting.

He set her down gently. 'Just follow me. It's easy,' he whispered in her ear, taking her hand and sliding his arm round her. He was barely half a head taller than her but he gave the impression of being immense and powerful.

At first she felt awkward stumbling over

her feet, but gradually she allowed herself to be guided by him. 'Relax,' he kept murmuring, 'it's easy.' The voice that had sounded so grating before seemed to purr rhythmically in time with the music, soft, seductive, Sinatra-ish. He was very light on his feet, almost as adept as her father.

'You're doing fine, just fine. We'll make a Ginger out of you yet.' He continued murmuring encouragement, persuading her she could do it. She knew it was all an illusion. She couldn't dance. She couldn't master the steps of formal routines and she hadn't the extrovert zeal required to improvise in the modern rock 'n' roll style. But for a few minutes Harvey Persky made her suspend her disbelief. She felt his arm tighten around her and didn't mind. As the Sinatra track finished, he pointed his finger up towards the light fixture to which a sprig of mistletoe was attached. He bent forward and seemed about to kiss her full on the lips then changed his mind and pecked her cheek.

She put up her hand as if to brush away the uncomfortable burning sensation of the kiss, which was barely a kiss at all. As she did so she became aware that they had all stopped singing and dancing and at first was convinced that she and Harvey were the centre of their attention. Impossible to think otherwise; the feeling she had experienced in Harvey Persky's arms—a mixture of pleasure and disgust—must surely have affected everyone else. But only Brad was looking numbly in their direction. And Toby, his mouth open and his eyes wide with distress as if he'd been witnessing a calamity. Which perhaps he had.

She felt foolish and tongue-tied and was grateful to be saved by the bell.

'It's Oliver,' said Val, hurrying to the front door. Her mother, flushed and cheerful, remembered she must baste the turkey but not before her husband had claimed a kiss under that damned mistletoe—hanging from the ceiling, so innocent and dangerous, thought Emmy. 'Gilbert!' Madge demurred but not very forcefully. She had suffered his morose preoccupation since the arrival of Harvey Persky and was glad for any little lightening of his mood.

'Oliver! Crawford! Happy Christmas! Glad you could come. What can I get you to drink?' The cheerful chatter of hospitality sounded to Emmy's ears oddly hollow.

Oliver's father Crawford was a portly man with a pinched mind to match his pinched face. But he was, Gilbert always insisted, the best brain in Clifton Coombe when it came to legal and financial matters:

a reputation that might have had something to do with the fact that he was a Mason and played a lot of golf with town councillors and others high in the pecking order of the town. He gave a constant impression of faint disapproval, not necessarily of Gilbert May, but of all his clients.

His son, on the other hand, was an outgoing young man who had inherited his father's professional acumen but none of his personal unlikeability. His looks were so darkly heroic that one might have taken him for the actor rather than Reggie, who was sturdily built with sandy-coloured hair and plain, square features that lacked the refinement of a sensitive soul. None of the May girls were unaffected by him, but only Val took his charm seriously; which was perhaps poetic justice, for too many young men took her charm seriously to no avail.

It was surprising that Crawford Ballantyne should have deigned to turn up to the Mays for Christmas drinks. His relationship with Gilbert was strictly business, yet today it was obvious that Gilbert expected him. 'I hear the show is going well,' said Crawford with an air of self-satisfaction. It was understood that he was referring not to any appreciation of the pantomime Gilbert had produced but to a very real appreciation of its box office receipts.

'Whisky,' he said, nodding at Harvey Persky as if he knew or at least knew of him.

He appeared to have forgotten his son who was standing awkwardly in the hall, his hand cupping the elbow of a girl in jodhpurs with a mane of flaming red hair and a strong, angular face that could be charitably described as horsy. Her ruddy, unprotected complexion threatened to look leathery with the passing of many more years on horseback exposed to merciless British weather.

Val was looking hard at the girl, unsure how to react. It was an unusual position in which to find herself. She sensed rejection and she felt affronted.

'I've brought Pamela,' said Oliver, as if they might not have noticed.

Val continued to stare at her, silently. It was Reggie who retrieved the situation, glaring at Val as he did so. He liked Oliver and often felt Val went way over the top. That was all right on stage: in private it could be downright embarrassing.

He warmly welcomed the girl, who didn't appear to be aware that she had created a scene, offered her some punch and introduced her to anyone she didn't know. Harvey was mesmerised, convinced that he had met a real English aristocrat; surely only an aristocrat would wear jodhpurs when she wasn't riding out.

Pamela Finch was not an aristocrat, but people did tend to regard her as such. She was the daughter of an old friend of Crawford's who had made a great deal of money after the war by smartly switching his factory from the manufacture of military aircraft parts to consumer goods, and it was generally accepted, although not acknowledged by Val, that she was the elder Ballantyne's preferred choice of bride for his son.

She was a pleasant enough girl who treated human beings much as she treated animals, which endeared her to Cissy. She was forthright, practical, totally lacking in imagination or, Val suspected, a sense of humour. When she'd first encountered the Mays she'd had to have jokes explained to her; since then she'd just laughed uncomprehendingly with everyone else, as she found the explanations more difficult to understand than the jokes themselves. The Mays baffled her: she couldn't conceive how anyone could be so serious about so trivial a profession as the theatre. But she kept her opinions to herself.

It had seemed that Pamela was a burden Oliver was forced to bear in order to keep in with his father whose lucrative business he was determined to inherit when Crawford's dicky heart did the decent thing and dispatched him to the hereafter. It was unimaginable that he should actually like the girl. Today, Christmas Day, he seemed unduly apologetic about bringing her as if he were trying to hide something he knew eventually he would have to divulge. His father, sublimely insensitive to atmosphere, saved him the trouble.

'Well, aren't you going to tell them, Oliver?'

'Not now, dad,' Oliver said irritably. He didn't want it to be thought that he was dictated to by his father even if, for expediency's sake, he frequently was. 'You're looking lovely, Val,' he said. The compliment, though probably meant, rang false. It was worse than if he'd ignored her, more like a pat on the head for trying.

She pulled the decadent housecoat that revealed too much tightly around her, wishing she'd taken her mother's advice. It was hard to compete with Pamela's jodhpurs which looked somehow appropriate and horribly healthy.

'Tell us what, Ollie?' she said in a steely voice, salvaging her dignity. She emphasized the 'Ollie' which she knew he hated. But she had a feeling that the question was irrelevant. She didn't need to be told.

'Can't you guess? He's engaged!' Reggie sounded triumphant. He enjoyed scoring points off Val, especially as Oliver had told him the night before in the pub and sworn him to secrecy.

There was a moment's stillness in the room as if in mourning for Val, like the two minutes' silence for the war dead on Remembrance Day, followed by the usual shrieks and cries of manufactured joy, the exclamations of pleasure, for the happy couple.

The future bride stood there vaguely bemused by all the attention which she supposed was intended for Oliver. His proposal had neither surprised nor particularly excited her but, on reflection, she'd decided she'd quite like to be married to Oliver and, as both her parents and his had impressed on them, the match would be very suitable. If she'd thought about it she might have questioned the idea of a union based on suitability rather than love in this day and age, but she wasn't a girl given to deep thoughts. She'd have to get married some time and Oliver seemed a better bet than most of the men she met. The fact that he obviously wasn't all that passionate about her didn't concern her much for it suggested that his demands would be minimal, leaving her lots of time for her horses and the hunt and the riding school her father had promised her as a wedding present.

During all this congratulation from the swarming Mays, who tossed extravagant delight around like misguided ping-pong balls, Oliver held her hand, engagement finger with its diamond and sapphire ring in full view.

'This calls for a celebration. Champagne!' With Gilbert it was any excuse for celebratory champagne and this was a more valid excuse than most. 'Get Aggie...' He turned to his wife.

'Aggie's visiting her sister in Barnet. We gave her Christmas off. Remember?' Madge sounded fractious. Housework she could tolerate, but cooking—Aggie's principal function—weighed heavily.

'Then I'll get it myself,' he barked back, unlike himself.

'I think it's wonderful, just wonderful!' The voice commanded another silence. It was Val. ('Practising to project to the gallery,' Penny hissed to Cissie, who enjoyed the joke but not the malice behind it.)

'Congratulations Oliver. Congratulations Pam. I know you'll be deliriously happy. And, Pam, I hope we're going to be great friends.' In the minutes since the announcement Val had decided to be not only a good sport but the best sport imaginable and terribly, terribly gracious with it.

She approached Pamela, who flinched slightly, and flung her arms around her. She noted with satisfaction the terror in Pamela's eyes at such an unseemly display of insincere affection.

'Oliver!' She held out her arms and he did what was expected of him, allowing himself to be embraced in a sisterly way. 'What are you playing at?' he muttered in her ear.

'Playing at? *Playing* at, Oliver?' she repeated very loudly. 'What *can* you mean. I'm just so very, very overjoyed for you.'

He stood looking flushed and silly. She really knew how to put the boot in, he thought. What amazed him was that she should ever have taken anything for granted. He'd never given her any reason to suppose that theirs had been anything but a casual and mutually agreeable affair and not a lot of that either.

'I must go and help mother—in the kitchen,' she said archly, ensuring herself a fetching exit.

Once in the kitchen she stabbed the carving knife into the side of the wooden welsh dresser and burst into tears. Madge watched her calmly. She was used to her eldest daughter's tantrums. If it hadn't been Oliver it would have been something else.

'Well, since you're here, you can help with the brussels.'

'Bugger the brussels!'

'Don't use that language with me, save it for your friends in the pop business. And when you've finished the brussels, you can wash your face, get into something decent and take in the champagne.'

'Bugger the champagne!'

'Suit yourself.'

Emmy poked her head round the door. 'Come on, you two. Get off, Toby!' The boy was behind her, his arms wrapped around her waist. He was giggling hysterically.

'All this excitement,' sighed Madge. 'It's not good for him. And it's not good for you, my girl, either.'

'Me?' said Emmy, acting bewildered although she had a shrewd idea what her mother might mean. Madge didn't miss much.

'You, young lady. I suppose that's half the trouble. It's young lady, now, not my girl.' She pointed the basting ladle at Emmy, dripping fat on the kitchen table. 'You may be grown up for your age. But you're seventeen. Think about that. I just don't want you—making a mistake.'

'Brad?' Val snorted. Having vented her anger she felt able to take an interest in

217

something other than Oliver's approaching nuptials.

'No, not Brad,' Madge retorted. 'Emmy knows very well what I mean.'

Emmy blushed. She did, too, know very well.

CHAPTER FOURTEEN
CHRISTMAS AFTERNOON 1957

'Well, *I* like her,' said Cissie firmly.

'You like anyone who knows one end of a horse from the other,' Penny goaded her.

It was a source of some surprise to almost everyone that they were twins. Twins were supposed to be identical and Penny and Cissie were identical in nothing but their birthdate. They didn't even look alike now. Penny was rather regal and queenly. Even when she was harmonizing with her sisters she always gave the impression of being a little too lofty to be a member of a singing trio. She'd inherited the Mays' striking looks while seeming to keep them in reserve for higher things, not flashing them around showily like Val. Cissie was pretty and birdlike, with a rather distant air. She played her part as a Mayflower with equable good humour not because she enjoyed it that much but because she knew she didn't intend to pursue it for long. And whatever the twins' reservations about what Gilbert insisted was their 'career' there was no denying that they had the May touch, the ability to reach out to an audience—in their case hordes of squealing teenagers.

When interviewed by *Picturegoer* or *Melody Maker* or *Woman* they always dutifully attributed their success in the charts to luck. It showed the right degree of modesty, and readers liked modesty in celebrities: it made that celebrity seem within reach of anyone with ambition. But the Mays knew that luck—like Mae West's goodness—had very little to do with it. They worked hard under Marcus Gammie and Gilbert's guidance, perfected their style, picked up the right songs for the time and watched their weight. 'Weight's everything,' Jessie Matthews, who was putting on a little at the time, lectured them once when she'd visited Rushey Green one memorable Sunday,

'I think she's nice, Pamela.' Brad volunteered, unasked. It was always his instinct to champion the underdog and Pamela Finch appeared currently to fit that role.

The day was not panning out as he'd expected. He was looking forward to spending some time with Emmy but she seemed to be all over the place. He couldn't think that she was avoiding him, not after the night before the opening of the pantomime. The dress rehearsal had gone so well and Gilbert had broken open the champagne. 'A little previous,' Madge had sniffed, but he'd insisted, just to give a lift to the company before the big day.

Brad, who wasn't a drinker, had had a glass too much and Emmy in her quiet, challenging way had looked so warm and nice. Not radiant like her sisters or Reggie's Isabel. But somehow approachable as she hadn't before.

At twenty he had had little experience of girls—a legacy of his sheltered Canadian upbringing—and he'd kept reminding himself that Emmy was barely more than a child and, more important, the daughter of his current employer. He'd learned that much in his brief association with show business: don't mess with the boss's daughter. It wasn't as if there weren't plenty of other inviting fish in the sea swimming around him enticingly: chorus girls, teenagers from the town who hung around the stage door for a glimpse of him, and even some of their mothers who had indicated clearly enough that their sexual favours might be available. On the whole the latter might have been a safer bet, older married women having the overriding quality of discretion.

But on that night he found himself looking at Emmy with new eyes. They'd been good friends since Gilbert had first invited him to join the company and the Mays had encouraged that. 'A nice, clean-cut boy,' Madge had said approvingly. Added to that he was good with Toby, which couldn't be said for some of her family.

Emmy had been the sister he'd never had and hadn't particularly missed. He'd rather enjoyed being an only child until he'd had to face up to telling his parents he was leaving home. But they'd taken it rather well which disconcerted him a little; he'd been braced for tears and protests.

He'd walked Emmy home that night. She hadn't resisted although she knew it was a mile and half out of town and he'd have to get back somehow. But in the event he hadn't had to get back until the early morning. They had kissed and cuddled in a companionable way during the walk until they'd arrived at the gate of Rushey Green. It was one of those crisp winter nights with stars twinkling away in the black sky and a full moon casting a glamorous, unearthly glow over trees and houses and faces nipped with cold.

To Emmy it had been like the extravagant backdrop for a love scene in a romantic film that everyone enjoys at the time and makes much of in retrospect.

Although she was a virgin she didn't rate her virginity very highly. In fact she didn't much think about it and she had been perfectly satisfied with her mother's sketchy outline of the facts of life, heavily populated by birds and bees. Val had been more explicit but as her account was coloured by her own slightly bizarre experiences she didn't give much credence to her sister's information.

But she knew enough to realize that Brad's kisses were no longer merely friendly and the thrusting bulge under his trousers that was pressing between her legs wasn't a wallet or a fountain pen. Equally she felt a sudden sense of arousal, as if her nerve ends were on fire and a moist throbbing in her vagina, like waking up suddenly after dreaming about Paul Newman, which she did quite often. It had seemed perfectly appropriate that they should sneak into her room through the side window and satisfy each other's needs on her chaste single bed. Although they could hardly call it satisfaction. But they'd 'done it' and, neither being very expert, they convinced themselves and each other that it was the most ecstatic experience imaginable. Emmy assured him that it hadn't hurt. Well, not much. Brad slipped out at four by the same window.

She had wondered whether she should talk to Val about it; Val being the least likely to lecture her on the hazards, quite apart from the morality, of going 'all the way'. She had had that lecture before from her mother when Madge had caught her and Brad fooling around—as it happened, quite innocently—in Emmy's bedroom some weeks before. This time there would have been some justification for it.

After a few days the memory of that fumbling night had receded and didn't seem important any more. And there had been the excitement of opening night and Harvey Persky's arrival and the restless feeling she couldn't shake that nothing would be the same again for the Mays.

But *she* was the same Emmy, just minus her virginity and that didn't show. Besides, if that was what losing your virginity was all about it hardly seemed worth the hullabaloo. Maybe Brad wasn't much good at it. But she did feel a little contrite about him. He seemed to be taking it all much more seriously, more perhaps from a sense of guilt than from any wild desire to repeat the experiment. When he sobered up the next morning he had to admit that, where

Emmy was concerned, he'd rather keep a friend and confidante than gain a lover.

All the same, Emmy knew she was treating him badly: barely thanking him for his present, refusing to dance with him, then letting Harvey whirl her off. She brooded on this for a bit while the others discussed the luckless Pamela Finch over more pre-lunch punch. The Ballantyne's and Pamela had left promptly at one. Oliver's meek compliance with his father's wishes lent credence to Reggie's conviction that he'd had the riot act read to him in no uncertain terms. Which, in Emmy's eyes at least, didn't cast Oliver in a very attractive light. She had a mental image of Harvey Persky's reaction to having the riot act read to him. Why, she couldn't think.

It has been a strange, unsatisfactory visit lacking much genuine festive jollity, and Emmy felt the announcement of Oliver's engagement had not been its principal purpose, more a kind of smokescreen. Gilbert, Crawford and Harvey had disappeared into the conservatory for quite a while; she doubted whether it was simply to escape from all the idle wedding talk.

'She's a bore,' said Penny. That seemed the general consensus. Val didn't speak but everyone knew her opinion on the matter of Pamela anyway. She had changed into an off-the-shoulder dirndl blouse, tight black toreador pants, slingbacked low-heeled pumps and looked very fetching. She also wore an eye-catching gold anklet which she had hinted was a secret present from Frankie Vaughan: a far more intriguing provenance than the truth that she had bought it herself in Bourne and Hollingsworth's jewellery department.

'She's very county,' said Madge vaguely. 'What do you think, Isabel?' It was one of the few times Isabel's opinion had been solicited in the May household. Mindful of their muted reaction to her, she wasn't sure whether to take Pamela's part or side with her future-in-laws. She opted for a diplomatic neutrality.

'Well—I hardly know her.' Which appeared to put an end to the discussion. In any case it was time to get Christmas lunch on the table and eaten in time to watch the Queen on television.

Gilbert, although he hadn't been born in Britain, was intensely patriotic. Deploring the unseemly scramble for the exit at the Adelphi before the national anthem he insisted it should be played before as well as after the performance, so that the monarch should get her affirmation of loyalty one way or the other.

'The Queen!' He raised his glass. 'God bless her!' He affected not to hear the giggles of his less than reverent family.

'God bless her!' echoed Harvey standing to attention, which surprised everyone although he said it with a perfectly straight face.

After that they sat around, full of too much food and drink, too idle to do anything strenuous like washing up and conserving their energies for the invasion of guests who popped in for Gilbert's traditional Christmas evening party.

Toby, half asleep, nestled close to Emmy on the floor by the fire. She felt pleasantly somnolent herself. Sooner or later she and her sisters would have to stir themselves to clear up the debris before the party, what with the indispensable Aggie visiting her sister in Barnet. But not yet. She closed her eyes and nodded off for a few minutes. When she came to Harvey and her father were swapping stories, entertaining the others. At least Harvey was doing most of the entertaining, prompting the occasional response from Gilbert, whose voice sounded strained and somehow unwilling.

But Harvey was in his element. He was doing what he was good at: being funny and ingratiating and feeding off the approval of an audience. But with Harvey that was not an end in itself as it was with the Mays. It was a means. But to *what* end? Emmy wondered. She was laughing like her sisters and Reggie at the tales of his and Gilbert's circus days. But why did she have the feeling that it would all end in tears?

'You don't mean there were *actually* bearded ladies?' Oliver temporarily forgotten, Val was flirting shamelessly with Harvey, rotating her ankle so that the chain glittered in the light from the log fire.

'Too right there were. Took quite a shine to your old man. Gertie! Remember grisly Gertie, Gilbert?'

'No,' said Gilbert suddenly. 'No, I don't. It's too long ago.'

Harvey took out a cigar, lit it carefully and rolled it sensuously round his pursed lips. He seemed to be measuring time to allow Gilbert's churlish refusal to play the memory game to create an uncomfortable silence.

'You're right, old pal,' he said at last. 'It's a long time ago.'

They all breathed more easily, grateful to Harvey for magnanimously relieving the tension. It was as if, thought Emmy, he were deliberately trying to drive a wedge between Gilbert and the May siblings who couldn't understand why their father of all people should spoil the fun. He was a manipulator and she loathed him for that, but she was no less responsive to

227

his manipulation than anyone else and it bothered her.

He stood up and patted his stomach, a pointless gesture for he always gave the impression of being lean and primed for action. 'That was some meal! Never tasted turkey like that even on Thanksgiving. How's about a walk? Emmy? Stretch your legs?'

Why me? she wondered. Why not Val? She looked to her father for a sign, any sign, of support. But Gilbert was punishing the logs in the fireplace, pummelling them viciously with a poker, the sparks flying dangerously on to the tiled surround.

The others appeared too indolent to care. It hardly seemed like Rushey Green on Christmas Day at all. It had always been a bustling, easygoing, somewhat chaotic household, full of chat, argument, showing off and mild misbehaviour, strictly within bounds: a Piccadilly Circus of people passing through or, more usually, staying into the early hours, the piano never silent.

But today there was an unaccustomed chill in the air, a listlessness, that permeated from Gilbert down to the rest of the family, which probably accounted for the fact that they had been prepared to waste even ten minutes discussing such a tedious subject as the merits or otherwise of Pamela Finch.

'Well, Emmy?'

He was standing over her, his hand extended. Why hadn't Brad thought of going for a walk first? she thought angrily.

'All right.' She made it sound surly and grudging.

'Don't!' It was Toby, shrieking, beside her. His hands were clasped tightly round her ankle. 'Don't go! I want to show you something. Come on, come *on.*' His sudden fury was turning to tears. 'E...mm...yyy!'

'Toby!' She used the lulling, soft voice she knew from experience would soothe him out of those wild, inexplicable tantrums. 'What's the matter?'

But he refused to be consoled. 'Emm ...yyyyy! Don't go!' he continued to wail.

'For God's sake,' sighed Reggie. 'It's Christmas,' he added for no particular reason. 'Come over here, Tobe. You can show whatever it is to me—and Isabel.'

'Besides, you mustn't cry,' said Emmy in that wheedling tone. 'Think of all the people who are coming this evening—Alf, Pat, the girls at the theatre and lots and lots of others. You don't want them to see you all miserable and crying.'

'I don't care,' he screamed. Madge came rushing from the kitchen.

'Who's upset him?' She looked round the room as if searching for a villain. None volunteered.

Before they were aware of what was happening, Harvey hoisted the boy over his shoulder and playfully mimed a spanking on his bottom. The howling ceased as suddenly as it had begun. Toby struggled free from Harvey's arms and sat quietly cross-legged on the floor. Emmy looked at his tear-stained, upturned face. He was gazing at Harvey with a fixed, locked-in expression, his eyes wide and blank.

She felt Harvey's hand under her elbow guiding her ahead of him.

'Young punk!' he muttered when they'd closed the door behind them.

'What do you mean?' she shot back. 'That's my brother!'

He grinned a charming, placating grin. 'It's just an expression. Just don't let him get to you. You don't have to pick up the pieces of his life, you know.'

Despite herself she knew she was again falling into the trap of being seduced by his persuasive powers that transcended the physical appearance of the man. A man, she kept reminding herself, who was old enough to be her father.

It wasn't especially cold, but it was bleak and grey outside in the garden. She shivered.

'Here.' He took off his jacket and draped it round her shoulders. It was still warm from his body.

'I don't want it,' she said firmly. 'I can get a woolly.'

'Sure you can. But why bother?'

They walked in silence for a minute or two towards the old shed. 'Dad's going to fit it out for Toby, where he can paint and do his things. He's down here all the time anyway. He likes being alone.'

'And what do you like, Miss Emmy?' He'd called her that the first time he'd met her and it didn't seem strange that he should revert to that mode of expression as if they were starting from scratch in what she assumed was their relationship. 'I mean, what do you want?'

'Dad says I have a good head for business. I'm no good at performing, singing, dancing, acting, like the rest of them. My mother was wonderful, too. We've lots of pictures of her and dad, and when we were little she used to do bits in the musical shows at the Adelphi. But then as we grew up and Toby came along she stopped performing and...' She knew she was rabbiting on stupidly, but it was all getting too personal. She felt flustered, unsure how to behave and talk seemed the best solution.

'I don't mean what Gilbert wants for you. I mean what do *you* want for you? Everyone wants something.'

'I—I don't know what I want.' And that

was the truth: she didn't. 'And anyway...'
She pulled away from him.

'I know. It's none of my damned business. Begging your pardon.'

She laughed out loud. Begging her pardon for a silly little cuss word. He'd come into their home, disrupted their lives and he was begging her pardon for that.

'You're right, it's cold. I want to go in,' she said briskly.

'No, wait. Feel in the jacket pocket. The right one.'

'I couldn't,' she argued. His jacket, his pocket.

'Please!'

Reluctantly she groped in the pocket and pulled out a thin, oblong, gift-wrapped package.

'Open it,' he said.

It was all planned, she thought; this walk, offering her his jacket against the cold. 'I don't want it,' she shoved it into his hand.

'Please,' he repeated.

She could hardly refuse again. She unwrapped the package, carefully un-knotting the gilt twine from habit because you never knew when it might come in handy again. Then she took off the tissue paper inside and uncovered a slim, vellum-bound volume. It was a copy of *Pride and Prejudice*.

'It's not first edition or anything like that. But it's old.' It was Harvey now who was flustered, which was so unusual that his discomfort made her uncomfortable.

'Look inside,' he said.

She opened the cover. On the flyleaf was an inscription in a copperplate hand. 'Emmelyne Disley. 1893. A Lady of Quality. H.'

'I found it in a second-hand bookshop in town.' His voice was husky.

'I wonder who "H" was?' she said. Emmelyne Disley and H. 'How did you know I read Jane Austen?'

'I saw a whole row of them on your shelves. You've probably got it, but this seemed to be waiting for you.' He was looking at her eagerly, waiting for her response and she wasn't sure she liked this new Harvey Persky. Or, rather, she wasn't sure she should like this new Harvey Persky.

She rounded on him crossly. 'What were you doing in my room?' He looked bewildered. 'I was passing one day and I saw the door open. I'm sorry...' Apologies didn't come easily to him, so he didn't elaborate. 'I couldn't miss it,' he went on. 'And besides your mother said you always had your nose in a book.' He paused, punching his fist in the air with frustration. 'Shit! I know what you all think

233

of me. A no-account slob from the States, a schmuck with no finer feelings. No class. No style. But I've bummed around enough in my life to learn a lot. And, Emmy, I ain't gonna bum around any more.' The veneer of refinement he'd been so assiduously acquiring during his stay in Clifton Coombe was stripped away. In that moment she glimpsed the boy from Brooklyn who had been brought up in the gutter and ended up in the circus, mucking out the animal cages, with Gilbert May. A yearning boy nursing a hopeless dream.

She didn't know whether to feel sorry for him or affronted. She settled for a chilling courtesy which she suspected would mortify him more than outright rejection.

'It's very kind of you, Harvey. Thank you. Now I think we should go in. I must help mother for this evening. What with Aggie away and the dailies who come in from the town...well you can't blame them not wanting to leave their families at Christmas...so you see there's lots to do.'

She handed him his jacket and walked purposefully towards the house, leaving him standing there. She couldn't resist glancing over her shoulder at him. He looked somehow forlorn and lost, then he shrugged on his jacket, flexed his shoulders like a feisty James Cagney itching for a fight and strode after her.

Outside the kitchen door she heard her mother and father talking. Their voices were raised.

'How much longer?' her mother was saying. 'It's been a week. And Christmas too.'

'Not much longer, Madge. Then he'll get a place of his own.' Gilbert sounded weary, resigned, as if the spirit had been drained out of him.

'And another thing, I don't like the familiar way he's behaving with Emmy. After all, she's hardly more than a girl.' Madge stopped suddenly. 'What do you mean, a place of his own? Here? In Clifton Coombe? Why? What's he doing here? I've been patient Gil, but...well, you see the effect he has on the family. He gives me the creeps.'

'You're exaggerating, Madge. He's just a guy I knew.'

'And what else, Gil? What else is he apart from being just a guy you knew God knows when?'

'He's nothing, Madge. But...but you might as well know I'm thinking of taking him on at the Adelphi as a sort of associate. That's what I wanted to talk to Crawford about, get it legal and...'

'Partner you mean? I can't believe this. What do you want with a partner, or an associate? You've run the Adelphi without any partners before. You must have taken leave of your senses.'

'Madge, he's got some great ideas. He knows the business. It's all changing. And he's got a lot of contacts in the States. He could be a big help.' He was pleading now, begging her to understand without asking questions. But she asked them anyway.

'Gil, there's something. What is it? Why are you giving in to him? Please tell me.'

There was a long silence. Then Emmy heard the sound of her mother weeping and her father making consoling noises. 'It'll all be right, you'll see,' he was murmuring. 'Trust me.'

CHAPTER FIFTEEN

'What *can* you mean, Terry Roberts? Of *course* she's in. I saw her at the window as I pedalled up the drive. And for heaven's sake—forgive me God!—spruce yourself up a bit, clean your fingernails...'

'I'm washing down the front porch. *If* you don't mind.'

'Yes, well...Emmy, Emmy! Emmy dear!'

Emmy groaned. She could imagine the speaker brushing aside the aggrieved Terry. He had sounded perilously close to losing his temper and she couldn't afford that the day before the funeral when she would be relying on his goodwill and co-operation.

Hastily she wiped her hands, smoothed her hair and emerged from the kitchen to confront her caller, a fairly convincing expression of pleasure on her face.

'Rose. What a lovely...' She caught Terry's sceptical eye. 'What a lovely surprise. What brings you here?'

Her visitor kissed her wetly on both cheeks, gripped Emmy's arm quite painfully in a gesture supposedly of sympathy, then surveyed her with a look of concern.

'I just wanted to tell you that everything is in hand. At the church. The flowers just as you wanted them. And the service. And music. Though, really—that entertainment song!...as I said to Arthur... Oh, but my dear, you mustn't let it bother you. If that's what you want. I was just wondering if there was anything I could do to help.'

Emmy tried to appear grateful. 'It's thoughtful of you, Rose. But really I can't think of anything. And the family will be coming down.'

The woman looked so downcast that she offered her a cup of coffee while she tried to think of some kind way of getting rid of her.

Rose Selby was the vicar's cousin who had moved in when his wife had died and then taken root. She was a good soul but something of a trial as much to the easygoing Reverend Arthur as to the victims of her relentless insistence on bringing succour regardless of whether it was needed or asked for.

She had a slightly scatty doll's face, pert and polished. Her bright, hysterical eyes were so large and protruding that they seemed about to pop out of their sockets. Her teeth, very white and prominent, looked false but probably weren't. When she spoke it was like a clatter of ping-pong balls in a colander, the words bouncing off each other with no sense of direction or purpose.

That she was irritating was bearable: that she so radiantly believed in her own intrinsic rightness was not. All the same, the unbearable was borne for one very good reason. To be fair (and Emmy was nothing if not fair-minded—in most things, at least) if Rose Selby hadn't existed she would have had to be invented. For all her aggravating little ways, she was indispensable both to her cousin and to his parish.

She ran errands, made sick calls, delivered handbills, chivvied the tardy in collecting for church charities, arranged children's outings and mothers' teas and was never short of a handy quote from the Good Book to cover any exigency. No task was too menial or trivial to escape her undivided attention.

She was, Emmy thought, one of a dying breed: middle-aged maiden lady of adequate means, boundless energy and a selfless devotion to doing good that consumed every waking hour. Rose belonged far more to the measured world of Emmy's beloved Jane Austen than to the tough, rushed life of the 1990s.

She sat, even now, sipping her coffee, those big, bold eyes boring into Emmy with absolutely no malice just the insatiable curiosity of one who feeds on the lives of others.

'He was such a dear man, your Toby,' she was saying. 'You must miss him dreadfully. But think how happy he must be now with his Holy Father. God—'

'I know,' Emmy interrupted, 'works in mysterious ways.' She supposed diving off the balcony of the Adelphi might be described as mysterious, although she doubted if that was what Rose had in mind.

'I'm sure he was wiser than anyone knew. Sometimes mental...I mean, simple people are. It's God's way of compensating them.'

'Like redundancy pay.' Emmy smiled, then covered her mouth with her hand so that Rose shouldn't see. The woman, after all, was merely trying to convey some comfort. The trouble was, however fine—and probably true—the sentiment, it always sounded so trite. Why the hell couldn't God have done some compensating during Toby's life? Like giving him the grip on reality that so eluded him.

'...in the cemetery.'

'What?' Rose had left God to his own devices and was on to another topic.

'It was just a few weeks before he died. I saw him in the cemetery. I was putting some flowers on the grave of old Mrs Haddy's husband. She's very infirm now, you know. It's the legs. But wonderfully game. It's just the steps that defeat her, so I always take her flowers—once a fortnight. She always insists on paying. I tell her a nice hardy pot plant would have a longer life. But she will have cut flowers. And I have to respect her wishes. Well, at her age. It's her right, isn't it?'

'What about Toby? In the cemetery?' Even as she asked Emmy wasn't sure that she wanted to hear.

'Oh yes. Toby. He seemed very preoccupied, as if he was sleep-walking. But of course he wasn't. Because he knew me. He said he was looking for his father's grave. So I said: Gilbert May. Naturally I knew it was Gilbert May. But I said it, the way you do. And then the oddest thing happened. He rounded on me quite fiercely saying, "March, march!" As if I'd said the wrong thing.'

'March,' murmured Emmy.

It wasn't a question but Rose took it as such. 'Yes, march, march! So I told him *I* didn't mind but if he talked to other people like that they'd quite likely tell him to march off somewhere else. Then quite suddenly he was his old, sweet self again. But I thought at the time it wasn't like him to be so rude.' She looked at Emmy for confirmation.

'No, it wasn't like him,' Emmy agreed. Toby would forgive her that one white lie.

'I suppose...' Rose began hopefully, inviting an explanation.

No, don't suppose, Rose, enough is enough. 'There is one thing you can do for me, Rose,' said Emmy brightly, changing the subject. 'I'd be grateful if you would take some wool and bits of fabric I've collected for the ladies at Sunny Hill. I said I'd bring them on my next visit. But I'll have to miss out this week.'

'Oh, anything, Emmy, anything. Anything I can do to help.' Rose was revived by the magic word 'help'. It was what she'd come for: to be of help.

'I'll go and fetch them. It's quite a

bundle, I'm afraid.'

'No problem,' Rose beamed.

Having anchored the bundle in the basket of Rose's bicycle, Emmy watched her purposeful progress down the drive, her sturdy legs pedalling furiously.

'That woman should be had up for aggravated assault.' Terry had finished cleaning the porch and was leaning heavily on the handle of the mop.

'That's not kind, Terry,' Emmy reprimanded him absent-mindedly.

'So, how many do you suppose will be coming back tomorrow? After the funeral?'

'The family I suppose. A few friends. The vicar. Flo Gosling's coming round to help with the catering.'

'Ham, tea, sweet sherry and God rest his soul,' Terry sneered, then, 'Sorry. By the way there's something I've got to tell you.' He tried to make it sound unimportant but he wasn't very good at disguising the truth.

'You're leaving,' said Emmy.

He frowned at her, perplexed. 'How did you know?'

'It's the only "by the way" I could think of. If it had been something really trivial you'd have said it straight out. So, when did you come to this decision?'

'Last night. Lorraine and I talked it over. She said it was about time I got myself sorted out.'

'She's right. But I'll be sorry to see you go.'

'Yes, well, you won't want me around any more.'

'It wasn't anything Mr Ballantyne said?' Damn Oliver!

He snorted. 'What? Old smart alec? Wouldn't give a tinker's for anything he said. No, Lorraine wants to go back up north. That's where she comes from. Her brother's got a garage up there and his girl's left, so she's taking over in the parts shop and she thinks he might take me on too. Mechanic. I'm not bad.'

'You're very good when you put your mind to it. Where will you live?'

'With Lorraine. We'll get a bed-sit or something. Beggars can't be choosers. We'll manage.'

She knew he wasn't angling for a handout. In all the time he'd been with her he'd never asked for anything but his due: board and a small wage. Maybe God, who seemed to be putting himself about this morning, was trying to tell her something.

'I could give you a loan. A few thousand. That way you and Lorraine might get a mortgage on a small flat.' I'm rich, she thought, well, relatively rich, according to Oliver. It was, she discovered for the first time, a rather satisfying feeling.

'I couldn't.' He sounded truculent as if affronted that she should even offer, even suggest that they wouldn't make out all right.

'Of course you could, Terry. Don't be silly. It's strictly a loan. And you've got to promise me that you're serious. Really serious about getting yourself together. If you don't like taking money you just send Lorraine to me and we'll sort it out between us. She's got a good head on her shoulders, that girl.'

'She's not my keeper,' he said brusquely, his pride bruised.

Whoops! thought Emmy. She'd forgotten how fragile the male ego could be, especially when it was attached to a young man whom society had never encouraged to have a high opinion of himself.

'I didn't mean it like that, Terry. Think of it as investment. My investment. An investment in your future.' She grimaced, realizing that she sounded like a party political broadcast.

But Terry seemed to take it as was meant. 'If you put it like that,' he said grudgingly.

He appeared to be at a loss for words so she relieved him on the necessity of searching for any. 'Just you think about it. Talk it over with Lorraine. No hurry. Now I'd better get on. I'm expecting my sister and Mr Hastings some time.' It was as good an excuse as any. She wondered what was going through Terry's mind. Was he pleased? Annoyed? Envious? He'd always seemed to like her, but maybe this would too clearly mark the divide between she who had and he who hadn't, the privileged and the deprived. Perhaps she'd never know. Perhaps she'd done the wrong thing. Perhaps he thought she'd forget all about it or be talked out of it.

'Terry. I won't go back on my offer. It's a promise.'

She didn't wait to hear his response, whether he was reassured or confused or both. She could imagine Oliver's reaction when she told him, as she would have to: he's taking advantage of you; of course he expected you to cough up some money when he left; why do you think he came to work here in the first place? And maybe he would be right. She'd bent over all her life to understand people but she'd always felt she was missing a vital link in the equation.

She supposed it was Rose and her cemetery story that had brought this on. She went upstairs and unlocked her bureau drawer. Underneath a neat pile of answered letters and paid bills her hand went unerringly to a medium-sized buff envelope.

Even as she touched it she felt a vibration as if the inanimate thing inside the envelope were alive with electricity. She had memorized it so completely that there was no need to inspect it again, but she did, as she always did, compelled by a curiosity outside her control. And, as she always did, she gazed instantly at the two boyish faces staring rakishly out of the faded sepia photograph. It had been taken in a studio, the pose as studied and unnatural looking as the dusty potted palm on a pedestal that was placed like a sentinel in the corner of the picture.

The two figures were obviously wearing their stiff Sunday best. Each had one arm draped carefully around the other's shoulders, while their spare arms cradled straw hats at right angles to the body. They appeared immensely pleased with themselves. For all its artificiality the photograph reflected the youthful bravado of two very young men.

'That's your dad and me on our first pay day. Barely fifteen, we were. We were so proud of those suits and those hats. Would you look at them? What dumb punks we were then.' She could still remember his words as he had showed her the photograph the day after he'd arrived in Clifton Coombe.

She didn't need him to identify them.

Harvey Persky slight, wiry with jet black hair and those same piercing eyes; and Gilbert taller, more elegant even as a boy with romantic features and floppy poet's hair.

'What do you think?' he'd asked.

'I don't think you look as if you liked each other very much,' she'd replied, reading more into the old photograph than was probably there.

'We were buddies!' he'd laughed. 'Buddies! Giddy March and me. What am I saying? March? May!' But it didn't sound as if it were a slip of the tongue and she knew she was right when she had seen the sudden apprehension in Gilbert's eyes when the photograph was produced.

Her fingers traced the outline of those young faces bringing the past uncomfortably to life so that for a few moments the present didn't exist. She started nervously as the telephone pealed and felt as if she'd been caught out in a guilty act. She stuffed the photograph back into its buff envelope and hastily returned it to its hiding place underneath the bills and letters.

'Emmy?' The voice at the other end of the telephone sounded anxious and a touch peeved.

'What is it, Ollie?' She knew it wasn't much of a greeting. She could at least have said, 'Hello.'

'I was just wondering how things were. I haven't heard from you in two days.' Not just peeved, but neglected too.

'Things have been fine,' she said considering her words. 'There's been quite a bit to do. The church, the undertakers, the press...'

'What press?' Peeved, neglected and alarmed.

'The *Clarion*.'

'Oh, well, that's all right.' Relieved.

'On the other hand I am considering an in-depth interview with the *Sunday Times* and tell-all exposé for the *Sun*.' She couldn't resist it. Oliver brought out the devil in her.

For a split second he wasn't sure whether to take her seriously. 'You wouldn't...? Emmy, you're joking. You *are* joking.'

'Of *course* I'm joking, Ollie. You're such a sitting target,' she said fondly. He always had been even when he was young and much fancied.

It took a while and a good deal of flattery to restore his self-esteem. 'I was phoning to ask you out to dinner tonight. Just a quiet dinner with Ellie and George Dixon and the Crenshaws. They were concerned about you.'

'That's nice.' She quite liked the Dixons and the Crenshaws, as much as she liked anyone in the plushier echelons of Clifton

Coombe's carefully stratified society.

'I know it hardly seems appropriate, the evening before the funeral. But we don't like to think of you all alone. At a time like this.'

If she heard that expression again she'd scream. At a time like this! Any support, advice or what in any other circumstances might be regarded as wanton interference could be justified 'at a time like this'.

'You make me sound like little orphan Annie,' she snapped, regretting it instantly. It wasn't fair to throw people's concern back in their faces. 'But I am grateful, Ollie. Do thank them. If you don't mind, though, I'd really rather not. And, besides, I'm not alone. There's Terry. Brad's here and Val is coming down today. In fact...' Why not? It wasn't such a bad idea. 'Why don't you come over for a meal tonight? It won't be much. But Terry and I can rustle up something edible. And we crack open a bottle of something suitable and be nice to each other.'

'Val! Brad!' She could imagine the worry lines forming becomingly between his eyebrows. He had always been uncomfortable around Brad and he could never be certain about Val: she was just as likely to ignore him altogether as to embrace him with open arms. 'I'm not sure...' he ventured.

'Of course, you are, Ollie. It's settled. Sevenish—no, make it eight. Besides, Ollie,' she lowered her voice 'it'll take my mind off things—at a time like this, you know.' (Write out on the blackboard a hundred times 'I won't make fun of Ollie,' she reprimanded herself.)

'I understand,' he responded gravely. 'Around eight, then.'

In the roomy, old-fashioned kitchen with its solid wood fitments and owlish Aga, Lorraine was cooking an imaginative casserole (everything but the left-over custard) for the freezer and Terry was gazing ruefully at a huge basket that had just been delivered at somebody's enormous expense by a parcel service.

'What am I supposed to do with this lot? Socking great crate of apples!'

Each one was carefully wrapped in newspaper. He handed Emmy the note that came with them in her sister Cissie's flowering hand. 'Toby so loved them and they're especially good this year. Courage, dear Em. Cis.'

'What does she expect you do do? Bury them with him?' said Terry, peering over her shoulder at the note.

'Eat them to his memory perhaps,' said Emmy. 'It's a lovely thought,' she added.

'Give or take a fiver I reckon you could have bought this lot ten times over in the shops for what it cost to send them.'

'You couldn't,' said Lorraine, flushed from shooshing the casserole. She glanced at the ranks of apples. 'They're James Grieve. They don't travel.' She spoke with enormous authority, brooking no argument.

With a finicky thumb and forefinger Terry selected a distressed fruit bruised in transit. 'Too right, they don't,' he sniffed.

'Terry!'

Lorraine turned to Emmy with a dripping ladle in her hand. She was the kind of big, broad-beamed girl who was usually described as earthy and she had about her an air of complete conviction in everything she said and did. She was the girl, thought Emmy, you would turn to in a crisis in the certain knowledge that she would have the answer. 'Terry told me you'd have some people today, so I don't mind staying and cooking a roast or something.'

'She's a good, plain cook,' Terry volunteered eagerly. It was obvious that he was totally mesmerized by her.

'*Can* it, Tel!' she said smartly. 'He told me about your offer.' She jerked her head at Terry while facing Emmy. 'He's not keen. Charity and all that. Funny when you think what a villain he is. But it sounds great to me. I'm not as fussy about accepting what's on offer as he is.'

'I'm glad you're the practical one,' said Emmy.

Lorraine nodded, acknowledging the fact. 'We'll pay you back. Gawd knows when. But we will.'

Emmy hadn't the slightest doubt of it. She'd trust Lorraine's word over a legally drawn up contract any day. But then, she conceded, 'for a sensible woman you can be woefully lacking in judgement sometimes,' as Ollie occasionally reminded her. She thanked Lorraine and worked out a scratch menu for the evening which she was quite sure the girl would discard in favour of something that suited her.

She supposed she should ring Cissie and thank her, too. Dear Cis! Always ready with the right gesture and guaranteed to get it slightly wrong. A load of less than peak condition apples she could do without. She was conscious of the wave of affection she always felt where Cissie was concerned. Of all her sisters, she was the one Emmy turned to most often.

'Would you say I'm not bad looking, Cis?' On that long-past Christmas Day she had asked her the question knowing she would get an honest answer. Madge would have been too maternally reassuring. Penny would have found the question amusing and given a cutting response. Val would first have wanted to know why she asked and have coloured her reply accordingly. With Cissie, though, honesty was taken for granted simply because she couldn't be bothered to be devious.

In the mirror in which she had been regarding herself, Cissie's reflection joined Emmy's.

'You've got a frank, clever sort of face,' she said after consideration.

'Is that good?' Emmy had prodded her.

'Hard to tell. If you're thinking of Brad—or that Harvey Persky—I doubt it,' she said with disconcerting prescience.

'Be quiet and buzz off,' Emmy said childishly. It wasn't the answer she'd expected or wanted.

CHAPTER SIXTEEN

Cecilia Collingwood, née Cissie May, heaved a deep pleasurable sigh. Nothing about nature offended her. Only people were a problem, and then not always.

'The high-rise apartment block! It's becoming quite ungovernable. I'll have to get Frank to do something about it.'

She was contemplating a tall, untidy

Escallonia hedge which marked out the territory of her cottage.

'The tits, you know. They nest there. Several families at a time. Very autocratic they are. Dreadful racket they kick up at dawn early in the year. But I haven't the heart to let Frank cut it hard back. I mean, they'd have to find another home next year. It wouldn't be fair. Not fair at all.'

Her friend and neighbour Major Eric Wittering, former Royal Corps of Signals, looked perplexed as he often did these days. By clinging to his wartime rank, though in name only, he could convince himself that life was just as it had been in those heady times when his brain was sharp, his opinion respected and his authority unquestioned. It was an illusion more easily fostered in the rural area of Kent to which he had retired than in the bustling urban environment from which he had escaped.

'What would *you* say, Eric?'

Cissie was one of the few people who bothered to ask his advice these days and he would not fail her. He ran his tongue round his dentures as if to make sure they were still there and then cleared his throat.

'Cut hard back,' he barked. 'Best in the long run.'

'I suppose,' she agreed reluctantly, then

allowed the matter to drift peacefully into the mental closet of things decided for future action. A large ginger tom wound himself round her trousered legs and purred suggestively. She ran her workmanlike fingers over his arched back. 'What's naughty Neil been doing?' she cooed. But Neil wasn't telling.

The major cleared his throat again. 'Chasing the ladies, I'd say.'

'And why not? A handsome mog like him! Another teacake Eric?' The major rescued the surviving buttery bun from the plate before a lolloping spaniel who answered to the name of Simon could get there first, shooting a withering look at the animal as he did so.

Cissie affected not to notice the contre-temps over the teacake, smiling her tranquil smile. She was a plump, placid woman who had completely shed all the appearance and affections imposed by show business in her early years as a Mayflower. She steered a stately progress through life unruffled by the squalls and storms that unsettle less evenly balanced human beings.

Troublesome babies tended not to cry nor yappy dogs to bark in her vicinity and quarrelsome couples suddenly discovered a sunny affinity with each other when she was around. It wasn't that she exercised some magical power of healing, merely that her own serenity prompted a reciprocal lassitude, as her now deceased husband Tom, who had been longing for an argument for the twenty years of their marriage, had known only too well. He had died, said some of their less kindly friends, from a surfeit of unexploded bad temper.

He had proposed to her partly because she represented the glamour and excitement that had been in short supply in the village where he was born and where he helped manage the family smallholding. She had accepted because he, in turn, represented the order and calm and comforting dullness of a life far removed from that of the Mays. But once this joint misunderstanding had been accommodated, they had rubbed along quite happily. Tom had continued to manage the smallholding until the day he died and their son Frank, fresh from agricultural college, had taken over; while Cissie lived on in the Collingwood cottage, part of which she'd opened out to house a display of rare Victorian toys that she'd collected over the years.

'You know, I'm really doing quite well.' Her voice came from the far distance, baffling the major yet again.

'Who said you weren't?'

'It's just an attitude. I don't think my sisters believe I'm very capable. Penny actually telephoned this morning and told me she and Harry were coming to collect me so we could go together to the funeral.'

'I'm sorry?' he said feeling he'd missed out somewhere along the line and fearing it was another of his lapses of attention.

'Toby. My brother's funeral. I'm quite able to get myself to Clifton Coombe.'

'Of course you are.'

'I always allow myself extra time to get lost on the motorway, so I usually arrive at things before everyone else. I hope Emmy enjoys the apples. It was just an impulse. But I wanted her to know I was thinking of her. Frank said she probably wouldn't thank me. He's so practical. What do you think, Eric?'

'Apples?' He'd lost her completely, but she didn't seem to mind.

'Daisy *will* look in on Neil and Simon and the rabbits when I'm away.' Daisy was Eric's obliging wife. 'I hate leaving them. But it's only for a day, maybe overnight.'

'Always at your service, Cissie,' the major, on surer ground, promised her. He levered himself to the edge of his chair, shot his gammy leg forward then hoisted himself upright. It was a lengthy operation punctuated by much puffing and blowing and assurance that he didn't need any help.

She gazed pensively through the small latticed windows at the hedge. 'The other morning I saw a hedgehog trotting along—just there.' She pointed in the direction of the rosebed. 'Lovely little fellow, right out of Beatrix Potter.'

'That's rare. Hedgehog in broad daylight.' He eased his weight on to his good leg.

She nodded. 'Hazardous too.'

'How so?'

'I was reading in the local paper just recently about a man who fell off his moped to avoid a hedgehog. Then the car behind ran over and killed him and swerved into a wall, wrecking the car and injuring the driver and passengers. A farm lorry had to pull up sharp and it shed its load of turnips all over the road. They say the traffic tailed back for ten miles.' She related the tale quite unemotionally as if bemused by the grisly yet perversely farcical inevitability of it all.

'Oh,' he said blankly. But she looked at him earnestly, obviously expecting some kind of response.

'Did—did the hedgehog survive?' he hazarded.

'Oh yes,' she said brightly. 'So he—the man on the moped—didn't really die in vain, did he?'

Sometimes Cissie's reasoning defeated him. 'On the other hand I don't imagine his wife saw it that way. If he had a wife,' he said.

'I suppose not.' Clearly she supposed nothing of the kind. 'Hedgehogs are an endangered species,' she murmured.

So, he thought, are men on mopeds. He wondered if she was having him on, but decided Cissie wasn't the sort to have people on. It was just the kind of bizarre happening that might very well occur in the country. He liked to think that he and Daisy had merged happily into village life but on occasions like this he wasn't so sure. He was all for conservation but there were limits.

'Thanks for the tea, Cissie. Most kind, most kind. I'll alert Daisy about the pets. I'll see she's around 0900 on the dot.' He occasionally lapsed into military lingo, old comforting habits dying hard. 'She's very fond of—of Neil and Simon.'

Neil and Simon looked at him with beady threatening eyes as if they knew they were to be abandoned for the day to the care of Daisy, who wasn't as fond of them as her husband insisted.

When they had seen him safely off the premises, Neil and Simon turned their backs on Cissie in a huff. Neil scooted through the cat flap and Simon settled himself in the warm chair the major had recently vacated.

Cissie looked around her with immense pleasure, as she did umpteen times a day. Even before she and Tom had set it to rights she'd loved the seventeenth-century thatched cottage which had been in the Collingwood family for generations. She hadn't even minded the scuffling in the reed thatch at night, even though she was much relieved to learn that it was birds nesting not rats infesting.

All the furniture had been Victorian or older—stripped pine cupboard and tables, button-back sofas, heavy carved linen chests, a massive oak bedstead in the master bedroom, woven rugs in autumnal shades on slate and wood floors. She'd enthused over the exposed brick walls and timber joists and enormous open fireplace, its mantelpiece festooned with pewter mugs and pottery jugs and family photographs fossilized in elaborate frames. All of it the Collingwoods had taken for granted when they weren't moaning about them for being dust-traps and labour intensive.

With a will and devotion that amazed Tom and his mother, who had thankfully moved into a modern, warm, easy-clean bungalow with all the amenities when her son married, Cissie embarked on a programme of polishing, restoring, scrubbing and painting. And when all the polishing, restoring, scrubbing and painting was done, she applied herself to the overgrown kitchen garden and the production of endless needlepoint cushion and chair covers and rural landscapes to hang on the walls. She embraced village ways as effortlessly as if she had been born to them.

She was in every way content. If she thought about her life in show business at all it was with a sigh of relief that she no longer had to live it. Tom Collingwood, a fan who had written to her so persistently that she couldn't ignore him, had come just in time.

More than once she had indicated to her sisters and Marcus Gammie that she wanted to give up, but she had allowed herself to see the error of such a move merely because it was easier than putting up an argument: despite the signs that their popularity was on the wane due to the radically changing style in pop music.

The Mayflowers, they persuaded her, were on the brink of major stardom. Look what happened to the Andrews Sisters in the forties! Marcus was planning a whole new image to launch them into the rock 'n' roll age, to which end he had engaged an obnoxious but knowing whizz-kid to manage them. No more bouffant frocks and sequins, but a sleek, slick, figure-hugging look, loads of dramatic black eye make-up and identical flowing wigs. (The wigs were Val's contribution.) Not to mention a different repertoire of songs with a big beat for the kids to dance to. And maybe they would introduce a backing group of musicians with guitars and a male singer, an Elvis type. That way they could package a whole show around the Mayflowers. They might even play Las Vegas or tour the troops with Bob Hope. Anything was possible.

Marcus was even working on another name for them. The Mayflowers sounded too prissy and cute. It had to be something more seductive, tougher.

'But if we're not the Mayflowers, why don't you find another trio of singers?' Cissie had, she felt, quite reasonably, enquired.

Their appalled expression had instantly silenced her.

But then came Tom, and she had a reason. It was Cissie who eventually nerved herself to precipitate the crisis that led to the break-up of the Mayflowers.

It had happened during what should have been a routine interview with the entertainment correspondent of the *Daily*

Mirror. They were all used to doing it: Cliff, Tommy Steele, Alma Cogan. A litany of tit-bits about their lives, their hopes, their ambitions, with just enough personal stuff to liven it up and convince the fans they were taking them into their confidence—which, of course, was the last thing they intended to do. The interviewer knew that, the stars knew that: the trick was to persuade the readers otherwise.

The May girls were good at this harmless deceit. They were quick and witty and, while conveying the impression that they believed in all the prime virtues and conducted themselves always according to the laws laid down by God and their parents, they were never boring.

Marcus had extravagantly booked a suite at the Mayfair Hotel for the interview and photographs. The session was drawing to its close.

To wind up, the correspondent asked what they felt was their biggest short-coming. A sceptical veteran of the sports pages and the news desk, he had successfully lobbied for a softer option in the entertainment department because the perks were better and the expenses less beadily scrutinized. He expected no great revelations.

Cissie volunteered the first reply, which

263

was unusual. Of the three of them she was the most guarded.

'I do have one insurmountable disadvantage in pursuing a career in this profession,' she said primly.

He jotted it down in shorthand reminding himself to jazz it up a bit when he came to write the piece. 'Insurmountable' and 'pursuing a career' were much too *News Chronicle* for the *Mirror* entertainment section.

'What's that, Cissie?' He looked no more than mildly interested, convinced he'd have heard it all before. When a starlet coyly admitted to a disadvantage it was invariably revealed to be an asset: like a prominent beauty spot or over-vital statistics or wonderfully wayward hair that most girls would die for.

'No talent!' she replied. Her face was as straight as the answer.

The newspaperman started to laugh, then stopped. 'You're serious?'

'Of course she's not serious,' Marcus jumped in nervously. He'd felt his hands go clammy the moment Cissie had spoken. 'It's a joke. Always joking, Cissie,' he continued even more nervously.

'No I'm not. I'm quite serious. I've no talent. Anybody could do what I do. Mostly a lot better. I just try to make the right noises, not to fall over my feet and watch what Val and Penny are doing.' She smiled very sweetly, relieved to have finally got it off her chest.

The interviewer, flummoxed by such honesty, was temporarily speechless. Marcus and her sisters were equally dumbstruck. You simply didn't air that kind of damning opinion in public. It was only later, when attempts had been made to smooth over the situation and everyone behaved as if Cissie had volunteered nothing more contentious than a mild disagreement about the reliability of the weather forecast, that it occurred to them she just might have tolled the death knell of the Mayflowers.

Despite Marcus's ingratiating, verging on the desperate, plea to the *Mirror* man to edit out Cissie's quotes, none of them was surprised when they saw them featured in the strapline of the piece. 'No talent': Cissie May. 'Anybody could do what I do.' It was just too good a scoop: trivial but readable. To compound the horror another newspaper launched a campaign to find a group of unknown 'anybodies' to rival the Mayflowers.

'How could you, Cissie!' raged Val.

'You'll have to ring him and say it's a joke,' said Penny, ever practical, but she wasn't over-bothered. She'd been having second thoughts about the Mayflowers,

265

too, since the young millionaire industrialist Harry Eardley had started courting her.

'We'll sort it out somehow,' Marcus had reassured them, but with no conviction whatsoever.

They all realized that a relaunch of the Mayflowers was out of the question now and in an odd way they didn't really blame Cissie. When they'd told Gilbert, he'd shrugged: 'It's only show business, you win some, you lose some: if it hadn't been that it would have been something else.' Although his line of thought seemed muddled, as sadly it so often did these days, his reasoning made sense. Show business was a merry-go-round. Nothing could unseat the stayers, but the majority fell off along the way after a couple of heady whirls.

Only Val had never quite forgiven Cissie over thirty years. But then Val still kidded herself she was one of the chosen.

'You'll miss it,' said Tom when they married.

'No I won't,' said Cissie. And she never had. Her son Frank had been all of eleven years old when he'd learned that his mother had once been in show business and then only when a boy at school, whose mother had been a fan of the Mayflowers, told him.

It was all so long ago. But Toby's death

had brought it back. Just a little.

With Neil and Simon padding faithfully behind her, Cissie walked through the cottage into the extension she'd had built for the toy collection. The council had put up an argument when she had wanted to open it to the public two days a week, but had given in when she'd said the proceeds should go to charity.

She had started collecting when she'd uncovered a treasure trove of dolls and mechanical toys discarded in the Collingwood loft and it had grown from that as she'd scoured the local antique shops picking up trophies when it was still possible to acquire them for a song. It had given her an added interest when Tom was out long days working on the smallholding, and when he died from a sudden heart attack it had become a comforting compulsion.

She looked around the cluttered little gallery with its rows of pink dolls' faces staring at her with their innocent glass eyes and rosebud lips: some moulded in china or wax and the rarest in wood and papier mâché. The teddy bears sat on their shelves asking to be hugged, the grandest of them—a couple of Steiffs—displayed most prominently. There were mechanical trams and steam engines and German-manufactured farmyard scenes with tiny figures that all worked at the touch of the right trigger and music boxes that played 'Goodbye Dolly Gray', 'Auld Lang Syne', 'Champagne Charlie', and any number of nursery rhymes.

She knew each one intimately and encouraged the children who visited to touch them, feel the quality of the workmanship and enjoy for just a few seconds a sense of ownership. She loved to see the look of wonder in their eyes as they fondled playthings quite unlike the plastic and electronic toys they possessed.

Neither Tom nor Frank had shared her passion for these treasures. Sometimes she felt they were more her children than Frank ever was. He had been a rather grim, long-faced boy with a prosaic turn of mind whose main interest in things was in calculating their value. He regarded his mother as an eccentric liability. He had married a sturdy girl who had shared his view and was rearing a tribe of equally sturdy children with as little imagination.

'You really ought to get proper security for this lot,' he advised on one of his duty visits. 'They could be worth a packet. That doll's house, for instance.' He pointed to the miniature Victorian residence that revealed a fully kitted family home including kitchen, bathroom and nursery with tiny figures and fitments to scale. 'Something like that was on the *Antiques Roadshow* and they put it at five grand.'

'It was your great-grandmother's,' she reminded him. 'If you think little Tracy would like it...?'

She was relieved when he turned down the offer, although he did make the point that the cash it might bring would come in handy. Perhaps at some stage she should recompense him for the family toys in which he had no interest. But she hated the thought of selling any of them.

'I know a dealer,' he said.

He would, she sighed. 'We'll see.'

But now she wondered whether she was being selfish. Frank was the way Frank was. She couldn't change that. But he worked hard and these days there was precious little profit in the fruit and vegetables he grew for market. You had to land a supermarket contract to make money and the tight margins were too stringent for a small producer like Frank who relied on casual labour for help.

Maybe after the funeral she'd think seriously about disposing of the collection, just retaining a few pieces to which she was especially attached. She felt Simon's moist, cold nose nuzzling her hand and bent down to pat him.

She picked up a child's-size porcelain

porter mug in the shape of a grinning clown. (Some ailing Victorian child actually had to drink porter out of it.) When she lifted the lid it played a Strauss waltz, to help the medicine down.

'What would you do, Toby?' ('It's not a Toby jug,' Frank had laughed at her. 'That's not why I call it Toby,' she replied. But he hadn't understood.)

'What would you do, Toby?' she repeated. 'You were always the wisest of us all. In your fashion. Poor Tobe!'

Simon, sensing her mood, whined. Neil, bored, took off on his own.

'Dinner—or walkies?'

The dog barked cheerfully. Either/or suited him.

CHAPTER SEVENTEEN
1 JANUARY 1958

'I swear to God I'll murder that man before I'm finished.' Patty Grace, the lead dancer in the *Dick Whittington* chorus, was known for her tantrums and usually no one paid much attention. But this time she was backed up, to a greater or lesser degree, by the whole company. 'A nine o'clock rehearsal call on New Year's *Day!*

It's unheard of in the theatre,' she said grandly with the authority of a trouper who claimed she had been born in a trunk, which if not strictly accurate was close enough to the truth. Her grandmother had been a Floradora girl and her mother had been one of C.B Cochran's young ladies. While letting it be known that appearing in pantomime at the Adelphi was merely a stepping-stone in her own career she was enough of a professional to give the show her best shot, which included throwing her weight around when needs must.

She was talking about Harvey Persky. Since his arrival in Clifton Coombe everyone was talking about Harvey Persky, or so it seemed to Emmy. He was that kind of man, arousing powerful feelings while doggedly refusing to be ignored.

When Gilbert had announced to the company that his good friend Harvey was joining him as associate there had been some surprise. Gilbert May had always been proud of going it alone since the time Madge and he had inherited the Adelphi on the death of her father. When he'd turned a ramshackle provincial variety hall into a tip-top regional theatre he'd been offered lucrative deals to amalgamate with more than one of the big music hall chains. But he'd always turned them down without even considering them. 'Give them

271

an inch and they'll take a mile.' No one quite knew what he meant by that. What they did know was that he relished being his own boss and he wouldn't abdicate that sovereignty for anyone. Until Harvey Persky.

The strange thing was that no one—not even Madge—doubted the legitimacy of Harvey's powers of persuasion.

Certainly he was fizzing with ideas for bettering the show, even the disgruntled Patty admitted that. He had worked the dancers ragged, sharpening their timing, streamlining the choreography, giving the show a Broadway gloss that might have been lost on the faithful Clifton Coombe audiences but not on the company. In a couple of weeks he had virtually taken over. The wonder was that Gilbert should meekly have allowed him to do so.

Harvey didn't seem to mind that in the process he had created bad blood. He had shrugged off complaints, arguments, even outright rows with the imponderable logic that that was show business. The atmosphere at the Adelphi was charged with tension, although Harvey had removed himself from the May household and had found himself a flat in town, financed by Gilbert.

'It's never been like this before,' Alf Gravely had sighed after one especially ugly set-to with Harvey. 'Don't know why your dad puts up with it,' he'd said to Emmy.

They all came to Emmy with their grievances. Of all the Mays she was closest to their father and since leaving school she'd become more involved in the administration of the Adelphi. For one so young, it was generally agreed, she had a good head on her shoulders.

Even Brad found Harvey's endless suggestions for beefing up his portrayal of the romantic lead exasperating. 'Think Howard Keel,' Harvey kept telling him. '*You* think Howard Keel,' he'd retorted, quite angrily for Brad. 'It's only a pantomime hero.' 'But he doesn't have to be a wimp,' Harvey had replied, meaning more than he said. 'It's not just wanting the girl, it's getting her,' he added and neither he nor Brad were in any doubt that he wasn't simply referring to his character's courtship of the winsome flower-seller in the show. Since Christmas Brad had seen less and less of Emmy.

'Dad, why do you let him walk all over everybody?'

Emmy and her father were sitting in Gilbert's office running through the accounts, which were healthily in the black.

It had been a sober New Year's Eve,

hardly a celebration at all. Val was still sore at being jilted by Oliver. Penny and Cissie, who at the best of times were not bosom chums, had had a flaming row about something trivial which neither of them could remember when their tempers were exhausted. Madge had suffered a migraine headache to which she was increasingly prone these days. Toby had just retreated into himself as he often did. And Reggie and Isabel had been invited to a rather posh theatrical party in London which, they pleaded, they couldn't honestly refuse, could they?

The guests who had dropped in found their high spirits evaporating in the subdued atmosphere and departed rather too eagerly as soon as they decently could after midnight.

'Patty's got a point,' Emmy continued when she received no answer from her father. 'You never expect the company to rehearse on New Year's Day.'

Gilbert May looked up at his youngest daughter with a worried frown. He was still a handsome man, with the lean, clean features of some debonair god sculpted in marble. In his youth, she thought, he must have been spectacular. No wonder he had swept her pretty mother, Madge Lavender, off her feet as irresistibly as he had 'worked' an audience in their music hall act. She had heard all the stories: how elegant he had looked in top hat and tails swirling Madge around the stage in those gauzy, beaded dresses she copied from Ginger Rogers: how charmingly he had sung the songs of Rodgers and Hart and Jerome Kern and Ivor Novello; how wittily he had delivered their comedy patter; and how deftly he had used his agile body to perform the acrobatic stunts he had picked up in the circus.

'The trouble with your father,' Jack Buchanan had confided to her on the last visit he made to Rushey Green, 'the trouble was he was too versatile, too good at everything. You have to specialize in this business. Sometimes I think he doesn't want to be famous.' She could remember that wonderful light, caressing voice which made everything sound like a love song and she could remember, too, how she had wept when he died not so very long afterwards.

'You don't understand, Emmy love.' Her father shook his head sadly as if all the fight had gone out of him. The change in Gilbert had bothered her. He was the same Gilbert May in every respect, except the spark that had been his special magic had been extinguished.

'I would, if you told me,' she urged.

'Harvey's a doer. You can see that for

yourself. The show's brighter, smarter...'

'But it's not *your* show, dad.'

'Well, maybe I was getting a little lazy, not open to new ideas.'

'I don't believe that. There's something else.' But he wouldn't be drawn. So far as he was concerned Harvey Persky was a breath of fresh air that the Adelphi needed—or so he said.

'What was he like, Harvey, when you knew him?' No matter how much she might want to change the subject it always came back to Harvey. He was like a perpetual itch that demanded to be scratched every so often.

'He was like no one I'd ever known before. As simple as that,' Gilbert mused. 'In a way I think he was everything I wanted to be: brash, cocky, ready to dare anything. He'd come from the school of hard knocks in Brooklyn one jump ahead of the law I shouldn't wonder, although he never said. I'd come from a small farming community in Kansas where folks went to church regularly, kept the ten commandments and barely ever visited the wicked city.' His eyes crinkled as he laughed and he seemed like the old Gilbert again. Maybe he shouldn't keep the past locked up inside him so much, she thought.

'So how did you happen to join the

circus? You talk so little about when you were young, dad.'

As soon as she'd mentioned the past she knew she had said the wrong thing. She watched his expression tighten and close in on itself. 'Kids' stuff,' he said as if that explained everything. 'I just wanted some excitement like boys do and then the circus pitched up nearby I asked for a job and they gave me one.'

'Didn't your parents mind?' she persisted.

'There were nine other mouths to feed and times were hard. No they didn't mind.' He sounded as if he regretted allowing her to bring up the matter.

'Is that all? They didn't mind? Or didn't you even bother to find out?'

'Emmy, I want to get these accounts out of the way before the show. If you want to help, help! If you don't, don't!' His tone was so sharp that she reacted as if he'd taken his hand to her, which he never had even when they were little and mischievous.

She refused to budge. 'Did you? See them again?'

'No,' he said angrily. 'Now leave me alone. What's got into you, Emmy?' He sensed the answer to his question and, calmer now, he looked at her gravely. 'You like him, don't you?' He didn't need to name a name.

Like! That wasn't it at all, she thought. Like didn't come anywhere close to describing the strange, reckless feeling she experienced whenever she was near Harvey Persky. But she couldn't explain that to her father, to anyone. She couldn't explain it even to herself. Instead, she shrugged.

'No—yes—a bit. I don't know. He's— like you say, dad—like no one I've ever met before.'

'Be careful, Emmy. You're so young. If I thought...' He was becoming angry again.

'There's nothing to think, dad.' But she recalled the Jane Austen Harvey had given her stuffed at the back of her bookshelves like a primed time bomb. His manner had been so different, strangely sad. She'd almost felt sorry for him and that, she knew, was dangerous. 'Why did he call you Giddy when he showed us the old photograph?'

He seemed to be debating an answer and opted for the easy one. 'I was christened Gideon. From the Bible. I changed it for the act when I met your mother.' He smiled as if it was of no consequence. 'Who ever heard of a song-and-dance man named Gideon.'

She knew that wasn't the whole of it. Some time, maybe, he would confide

278

in her, but not now. 'I like Gideon,' she said.

'That's nice.' He looked weary and waved his hand away from him. 'Cut along, Emmy. Tell your mother I won't be home before the show.'

She paused at the door to his office, hoping he would call her back or say something to reassure her that everything was all right between them. But he seemed to have forgotten her already. He sat, sunk low in the swivel chair, his eyes fixed blankly on a poster from some bygone show, his long, thin fingers cupping his chin. There was a look of desolation about him as if his world had suddenly been turned upside down.

'Gideon! I demand an accounting.'

As his father's voice came back to him in memory across the decades he felt himself stiffen to attention. It was a voice that thundered from the pulpit three times every Sunday and lost none of its fear-inducing awe in the privacy of the family parlour.

The Reverend Elias March was a Presbyterian preacher of the old school who had no patience with the new reformist thinking in the church, which he regarded as the work of the devil. He terrorized his parishioners, mostly simple farm folk and small tradesmen, who held him in high esteem for that very reason. Living a hard life dictated by the vagaries of the climate, the crops, market prices and the hollering and meddling of the politicians in the state capital and Washington, they found Elias March's solid certainty about reward and retribution a comforting rock in a shifting landscape.

He believed implicitly in the cleansing threat of hell-fire and damnation for sinners. And on that terrible day in 1925 his third son and sixth child Gideon was a sinner almost beyond redemption, certainly beyond his father's comprehension.

He stood tall and menacing, his back to the fireplace, his hands clasped behind him, his eyes blazing and his great, black-suited body quivering with rage.

'You have shamed this family. In the eyes of our people and the eyes of the Lord.'

Gideon hadn't quite seen it that way. He had done what other boys in those isolated communities did. He had broken out. It was just too bad that he was the preacher's son. He had played hookey from school and hopped a freight train to the bright lights of Kansas City.

He had dodged the railroad police, slept rough in the city and then spent an agreeable day wasting his hard-earned pocket money on hot dogs and a ticket to the vaudeville theatre. At fourteen he was tall for his age and he pretended to understand the leery jokes of the red-nosed comedians, laughing more heartily than the beefy men around him to show how smart he was. Then there were the singers and the dancers and the long-legged showgirls wearing nothing very much with spanking style and he knew beyond any reasonable doubt that this was where he wanted to be. And that swell, clever, dazzling fellow with his pomaded hair who serenaded the girls and executed such fancy footwork to the jazzy melodies of the time, that was *who* he wanted to be.

It was the icing on the fruitcake of a glorious, liberating experience. Even the grimy hobos in their torn and tattered clothes on the freight train had shared their bread and sausage with him and taught him how to jump from the wagon before it rounded the bend where the guards would be waiting with their mallets and whacking sticks and, some of them, guns. He had sampled moonshine liquor and been propositioned by a bosomy lady in red who was older than his mother. He had had a great time.

But it had to end. The police had rounded him up with a bunch of other boys hanging around the railroad depot and sent him home: a kindly social worker had, despite all his frenzied protests, taken what she deemed to be pity on him, telephoned the feed and grain store that passed on messages to most of the community and bought him a regular train ticket home. The guard on the train had strict instructions to see that he got there and was delivered into the hands of the Reverend Elias March.

Gideon had figured it was all worth the punishment he would get, especially now that he knew what he was going to do with his life. He could ride every adversity in the certain knowledge that his day would come.

In that frame of mind he faced up to his father's fury, cherishing the memory of Kansas City that nothing could take away from him.

'Take your hands out of your pockets, boy! Your brother and sisters are good and obedient creatures. You are the cross I have to bear. You neglect your studies and your chores. Look! Your poor mother is distraught.'

Thus ushered into the argument his poor mother felt obliged to make a contribution although she had made it a practice to leave the chastizing of her offspring to their father. 'Elias! Don't be hard on him,' she said to no effect and then abandoned Gideon to whatever fate

Elias March decreed was fitting. She was accustomed to not being listened to by her husband and had long since given up trying to intercede on her wayward son's behalf.

'Are you truly penitent, Gideon?'

Gideon swallowed hard. 'No father.'

'Then you shall be locked in your room until you are and until I decide a seemly punishment.'

But his rage was finite and now it was spent. He held out his hands like a broken man begging for mercy.

'Join me in prayer, my son, for the good of your soul and we will put all this wickedness behind us.'

Gideon couldn't suppress a smile. He was afraid of his father but, even in his fear, he appreciated what a good show he was putting on for his benefit.

'Why are you laughing, boy?'

'I was thinking father that preaching ain't so different to performing on a stage.' It was out before he could contain it and he was amazed at his own cheek.

'How *dare* you compare me—a man of God—with that trash!' Elias March raised his huge hand and aimed at Gideon's head. The boy managed to duck, but the blow caught his shoulder and sent him flying across the room.

'Upstairs! This instant!'

'Oh my!' said his mother feebly. 'You haven't hurt him?'

Gideon stood up, massaging his bruised shoulder. 'Not much,' he asserted defiantly, turning on his heel and banging the door behind him.

'Did he ground you?' His younger brother Benjamin had been eavesdropping outside as usual.

'What do you think?'

Ben surveyed his brother with a broad grin on his freckled face. 'You asked for it. You just don't know how to handle the old man right. It's easier than you think,' he said sanctimoniously.

Gideon cuffed him round the ear and they exhausted themselves wrestling with each other in the absent-minded way that invariably settled their differences.

'Enough, you two!' Their mother not only had eyes at the back of her head but hearing that could penetrate walls.

'I don't care what he thinks of me, Ben,' Gideon grumbled. 'He's a pious old bigot and I'm not putting up with it much longer.'

'What's a bigot?'

Gideon ignored that.

'What say, Giddy? You taking off?' his brother probed eagerly.

'Never you mind. But don't you go telling him.' Gideon made a fist and thrust it under his brother's chin. 'Promise!'

'God's honour!' Ben crossed his heart.

'Jesus! Leave Him out of it.'

Ben sucked in his breath at such audacity. Fooling around was one thing but blasphemy, in a preacher's home, quite another.

All the time Gideon was serving his time of punishment—no pocket money, extra chores in the house and yard, cleaning out the chicken coop and denied all social contact and any kind of reading material other than the Bible—he was planning his escape. It would, he decided, take place on the last day of the county fair which everyone in the community attended, except for dyed-in-the-wool sinners like Gideon who were confined to barracks.

When the Marches were out of the house at the fair he would set out on foot for the highway and hitch a ride across the state line. He'd seen a poster in a drug store advertising a travelling circus which was pitching up near Fremont in Nebraska. Circuses, so he had been told, were always on the lookout for strong, healthy cheap labour to manhandle the tents and equipment and muck out the animals, with no inconvenient questions asked. The thought of putting a couple of hundred miles between himself and Elias March cheered him up enormously through the dreary intervening days.

Maybe God had decided to turn a blind eye: everything worked according to Gideon's plan much more easily than he had dared to hope.

The circus was far less glamorous and spectacular than the poster promised but the manager, who doubled as the ringmaster, had been let down by two roustabouts who had been jailed in Fremont for being drunk and disorderly and in possession of stolen property.

'Can't trust anyone,' said the manager, chewing on an unlit stogie as he sized up Gideon for signs of unworthiness. Apparently Gideon passed the test.

'What's your name, son?'

'Gideon March.' As he said it he wondered whether he might regret being so honest. 'May,' he corrected himself.

'Well, make up your mind. March. May. June. July. What the hell! Gideon. Giddy! You look strong enough. How old are you?'

'Eighteen,' he lied.

The manager smiled sceptically. It wasn't a pretty sight. He had a broken nose which gave the smile a skewed, threatening look. 'Not in any trouble with the law?'

'No sir.'

'No sir, no sir!' he mimicked. 'The name's Barney. You do as I say and you'll be all right. If you don't you're out. You can bunk in the wagon with the other boy. Three dollars a week, three meals a day.'

'The other boy' was lounging in the door of the manager's trailer. He was a scrawny lad with knowing eyes, nearly a head shorter than Gideon. 'I'll show you where to stow your stuff,' he volunteered. 'I'm Harv. Harvey Persky. Just so long as you remember I was here first, so I'm the boss and we'll get along fine.' A kind of fellowship was established.

Sitting in his small, familiar office at the Adelphi, Gilbert May shook his head. It did no good. Remembering. That boy who had once been Gideon March no longer existed.

But Harvey Persky did. He had just finished putting the chorus through their paces, leaving them limp and resentful.

'That's better,' he said. 'It's still only one step up from lousy, but better.' For some inexplicable reason they seemed to warm to his grudging approval.

Emmy watched him from the stalls, her unnerving conversation with Gilbert still fresh in her mind. She watched him walk up the aisle towards her with a swagger.

'It's *you!* It's all *you!* It's all your fault,' she flung at him, knowing she was making no sense but not caring.

'Emmy!' He sounded perplexed and hurt.

She felt his hands gripping her elbows tightly and then, alarmingly, his mouth hard on hers. She found herself responding, wanting the kiss to go on and on. But just as abruptly he wrenched away from her.

'I'm sorry,' he said. 'I shouldn't have done that.'

She shook her head, confused and at the same time excited as she had been on Christmas Day when she had danced with him. Ashamed, too, that for a moment she had felt nothing but the longing to lose herself in the arms of this man who was so alien to everything she had previously experienced.

'Emmy, I'd never harm you or your family. You have to believe that,' he said. 'At first...well, it's different now. I guess you could say this is my last throw of the dice. My life's been one big crap game and since coming here I see... Hell, I don't know what I mean.'

All she knew about crap games and throwing losing dice was what she had seen at the pictures. But she caught his drift and marvelled that this rough and ready chancer was really much more of a romantic than she was. She touched his cheek almost as if he were a child, maybe Toby, who needed reassurance and comfort. Then she turned on her heel and left the theatre.

From a box at the side of the stage Toby May curled himself into a ball, nursing his knees in his arms, tears streaking down his cheeks.

'I hate him, I hate him, I hate him!' he kept repeated softly.

CHAPTER EIGHTEEN

Tonight, thought Emmy, I shall be very splendid. She felt rather pleased with herself and surprisingly strong, considering all that had happened that day. Strong and sure and serene.

She had laid the table just as Gilbert used to insist it should be laid when they were entertaining special guests. With the best crystal, the Royal Worcester dinner service, the Mappin and Webb cutlery, the embroidered tablecloth and napkins from Hong Kong, worked in the minute 'forbidden stitch', which had been lovingly preserved unused in tissue paper since her father died. She had spent more time than she should on the flower arrangement centrepiece and had gratefully accepted Oliver's offering of two bottles of exceptional claret and two of decent Chablis.

She wasn't too sure what they would eat as Lorraine had been quite peremptory when she had consulted her about the menu. Taking her cue from Mrs Bridges in *Upstairs, Downstairs* she had muttered darkly about 'interference in the kitchen' and threatened to leave Emmy to it if she persisted.

Even Terry had reluctantly agreed to smarten himself up for the occasion and to try to hold his tongue if someone uttered an opinion that ran counter to his own.

It was all like a glorious, silly charade. The only ones who were playing themselves were eyeing each other warily over an aperitif downstairs in the sitting-room, vaguely uncomfortable at the celebratory tone Emmy had set for the night before Toby's funeral.

'She's taking her time,' grumbled Val. 'After all, it's only family. Well, sort of.'

She looked round expectantly for signs of agreement. But Brad was pensive; Frances, who had arrived unexpectedly, was edgy; Oliver was brooding about something quite different; and Flo Gosling, who shouldn't have been there, was wondering why Emmy had insisted she stay and was busily trying to hide her feet in their worn trainers under the long, ethnic patterned skirt.

She was behaving, Emmy reminded herself, like one of those grand hostesses in drawing-room comedies who makes her entrance at the end of the first act, expecting a round of applause, just as her guests have finished assassinating her character.

She smiled mischievously at her reflection in the mirror. Why not? Just for once I'll be a star.

She'd arranged her hair in a chignon at the back anchored with one of her mother's amethyst-encrusted combs. She'd bothered to use blusher and lip gloss and eye shadow. The old gold pendant earrings and choker sat well with the midnight blue velvet dress that minimized her size sixteen figure without robbing it of its more flattering curves. Of course it was old-fashioned: she couldn't remember that last time she had given it an airing, possibly to one of those pompous Conservative dinner dances Oliver occasionally roped her into. But that didn't matter. Tonight it felt right and suitable.

Suitable for what? she wondered. She hadn't yet thought that through. She only knew that in the next few days decisions would have to be made. But they would be her decisions; not decisions based on prudent advice or fraternal opinion or informed judgement.

On that day barely more than a week ago Toby had liberated her. Maybe in his strange way that was what he had intended. He had presented her with the freedom not to do the right thing. Now, this minute, the right thing would be a decent show of grief and respect for the dead—or what is perceived to be respect for the dead.

But she could no more summon up that false bereavement now than when she had mourned for Gilbert, who had died within himself long before he breathed his last, or for Madge, who had emotionally buried herself with him and lived out the rest of her life suspended in a twilight limbo. 'Don't you care?' they'd said, the family, friends. 'Of course I *care*,' she'd replied. 'But caring is different.' They hadn't understood.

Does that make me a monster? she asked the woman in the mirror. Surely not! But even now a nagging ache reminded her she was no stranger to that grief that conceals guilt. As clearly as she could recall the image of Toby's twisted body on the floor of the Adelphi she could see the look of wounded surprise on Harvey Persky's face as he lay lifeless on that same spot.

Maybe now, too, she would be free of the memory of Harvey Persky.

Five pairs of eyes turned towards her as

292

she entered the sitting room. There was a silence, awkward, as if a stranger had come among them and none of them was quite sure what was expected.

Then, cutting the silence, a murmur of approval from Brad. 'You look stunning, Emmy.'

She smiled, stunningly, in the character she had chosen to play that evening. Searching for something gracious to say, she realized that the role might be beyond her experience. She wasn't used to compliments, except for the insincere kind that floated around politely between women who knew perfectly well that they didn't deserve them.

'What? This old thing?' She fingered the velvet dress with a nervous laugh and cursed her clumsy response.

No, really, stunning! they all assured her.

'*You've* taken a lot of trouble—for family.' Val was not about to be lavish with her praise. She was feeling disgruntled and she intended to go on feeling disgruntled for quite some time.

She had come down to Rushey Green that morning full of the milk of human kindness, prepared to comfort where comfort was needed and sympathize when sympathy seemed appropriate and help, although not too much of that she hoped. She wasn't much good at funeral arrangements and she had no idea what would be required in accommodating friends and family afterwards. In any case Emmy and that boy Terry and that peculiar Flo Gosling appeared to have everything very nicely in hand. She wasn't at all put out when she learned that Oliver would be coming to dinner. She had never quite got over the faintly flirtatious hope that they might be a couple.

Then, as she was unpacking her overnight case, she had spotted on the side table by the bed a copy of the *Clifton Clarion* with its black and white photograph of Toby's family mural on the front page in which she and Penny and Cissie were depicted as chimpanzees.

She stared at in horror, not bothering to read the text underneath where Marian Fancey liberally misquoted Emmy on her memories of Toby and the May family.

When she had more or less got over the shock, but not the rage, Val directed her bad temper at the obvious miscreant, Emmy. Her sister, she convinced herself, had deliberately left the paper on the side table, knowing how much it would offend Val.

'Emmy!' She barged into the kitchen where Emmy was deep in conversation with a large, slutty-looking girl. She waved the paper aloft like a weapon. 'What's this?'

Emmy looked up, amiably. 'It's the *Clifton Clarion*,' she said.

'I can *see* that. How did they get that photograph? That's what I want to know.'

'I took them down to the workshop in the garden where Toby did his painting and I showed it to them.' Emmy teased out the words slowly as if she were speaking to a slightly retarded child.

'Why didn't you consult me—us—first? You'd no right, Emmy, you'd no right.' Val wasn't sure whether she was more outraged at Emmy's attitude to her now or at her brass cheek in exposing the mural to the press without family permission. 'We'll be the laughing stock at the funeral tomorrow.' She had visions of hundreds of so-called mourners in the church stuffing handkerchiefs in their mouths to suppress their mirth. 'Reggie will be furious, so will Penny. What's so damned funny?'

Emmy was grinning unrepentantly. 'You, Val. It's only the *Clarion*, for heaven's sake, not the *Sunday Times*. And this is only Clifton Coombe. The people who know us probably won't be surprised and those who don't won't care anyway. It just seemed more interesting than a tedious interview with me. By the way I *didn't* say you were bossy.'

'You said I was bossy?' Val peered at the article underneath the photograph but couldn't make out much because, as Emmy pointed out, she wasn't wearing her eyes.

'No, *I* didn't. I said you were "glossy". You were, you know. Still are. The reporter must have misheard me.'

Val rummaged in her handbag for her reading spectacles and scrutinized the offending text. 'Oh, my God!' she said finally. 'Well, that's it, isn't it! That is *it!*'

'What?'

Val told her about the fifties nostalgia programme for television featuring the middle-aged Mayflowers. But the connection between the *Clarion* piece and the TV show escaped Emmy.

'I can't see why this should make any difference. It might even whip up some interest.'

Val considered that aspect. She conceded that people were funny these days in their appetite for the bizarre slant on show business personalities.

'Come on, Val!' Emmy nudged her sister in a comradely fashion as she did when they were young and Val was having one of her passing tantrums. 'Where's your sense of humour? Don't be such a tragedy queen. There's a lot more important things to consider.'

'Like what?' said Val, sensing Emmy had something to tell her that might not be very pleasant.

Emmy debated whether it was quite the decent thing to talk about Robbie behind his back to his mother. But at least it should concentrate Val's fanciful mind. All things considered, Val took it very well when she told her about Robbie and Deb and the baby. 'I suppose I'm betraying a confidence. But he would have mentioned it tomorrow anyway. Not perhaps the best time.'

'Mentioned?' Val smiled. 'You think it was worth a mention, then?'

'You know what I mean, Val.'

'Yes I do,' Val conceded. 'We, Robbie and I, haven't had the easiest of relationships. Deb—of all people!' She was silent for a moment or two contemplating Deb-of-all-people. 'You know, Emmy, I think it will be good for him. Good for both of them. I just hope they don't go mad and get married. I wouldn't recommend it.'

'Well, you're one of a kind, Val.'

Val deposited her spectacles in their case and took a good long look at herself in the mirror, sucking in her stomach and her cheeks simultaneously. 'Yes I am,' she decided. 'One of a kind. But I still haven't forgiven you for that *Clarion* thing,' she cautioned.

Emmy could see that she was still chewing it over that evening from Val's grudging comment on her appearance before dinner.

'Very nice,' said Oliver who could do much better in the flattery department.

Oh Lord, thought Emmy. Ollie too. More ruffled feathers.

'You've *what?*' he'd said when she had told him about her offer to Terry and Lorraine.

She'd expected some outburst of the sort and was determined to remain unruffled. 'Read my lips, Ollie! I've told Terry that I'll stake him and Lorraine until they get settled up north. And don't tell me I can't because I can. And what's more I made the same offer to Flo Gosling, only she refused, turned it down.'

'And I suppose you'll go on handing out spare cash to every blind beggar with a cap in his hand until there's nothing left.'

He was as close to being apoplectic as she had seen him since the opinion polls had predicted a Labour victory in the last election. In Oliver's morality promiscuity with money was infinitely more reprehensible than promiscuity of the more traditional kind.

'It's my money now. Isn't it?' she replied calmly.

'Emmy, I really do advise you most strongly...'

'Please don't, Ollie. Money's like manure. The only time it does any good is when you spread it around,' she quoted shamelessly from some play she'd seen or saying she'd read, knowing it would infuriate him further. Then she reined in her levity. ('I must be nice to Oliver. I must be nice to Oliver,' she mentally repeated. How could she possibly consider spending the rest of her life with a man she had to keep reminding herself to be nice to—even, that is, if he asked her?)

'I know you have my welfare at heart, Ollie—dear,' she added, which seemed to mollify him. 'You don't want me to be foolish. It's just something I want to do. It's not a fortune I'm throwing away, just a little bit to help a young couple over a sticky period. Maybe they're not the most deserving young couple. I grant you that. But they're my young couple. As Gilbert used to say: if you're lucky enough to be able to afford to be generous then help the needy you know first. Would you seriously be so cross if I'd told you I was donating a huge sum to the bottomless pit of some big registered charity where the outgoing on the cars for paid officials would stake a hundred Terrys and Lorraines?'

'You're being childishly simplistic and very unfair to registered charities,' he deflected the argument.

'I know. And you're being very unfair to Terry—and to me.'

They called an edgy truce, but that grudging 'Very nice' from Oliver reminded her that that was all it was. A truce. It was quite possible that hostilities would resume after the proprieties of the funeral. Perhaps it was just as well Flo had refused her offer, otherwise Oliver would have been totally inconsolable.

They'd been sorting out Toby's old clothes for the Spastics and Age Concern and preparing stuff for the freezer for the following day when Flo, almost shyly, had sprung her surprise.

'I expect now I'll be able to afford a little more for the *Wave*,' Emmy had been saying.

'You're selling Rushey Green?'

'I'm not sure yet. But Oliver tells me that the trust fund for Toby will revert to me and there's quite a bit of cash involved.'

Flo held up one of Gilbert's old blazers that Toby used to wear on his trips into fantasy. 'Spastics or jumble?'

The cuffs and lapels, Emmy noticed, were frayed and the elbows and pockets threadbare. 'Jumble.'

'You needn't bother about the *Wave,* Emmy girl.'

'You've found a millionaire benefactor?'

'No. I've come to my senses. It took long enough. But after you left the other day I got to thinking. Why am I hanging on in this town I never liked even when I was a kid? Just to be a thorn in the side of my parents. That's the truth.'

'Can't you—well, make it up with them?'

Flo bundled an armful of worn but clean shirts into the jumble sack. 'I have. I went to see them. And I mean *see* them. Emmy, they're getting old and they have this terrible pride. I can understand now how I must have bewildered them. Nothing in their lives had prepared them for me. When I told them I was leaving Clifton Coombe, it wasn't that they were pleased, it was just that they seemed easier. And they started behaving like parents, worrying about how I'd get on, where I'd go, what I'd do for money. Then I lied, saying I'd visit regularly—a real whopper!—I was turning over a new leaf. I think they have visions of me wearing proper tweed suits and Peter Pan collars and having my hair permed and getting a proper job in a proper office. All lies! But the main thing is they believed it. So I can leave town with a clear conscience. That is, as clear as anyone's conscience can be, especially mine.'

'Where will you go?'

'There's a women's group in Wales I've been in touch with on and off. Very go-ahead and active. They're organizing crèches for working mothers in local factories, a home for battered wives, lobbying on behalf of part-time workers. All the stuff I care about. And they want to bring out a weekly news-sheet, airing issues, raising political awareness. The job's mine if I want it. It doesn't pay much, hardly anything in fact. But it's worthwhile and I can do it. I'll be sorry to close the old *Wave* but in its way it served its purpose—and mine. I suppose it's a selfish way of looking at it, abandoning everything I fought for down here.'

'Not selfish,' Emmy reassured her. 'Natural. You want to feel comfortable with yourself. And I always told you you would never be that all the time you remained here. Besides, you did a lot of good, even in Clifton Coombe. Still, I'll miss you.' She stopped sorting Toby's old clothes into piles. She was grateful to Flo for giving her something to think about other than the task in hand. There was something so final about disposing of a dead person's wardrobe, like paying the very last of your last respects.

'I'll miss the *Wave* too. What *will* you do for money?'

Flo didn't seem all that concerned. Now that she'd come to a decision she appeared almost light-hearted. 'I've a bit saved and if anyone knows how to fiddle social security I do. I've advised enough students and single parents.'

'I'd like to help, Flo. A little something weekly.'

'I knew you'd say that, Emmy. That's why I'm refusing. Maybe I wasn't lying all that much to my sainted parents. Maybe I am turning over a new leaf.' She examined a candyfloss pink and white striped cotton shirt of which Toby had been particularly fond. 'Can I have this? To remember him?'

Emmy nodded. 'Anything.'

'Just this. I intend travelling light. No excess baggage. Emmy, I'm going to make it on my own. I feel it. I know I can. I've even given up booze and sponging layabouts.' She grinned. 'But don't take that for a pledge. Spare me some minor vices.'

She wished she had had more time to herself to digest Flo's news. Much as she had urged her to turn her back on Clifton Coombe, Emmy hadn't really believed Flo would ever take the plunge. Now that the decision was made, Emmy had a strong

303

sense that the structure of her own life was being chipped away and that Flo's imminent departure would leave another unpluggable gap.

'Emmy!' She was sitting staring into space in Toby's workshop at the bottom of the garden when Brad arrived. 'You look preoccupied—no, melancholy. Silly!' he apologized. 'Of course you're melancholy. The funeral.'

She felt a rush of warmth and gratitude. She had forgotten what a soothing influence he always had on her. Even now, facing his own grim future, he was more concerned for her.

She took his hand, feeling the sympathetic pressure of his long, bony fingers. 'It's not that, Brad. It just seems that Toby's death has unlocked so many doors and I think I'm a little scared of going through them.' She didn't bother to explain, knowing that Brad unerringly understood.

'You have to think of yourself now, Emmy.'

'What I'd like to think, Brad, is—'

He stopped her abruptly. 'Pity I can do without.' But he said it kindly, not as a reproof.

'I wasn't offering pity.' She wondered whether it was too late to offer anything else.

He was looking at her as if reading her thoughts. 'You never believed I loved you, Emmy, did you?'

She shook her head. 'No.'

'You were wrong. In my way I did. Even though it wasn't enough. I know I'm not Fran's father,' he said suddenly. 'At least I'm pretty sure. But it doesn't matter now.'

'Let's just say there's a strong element of doubt,' she admitted. 'But why did you let Fanny believe you were?'

'She hates being called Fanny.'

'I know. It's a bad habit of mine. One of many. So, why did you encourage her to believe you were her father?'

He was staring at Toby's mural and at his other strange, striking paintings scattered around. 'They're so wild: weird and yet very real. Every time I look at them I see something different.' He studied them for a long time, then answered her question reluctantly. 'I suppose I didn't want her to think her father was a vicious man who died a violent death.'

She experienced a sense of shock. She hadn't expected him to be so direct. 'Harvey wasn't vicious. He just never felt easy in his own skin, so he made life difficult for everyone else.' Emmy smiled wryly. 'I have to say Fanny's a lot like him.' And it was true. Fanny had Harvey's drive and charm, and ruthlessness, too: his ability to introduce an unsettling atmosphere into what would seem on the surface the most settled of situations.

'She's here, Emmy.'

She raised her eyebrows. 'So soon?'

'I left her in the house with Val.'

'In that case I'd better go and sort them out before they start winding up Terry and Lorraine. Very low fuses, those two—all four of them in fact.' She lent forward and kissed Brad tenderly on the cheek. 'I've never deserved you, Brad. Maybe that's why I've resented you all these years. You remind me of my shortcomings. Pax?'

'Always pax!' He lifted her chin with his forefinger and peered into her eyes. 'Why do I get the feeling there's something you're not telling me?'

'Later, Brad.'

'It's not Oliver?'

'No, Brad. It's not Oliver,' she said, amused that such a thought should cross his mind.

'Why do I get the feeling there's something you're not telling us?' said Frances abruptly as they were sitting over the remains of Lorraine's excellent dinner, finishing the claret and wondering whether the occasion demanded high seriousness or just an amicable exchange of trivial views.

My, my! thought Emmy, am I that transparent or have Brad and Fanny been swapping dialogue?

Despite the tension it had all gone rather well, she'd considered. After an initial uneasiness, Val and Oliver seemed to relax in each other's company. Flo and Frances became quite heated, but amiably so, about women's rights in the Third World. Brad was—well, Brad. Emmy looked at him, pale, drawn, toying with the food but careful not to draw attention to his lack of appetite: they exchanged a warm, secret smile.

Lorraine was lavishly complimented on her roast crown of lamb and an immaculate cheese soufflé.

'Amazing!' enthused Oliver. 'How did you learn to cook like this?'

'From a cook book, of course,' was her surly reply as she turned on her heels in a huff and left them to it.

Oliver looked bewildered. 'I only asked.'

'What a bloody snob you are, Ollie!' Emmy reprimanded him. 'Why shouldn't she be a good cook? I imagine no one told her it was supposed to be difficult.'

'That's deep,' said Val.

'No it isn't. It's a fact. The world's too free with reasons why we shouldn't take risks.' Emmy felt her cheeks flush with wine and embarrassment. What on earth had made her say that?

She had a feeling that clever Fanny would pick up on it.

'Is there something you're not telling us?' repeated Oliver apprehensively. Terry's handout was shock enough for one day.

'Well, yes, actually, there is.' Emmy drew a deep breath and busied herself meticulously refolding her napkin into a water-lily shape so that she wouldn't have to meet their eyes. 'Marcus Gammie telephoned this morning. He's bringing a friend of his who runs an art gallery down at Rushey Green.'

'Since when have you been so thick with Marcus?' Val interrupted.

'What's that got to do with anything?' snapped Frances, who believed in the first things first. 'Well, go on, mother. And—?'

'And there's the prospect of an exhibition.'

'Of Toby's terrible, insulting paintings? You're joking,' said Val. 'No, you're not, are you?'

'No, I'm not. I shall help organize it and provide the biographical notes for the brochure.'

'You mean like stripping the family naked!'

'No, *not* like stripping the family naked, Val,' she said irritably. 'Stop being so melodramatic. Anyway it will be for charity.'

'Which, I may remind you, begins at home.'

'Val!'

'Well, I think it's a wonderful idea, Emmy. All that talent should be recognized.'

Trust Brad, she thought, to back her up. And Flo too.

'Have you really thought this through seriously, mother?' said Frances dubiously.

'No, I haven't. That's what's so good about it.'

'What if he—this art fellow—doesn't think they're worth it?' said Oliver.

'Oh he will. Marcus is certain. As a matter of fact he's already seen them. He came down with Marcus months ago, before Toby died.' She unfolded the water lily and placed it in her lap, well pleased with herself. 'Now if no one wants to eat the rest of that Brie I will, before it runs all over the cheeseboard.' She looked over at her dumbstruck sister and burst out laughing. 'Oh, Val, if you could see your face!'

CHAPTER NINETEEN
8 JANUARY 1958

'I don't know what to do about him, Emmy. He won't eat. He barely sleeps. He just sits in that wretched shed, drawing those awful pictures. I'm at my wit's end. Ever since...'

Her normally placid mother looked distraught and wretched. She kept her worries from the rest of the family because they had a job to do being bright and glamorous and mustn't be bothered. The show must go on (although no one had ever successfully explained to Emmy why) and it would never do to let the public glimpse the private trauma of the Mays who always prided themselves on putting on such a smiling, untroubled face for those outsiders traditionally regarded in the music hall as 'civilians.'

But Emmy was different. She was the May who didn't need to be sparkling on stage every night, and therefore didn't have to be protected from the realities of the May household. Her mother could confide in her, rely on her to keep secrets.

'Your father doesn't seem to understand,

want to know. He's in another world these days. And the doctor—Emmy...!' She tried to contain her tears but they trickled down her cheeks one by one in mournful progress streaking her careful make-up. (She was always fussy about keeping up standards.)

'Emmy, he thinks if he goes on like this we'll have to think about putting him in a home. He thinks it would be best for him. I couldn't bear that.'

'Don't cry, mum,' murmured Emmy knowing it was as useless a remark as counselling someone to stop worrying. She hugged Madge to her and sure enough the trickle became a flood.

'I hadn't noticed,' she admitted. And it was true. She hadn't noticed much of anything over the past week, not even the strange, solitary young brother who had always depended so much on her in the past. She had been living in a daze, bemused, exhilarated and angry with herself, too. This was not the way she, Emmy May, behaved.

Val would tell her she was in love. But Val put any deviation from the norm down to being in love. It happened to her all the time. Emmy wasn't sure she believed in that kind of love. If she had she'd have fallen for Brad who was ready and willing, though not, she suspected from her

311

admittedly strictly limited understanding, very able. Certainly he was desirable, as the number of squealing Clifton Coombe fans that haunted the Adelphi stage door every night testified.

There was nothing particularly desirable about Harvey Persky. Not desirable at all in the accepted sense. But since his unexpected arrival in the town less than a month ago she had felt more truly a person in her own right than ever before. No longer the 'other one' in the May family, she was, she knew, in Harvey's eyes *the* one.

Common sense, of which she had always had an overabundance even as a child, told her it was all wrong. He was thirty years older than her. He was uncouth, ill-mannered, self-seeking, hardly prepossessing and she feared, but did not dare to ask, that the hold he had over her father was more than merely long-past friendship. His clumsy gestures, like the Jane Austen at Christmas and his hosting of an embarrassing party at the Metropole in Brighton, were almost pathetically planned to please, but he hadn't the grace to carry them off with style. In contrast his dealings with the Adelphi company were so insensitive that he had succeeded in destroying the happy amicability that Gilbert had always fostered, even though the box office receipts had increased dramatically. Several cast members had walked out in a huff and been replaced, it had to be said, by better, more professional, if less likeable artists. And Gilbert had let it all happen. When he was challenged he said it was for the best and perhaps, Emmy found herself thinking, it was.

But none of this mattered when she examined her feelings for Harvey. Despite all of his shortcomings when she was with him it was as if he exercised some kind of of strange spell over her with those mesmerizing eyes that seemed to X-ray the woman inside the girl: the woman in Emmy only he could release.

Ever since he had kissed her she had known there would be no going back, no retreat in their kindly relationship. Each morning she awoke with a sense of suspense, uncertainty. She wished she were as experienced and nonchalant about sex as Val.

But Harvey seemed to be avoiding her, treating her with casual courtesy in company while making sure they were never alone. She half hoped and half feared she had read more into the kiss then he had meant.

Until one morning when the Adelphi was still and quiet as if holding its breath before the eruption of activity later in the day. She had taken to arriving early just to enjoy the calm that seemed to settle her emotions, away from the family and the others.

She was passing a prop room backstage which Gilbert always insisted on keeping locked, when she noticed the door was half open. She heard a sound and peered inside.

'Beautiful! Don't you think?' He spoke gruffly, sounding embarrassed at somehow being caught. At what?

'You scared me,' she said. But he hadn't.

'She reminds me of you a little. Those eyes.' Harvey was holding a cast of an Egyptian head, one of a pair they sometimes used as set decoration. Nefertiti perhaps, or some Birmingham factory's cheap impression of Nefertiti.

'It's just plaster.' Her throat was dry and she felt that throbbing sensation she always felt now when she was with him, as if her whole body were about to explode.

'I often come here, looking at things, imagining how they'd look on stage. I know it's mostly trash. But all you need is a little magic. Lights, colour, audiences. Magic! That's what your father does. Makes magic.'

He had never spoken so eloquently about Gilbert.

'You too,' she said softly.

He shrugged. 'Sometimes. With me it comes harder.'

He appeared suddenly forlorn as he had that Christmas afternoon in the garden at Rushey Green. She wanted to comfort him. But more than that she wanted to feel his arms around her again.

She took the Egyptian head from his hands and, without thinking, let it crash to the floor. She looked down at the scattered pieces of plaster, perplexed by her own act of vandalism.

'Why did you do that?' he asked, more as a formality, for he hadn't seemed surprised by her action.

'I don't know. I—I didn't want you comparing me to that—that thing.' She gazed accusingly at the shattered head. She was so close to him that she could feel his breath on her cheek.

'Emmy!' he whispered, 'if you don't go now...'

'I know, I know.'

He cupped his hands round her face and forced her to look at him. 'You're just a kid. How can you understand what I'm saying?'

'I know, I know,' she repeated. 'And I'm not a kid—not any more.'

As he wrapped his arms around her she thought: this isn't the way it's supposed to be. No romance, no music, just a grubby old room at the back of the theatre and a man she barely knew who was more than twice her age.

But she didn't care. She didn't even care that their sweaty, frenzied lovemaking, rolling around on the dusty floor of the prop room, had satisfied neither of them. She knew that wouldn't be the end of it.

And the next time, in the flat he had taken in Clifton Coombe, he had been gentle and solicitous yet passionate as he initiated her into the pleasures of fulfilling her own desire as well as his. He was a skilful lover and she understood now why Brad's awkward fumblings had been such a let-down.

She had told no one, hugging the secret to herself, partly because she didn't wish to share the thrill of it and partly out of shame for being so easily seduced by a man reason told her she should distrust.

But it was too late now and she had to admit that Val, in her usual sassy fashion, had been right: once you'd got the hang of it it was one of life's great enjoyments, like oysters and caviare and champagne and New Year at the Savoy and seeing your face on the cover of *Life* magazine. Emmy would have put it differently, but then Val's pleasures tended toward the superficial.

'Are you listening, Emmy?' Her mother was looking at her, puzzled and still tearful.

'I'm listening, mum. I'll go and see Toby.'

'Please Emmy. You're good with him. Better than anyone.' She blew her nose loudly and scrubbed her cheeks with her handkerchief. 'Emmy, I don't want to lose Toby. It would break up the family. I've thought about that a lot lately.' She paused, then continued nervously. 'I've thought a lot about you, too. That man! I worry. He seems—well, he spends a good deal of time with you. It doesn't seem healthy—him—a girl like you.'

'Don't!' said Emmy, too harshly, anything to stop her mother quizzing her about her relationship with Harvey. 'I mean,' she went on, less abrasively. 'Don't worry. There's nothing to worry about. I promise.'

'I hope so,' said her mother doubtfully.

'I'll talk to Toby now. And *stop* talking about breaking up the family. The Mays are—well, the Mays are invincible. That's what dad always says.' But not lately, she thought.

'You're a good girl, Emmy.'

Emmy smiled, not feeling good at all.

'What is it, Toby?'

He was sitting cross-legged on the bare

wooden floor of the old hut stabbing fiercely with his paintbrush at a sheet of drawing paper laid out before him. He didn't look up at her approach.

'What's that you're painting?'

He went on sploshing the angry reds and oranges and purples across the paper, the colour running wetly and merging at the bottom to form a bubbling base for the abstract rage he was expressing.

'It's him—and you,' he mumbled finally. Then he lifted his arms and pummelled her skirt, splattering it with paint. 'I saw you, Emmy. I saw you with that man.' He continued to lash out at her and she didn't try to stop him. Then, exhausted, he threw his arms around her legs and pinned her tightly to him, sobbing into her skirt. 'I saw you...I saw you...' he kept moaning.

She lifted him up and hugged him, smoothing her fingers through his hair and rubbing his back in a circular motion which always seemed to comfort him, aware that she had no comfort to give him. If he had seen her and Harvey she couldn't lie to him. She'd never lied to Toby even to calm him down. Somehow she always found a palatable truth to disguise an unpalatable fact.

'You don't like him, Emmy? Emmy, you don't?'

She looked into his eyes. They were

beseeching her to reassure him and she consoled herself that he had asked the wrong question. Like was not an emotion that entered into her feeling for Harvey. Desire, passion—maybe even love. But if she were honest, she did not like him.

'No, Toby,' she said. 'I don't think I like him.'

He examined her face earnestly. 'Truly?'

'Truly.'

He closed his eyes, seeming contented, and nestled close to her. She hummed softly in his ear, nothing identifiable as a song, just a melody they'd made up, and he joined in putting jabberwocky words to it that made no sense but had a kind of rhythmical impulse. They remained like that for a while, their arms locked around each other, humming and singing their shared song.

'Mum says you're not eating. That's silly. Promise me you will.'

He nodded. 'I've missed you Emmy,' he said sleepily.

'But I've been here, all the time.' She knew what he meant though.

'You won't see him, Emmy.'

She stiffened slightly and he sensed it. 'But he's dad's friend, Toby.'

'He frightens me,' he said.

Poor Toby, she thought. Everything frightens him: the postman with the limp;

the theatre tom that snarls like a tiger; the boys who hang around the street corners in town and jeer at him; the girls behind the counter at Woolworth's who think him puny and daft.

You mustn't let them see it, she'd always told him. There's nothing to be scared of.

'You mustn't let him see it,' she said now and then wondered why. Harvey was no threat to Toby. 'There's nothing to be scared of. He—he thinks you're very clever. Your paintings.' She wouldn't even try to convince him that Harvey had any warmer feelings for him.

'Reggie says he looks like a gangster. George Raft, he said. A gangster.'

She blushed, glad that Toby couldn't see. 'Reggie doesn't know what he's talking about.' But Reggie did, she conceded. Harvey did look a little like George Raft. And who was she to vouch that he hadn't been a gangster in his time?'

'All better now?' she said abruptly.

He didn't answer but gripped her hand so firmly that his fingers left indentations on the skin.

Who was Harvey?

The question nagged at her after she had delivered Toby, admitting to an appetite, to his mother.

'Who is Harvey Persky?'

Her father was watching the matinée from the back of the stalls, enjoying it all—the jokes, the tricks, the song and dance routines and the banter with the children in the audience—as if it were freshly minted. For a while whatever was troubling him seemed forgotten and Emmy cursed herself for blighting those blessed moments of forgetfulness.

He swung round startled, as if he were expecting some kind of retribution. Then he registered that it was only Emmy and turned back to the stage.

'You know who he is,' he whispered but not quietly enough to prevent a testy chorus of shushing from the back rows.

'Dad, you've seen this a thousand times before. You owe us, me, an answer,' she persisted.

'Not here, Emmy,' he said, smiling placatingly at a glowering face from the back row demanding hush.

'Then outside,' she hissed, dragging him by the sleeve through the swing doors into the foyer. 'Let's walk.'

He looked at her and sighed.

'I owe him, Emmy,' he said at last.

They were walking in the municipal gardens across the street from the Adelphi. There was no one else about. It was too chill for strollers and lovers and a mist from the sea blended with the dusk of evening to cast a dank, gloomy cloak over the bare trees and neatly landscaped beds waiting for a spring planting.

She shivered but not from the cold.

'You'll catch your death,' he said. The very English expression had an alien ring and she noticed how very American he still sounded, noticed too that in a way he was as much of a mystery to her as Harvey. Perhaps even her mother didn't truly know him.

'I'm all right,' she said. 'What do you mean, you owe him? Owe him what, how much?'

'I let him down. A long time ago. It's not something I'm proud of.'

She heard the crunch of their footsteps on the path on which the frost was already beginning to form. She didn't speak, sensing it was better to let him tell the story in his own time.

'After I left home my father tried to track me down. It took some time because he refused to ask for help from the authorities as any normal parent would do, too pig-headed to admit he's failed as a father I guess.' He lifted his hand and rubbed his forehead. 'You don't want to hear this, Emmy. It's not even important.'

She stopped and turned toward him, shocked. 'Not even important, dad? How can you say that? You haven't been the same since Harvey arrived. You take him on as a partner, let him run the show and I don't know what else. Dad...' There was a catch in her throat and she had to swallow hard before she could continue. 'We need to know. I need to know,' she whispered urgently.

He took her hand in his. 'Don't get too close to him, Emmy. He has all the charm in the world when he feels like it. I've seen you and him and I know I should have said something. But I always vowed, after my father, I'd never dictate to my children, just bring them up sensibly enough to make the right decisions, or so I hoped. But now I wonder if that's fair, if I wasn't just fooling myself. I wanted so much for you all.'

She wrestled her hand out of his grasp. Even though she had begged him to tell her she suddenly dreaded what he might confess about Harvey, about himself. Why couldn't she love freely, without conflicting loyalties, like other people? If, indeed, what she felt for Harvey was love.

'Dad, don't!' She couldn't bear to hear him, judging, questioning himself. He'd always been so rock solid, so certain, so sure. Other children in Clifton Coombe had flawed fathers, but not the Mays. When you announced that your father was Gilbert May you felt you were walking around with an invisible halo, a favoured offspring.

But she knew it was too late to draw back. She had to hear the truth. Her father's truth.

'Harvey discovered that someone was asking around about a Gideon March. He was good at ferreting out things like that. There were a lot of small circuses in those days in the Midwest, a magnet for runaways. When he told me I figured it wouldn't be too long before my father caught up with me and nothing, *nothing* would make me return home to that house and that endless preaching of his.' Even now the bitterness in his voice was disturbing.

'That was your real name. Gideon March—not May?'

'I changed it when I hightailed it across into Canada. Harvey gave me the address of a pal of his in Toronto, helped me get a job. I said I'd wait for him to join me while he put up a smokescreen...'

'A smokescreen?'

Her question pulled him up with a jolt and he pondered it carefully, seeming to want to draw back but knowing he couldn't, not quite. 'A smokescreen so they couldn't follow me.'

She wanted to ask who 'they' were if his father had pursued him alone, spurning help in his search, but she resisted, sensing that Gilbert would clam up if taxed too far.

'I worked my way east to the border, turning my hand to anything—crop picking, dish washing, you name it. There was a lot of action there then, smuggling bootleg liquor into the States and one small-time operator hired me as a look-out. Given a push I could have taken up a life of crime, I suppose, and ended up behind bars or at the bottom of Lake Erie with a bullet through my head. I told you, Emmy, there's a lot of my life I'm not proud of and I've been trying to make up for it ever since.' He gave a short, humourless laugh. 'Anyway, I decided I was too chicken for crime and I managed to slip over into Canada and make my way to Toronto. The address wasn't much more than a flop-house and Harvey's pal's idea of a job was pimping for a local whorehouse.' He stopped suddenly as if seriously listening to himself. 'Oh, my God, Emmy! I never thought I'd be saying any of this to you, to any of you. Promise me you won't repeat it—to your mother, the others. They mustn't ever know.' He had the same expression as Toby, silently pleading for reassurance from her. Why her? Why always her?

She linked her arm in his. 'They won't

ever know from me, dad. But maybe they've a right...'

'No.' He shrugged away from her. 'No, never. I'm not that boy any more. I'm Gilbert May. I've made something of myself.'

'And you didn't wait for Harvey in Toronto,' she guessed. That was what was eating into him, the betrayal of a trust, more than all the rest.

'That's right. I just took off. And, Emmy, the worst of it is I didn't even give it a second thought.'

'You were just a boy.'

'But I should have...! What the hell, I didn't. I was lucky. I joined a travelling vaudeville troupe, learned the song and dance routines, added a few ideas of my own. There was a lovely old lady named Lily in the show; can't even remember her other name. I guess she taught me just about everything: how to project myself, how to use what talent I had to the best advantage, how to dress, how to speak...'

'How to dazzle?' she prompted.

He laughed again, not abrasively but with genuine warmth for a lady named Lily to whom he owed the life of Gilbert May. 'She gave me my name and when the chance came to come to England she urged me to take it, gave me some contacts over here. A friend fixed me up with some convincing-looking papers and a passport. And—and that's the story of my life.'

'What happened to Lily?'

'I never knew. I was too busy making my own way in show business. I wrote a couple of times but there was no reply and the troupe had disbanded.'

'What was she like, dad?'

'Very regal, grand. A great beauty in her day. She'd been on Broadway but, like a lot of entertainers, had fallen on hard times. She used to appear in sketches with the comics in the troupe. She was the high-toned stooge, like that actress in the Marx Brothers films. When I knew her better it hurt me to see it. But she didn't mind. "It's all theatre," she'd say. "If you can hold an audience it doesn't matter whether it's slapstick or *Hamlet*, you're someone of value." I suppose you could say she taught me to value myself. And so, too, in his way, did Harvey—that skinny, crafty, slum kid. I've always felt badly about him. I guess I didn't realize how much he wanted us to be a team. "You've got the class, Giddy, I've got the brains. We've got it made." But I never waited to find out what "it" he had in mind. I never gave him a chance.'

He looked at his watch. 'I've got to get into costume for the finale, Emmy.' He put his hands on her shoulders in a

327

conspiratorial gesture. 'Our secret?'

She nodded, feeling privileged that he'd told her so much about himself while at the same time repressing a nagging suspicion that he hadn't told her the whole of it.

She wandered the town relentlessly, the secrets of her father's past racing through her mind yet somehow not quite connecting, until she found herself outside the new apartment block where Harvey had taken a top-floor flat. She'd been there a couple of times but he hadn't felt easy about it. 'This isn't the place for you, Emmy. No class.' Class! She smiled. Gilbert and Emmy May. Class! 'I want something better for you.' And he'd said it so earnestly, as if he were trying to commit them to a life together.'

Her sisters were convinced he was keeping a woman there. And when she had spotted him patting Ruby—one of the girls in the show—on the rump and saw her sly wink in return, she remembered Penny primly likening him to a certain famously sexy musical comedy star who didn't feel he'd given of his best if he hadn't gone through the chorus within three weeks of rehearsal.

'Mark my words, he's randy. All short men are,' she'd announced with great authority.

'Too true!' said Val, rolling her eyes,

with even greater authority.

When Emmy had taxed him with it he not only hadn't denied it but was plainly surprised that she should couple his feelings for her with his pleasure at helping himself to what was on offer in the chorus line. She knew she should have felt humiliated, demeaned, yet, paradoxically, it had added to his attraction. She wasn't one of a crowd. She was special.

'When this is over I'll be myself again,' she'd told him, reassuring herself. But she couldn't foresee that time and neither could he.

She rang the bell, not expecting him to be there and, when he opened the door, she almost turned and ran.

'I don't know why I'm here,' she said nervously.

'You're cold. What are you doing, walking around in a thin jacket like this?' He sounded quite paternal.

He took her into the sparsely furnished living room, sat her down by the gas fire and started rubbing her hands and feet. She tried to suppress the tingle of excitement his touch always generated in her.

'I've been talking to Gilbert. He told me about you—and him.'

He looked up. 'All of it?'

'I'm not sure.'

'I'll get you a brandy.'

'I'd rather have tea.'

He grinned. 'Then you'd better make it. English tea is still a mystery to me, warming the pot and all that stuff.'

'So what did he tell you?' he called to her as she busied herself in the tiny, purpose-built kitchen, putting on the kettle and finding a caddy of tea-leaves which he seldom used but felt was a necessary accoutrement of the Englishman's home.

'That he let you down in Toronto, not waiting for you to join him.' She looked around the bare, tiled walls of the kitchen. 'When are you going to furnish this place properly? It could be quite nice with some pictures and bits and pieces.'

'I've told you. It's just a place to flop down. It's not for ever.'

She opened the drawer by the sink looking for a spoon and a strainer and her hand strayed to a garishly printed circus programme stuffed underneath the cutlery container.

'Is this the circus you and dad worked in together?'

She thumbed through the pages with their crude photographs of circus acts. As she did so a yellowed newspaper clipping fell out on to the work surface. Her hand, she noticed, was trembling when she picked it up. The kettle of boiling water started screaming on the gas ring and she took her time turning off the gas and filling the tea pot.

I don't want to read this, she told herself. It's not my business. I shall put the clipping back in the brochure and forget it. But she knew she couldn't. Not now.

It was dated October 1925, and was from a Nebraska newspaper. The headline took up almost as much space as the text: 'Kansas Minister Murdered in Fairground'. The rest of it was more speculative. Presbyterian minister Elias March had been found dead, his skull crushed, hidden on a dump near the site of a circus that had recently left the area. It was known that he was searching for his son Gideon who had run away from home and worked for a time as a rigger at the circus. Witnesses had heard them engaged in a heated argument. The son had since disappeared, but the Nebraska police had put out an all-points alert to locate him. His weeping mother had told this reporter, 'He was a fine boy, but he and his father never did get along real good.'

She stared at the clipping as if it were a living, malevolent thing. She felt it burning her fingers and sending arrows of pain through her body. When she dropped it on the floor, she still couldn't take her eyes off it.

Lies. Gilbert. Harvey. Both guilty. Both involved in this conspiracy of silence. What more lies were they capable of? But she was too numbed with shock to think coherently.

'Emmy!' He was standing in the door to the kitchen, but she continued to stare stupidly at the innocently evil piece of ageing newsprint. And she knew she was looking at that missing piece in the jigsaw of her father's life.

She turned towards him and lunged at him, pummelling him with her fists. 'This is what you came for! Blackmailer! Blackmailer!' she sobbed.

He tried to restrain her. 'Emmy, listen, for Christ's sake, listen!' he said urgently. But she was past listening to anything other than the certainties in her own mind.

Then, somehow, she was out in the street again, running and stumbling, oblivious of everyone and everything. When she fell she picked herself up not caring or even noticing that her face was cut and her knees grazed.

And all the time she heard him calling from the open window of the flat on the top floor. 'Emmy! Emmy! Emmy!'

CHAPTER TWENTY

The Reverend Arthur Selby cast his eyes appreciatively over the assembled mourners. He hadn't seen such a large congregation since BBC Television had selected the parish church of Clifton Coombe for a recording of *Songs of Praise*. The event had brought out the pious, the would-be-pious and the pious-only-when-it-showed in such huge numbers that they spilled out into the churchyard where the hymns had to be relayed to the overflow through loudspeakers. It had on the whole been quite a feather in his cap, even eliciting a grudging compliment from his singularly phlegmatic bishop, despite the complaints of regular worshippers who grumbled that the congregation had been non-representative and that seventy-five per cent of those who sang so lustily and beamed such holy faces at the cameras never went near the church except for births, deaths and marriages.

Although a devoted man of God he was also very much a man of his times. He was not so naive as to suppose that everyone attending the funeral service for

Toby May was there out of genuine affection or respect for the dead man. In fact a lot of those he could name had been anything but benevolent in their strongly voiced feelings about his eccentric behaviour and the desirability of having him put away—'for his own good, of course.'

On the other hand it wasn't every day that you got to share prayers with celebrities like the distinguished actor Sir Reginald May and Lady May and the financier Harry Eardley and his wife Penelope, who with her sisters had formed the Mayflowers singing group, and the once very famous Hollywood star Brad Hastings. Not to mention the one you kept seeing in bit parts and commercials, Valerie May, and Emmy May's daughter Frances who was very big in television. Rumours that royalty might put in an appearance had regrettably proved to be unfounded.

There had been more than a little media interest in the funeral and the circumstances of Toby's sudden death in his father's old theatre. It was amazing how many very best friends of the Mays reporters from national newspapers and regional radio and TV had managed to find propping up the bars of local pubs, serving behind the counters of local stores and living in retirement on bungalow estates by the sea, all anxious to be interviewed.

Arthur Selby wasn't the only one to survey the scene in church with satisfaction.

'It's a jolly good house,' whispered Emmy. She hadn't expected that the service and Arthur Selby's simple, well-chosen words of comfort and belief in the after-life would be so affecting. She was overcome by the sense of loss she had rigorously denied herself, even derided, since that calamitous day at the Adelphi just over a week before. She had accepted the fact that Toby was gone and with him a substantial part of her life, but now it was an aching reality. All the same she was determined to keep up a cheerful front for his sake. 'Toby would have enjoyed a big box office send-off like this.'

'You're incorrigible,' Brad whispered back.

'Of course. How much do you think Penny's hat cost?' It was an elegant funeral number in black Bangkok straw with a large sweeping brim garnished with a complementary ribbon in graded shades of grey. 'Enough to feed a starving village in Africa for five years?'

'Bitchy, too!' It wasn't a criticism, or even a considered comment: he understood very well what she was going through and her need to suppress her feelings in public until she could indulge them in the luxury of privacy.

She grimaced. 'It's all coming out—after all these years,' she intoned in a mock sepulchral voice. Her gaze fixed on the ceiling of the church. 'It's gone!'

'I guess he's seen what he came to see.' He knew what she was talking about. A portly pigeon had resisted all efforts to reject it and had observed the proceedings perched high on the buttress about the nave, emitting now and then a throaty chorus, especially during Miss Fraser's lively rendition of 'That's Entertainment' on the organ. There had been an audible gasp from those mourners who recognized the melody and a puzzled murmur from those who thought it some newfangled setting of a familiar hymn.

'Of course it's Toby—the pigeon. I like to think that birds are way stations for the spirit on the journey to the hereafter. Don't you?'

'I've never thought about it.' He looked askance at her.

'Except I always figured Toby for a robin or a finch.' She frowned. 'Don't worry. I'm quite sane. Just fanciful.'

'How fanciful were you being last night—about Toby's exhibition?'

'Oh, quite serious. In fact Daniel Boisseau came down with Marcus—oh, months, a year, ago. He was very impressed. An original. A primitive. A less scary Francis Bacon. You know how they talk. He didn't even mind that Toby slunk into a corner and wouldn't speak to him. Nice man!' She thought it was a strange discussion to be having during the service for her dead brother while all around them were trying to look as if they were in deep communion with God on the subject of the dear departed's soul. She fingered the white cardboard Order of Service in front of her: Toby Alexander Gilbert May: 1945-1991. A life! She brushed away a tear angrily and then felt Brad's comforting arm round her shoulder.

'It looks so clinical, tidy,' she murmured pointlessly.

'Buck up!' he whispered, then, changing the subject. 'Daniel Boisseau! That is serious. Not just one gallery but branches all over.'

He was right. There was always a bright side. Maybe in the long run Toby would be the best remembered May of them all. 'He couldn't persuade Toby then to be parted from his paintings, let alone display them in public,' she said under her breath as the organ swelled triumphantly into the last chorus of 'Onward, Christian Soldiers'. Above the roar of the congregation raising their voices in delight at knowing the words and letting their neighbours know they knew them, she felt she could hear Toby's sweet, treble voice expressing some inner solace in the hymn he so loved. 'I don't think he'd mind at all now. The paintings! And the diary!' She hadn't meant to say that. Not yet anyway. Maybe Brad hadn't heard.

But he had. 'Diary?' His query was lost in the final thundering forecast of the 'Cross of Jesus Going on Before'.

There was a silent moment of prayer, then a rustle of expectation.

'Right!' She braced herself to walk down the aisle and into the throng of family, friends and plain, ordinary sightseers. 'It's show-time!'

A sudden shower brought out the umbrellas by the graveside. Emmy shared hers with Alice Gravely who was muttering over her prayer book, which surprised Emmy who hadn't taken her for a churchgoer. Val, who had elected to play Lady Bountiful that day, was holding a vast, multicoloured striped job over herself, Betty Burstyn who ran the newsagent's and her son Trevor who had a vested interest in Toby's death.

Reggie and Isabel were huddled together with Penny and Harry Eardley. Apart from Harry, who appeared to be enjoying it all hugely, they seemed vaguely uncomfortable at being obliged to be part of what was in truth a motley crowd. Oliver Ballantyne and Frances were perfectly acceptable. Cissie, in her woolly hat, was bearable. Brad less so. Marcus Gammie and a man they'd never seen before were quite proper, although Gammie might have done better than an elderly Prince of Wales check suit, psychedelic tie and pink shirt. Lining up behind them were the town worthies who had come to be seen to pay their respects.

Ranged opposite them on the other side of the grave were those of more doubtful social standing. Flo Gosling, who had exchanged a light ethnic skirt for a darker ethnic skirt. Terry Roberts and Lorraine in decently sombre black but sporting defiant red scarves in memory of Toby. The cousins—Robbie Hesselman, Deborah May and Martin Eardley—eyed their parents across the great divide, knowing themselves to be more at ease than their elders.

Bringing up the rear the *Clifton Clarion* was doing the funeral proud with a full contingent of reporters and photographers, as well as Harry Catchpole who had been sent along to comment on the flowers and wreaths; no one else was trusted to differentiate between a lily and an iris.

When the rain stopped Emmy noted with some satisfaction, which she recognized as shamefully mean-minded, that a small puddle had accumulated in the curve of Penny's straw brim. She wondered whether she should tell her about it or just let it trickle down her neck in its own good time.

'I think that went very well, don't you?' Rose Selby beamed. A well organized funeral (or wedding or christening, come to that) gave her such pleasure that she was occasionally guilty of forgetting the purpose of the exercise.

'Apart from that song—entertainment! People didn't understand. Still...'

She left the comment open-ended, waiting for Emmy to finish it.

'Still—it was very nice,' said Emmy. 'Arthur was splendid. I must thank him.'

Rose beamed even more brightly. 'He was, wasn't he?'

Alice Gravely paid no attention to the niceties. She was studying the flower-festooned casket as if expecting a second coming.

Emmy touched her elbow. 'I hadn't realized how little he was,' she said.

'Well, you know what they say about small packages,' said Alice, wiping her eye. 'I don't think I'll come back. To Rushey Green. Though it's nice of you to offer. Can't stand all those Mays.' Her weepy old eyes suddenly twinkled. 'Don't age very well, do they?'

'Think not?'

'Age is a bastard anyway,' said the old lady. 'I can make my own way back.' She irritably refused Emmy's extended hand. 'You've got enough to do.'

There were some moist eyes as they left the churchyard but the overwhelming feeling was one of relief. It's not ignoble, thought Emmy: after that terrible sense of parting as the coffin was lowered, she was aware of a kind of peace, however temporary, that she assumed the others shared.

'Damn!' cursed Penny as the puddle of rain dripped down her neck.

'It's a lovely hat,' said Emmy.

'Where's yours?'

'Haven't really got one. Just a scarf. It does, these days.'

'Standards!' sighed Penny, ignoring her husband Harry's chortle of derision.

'Lady Eardley?' Marian Fancey from the *Clarion* nodded at Emmy but was concentrating on bigger game today.

'Not yet,' quipped Harry, winking at

Emmy. 'Although the old girl does rather delude herself sometimes.'

Penny cast a withering glare in his direction.

Marian Fancey, looking flustered, finally made the connection. 'Sorry, *Mrs* Eardley.' But she'd forgotten the question and ad-libbed lamely. 'It must—must have been a great shock to you—I mean, your brother's death.'

Penny paused at the door of the Rolls, smiled a sorrowful smile for the photographer Norman Jessop, and decided to be gracious. 'We all loved Toby deeply,' she said sadly.

Emmy left her to the tender mercies of Marian Fancey and looked around at the departing mourners approvingly. All the Mays, playing their parts to perfection. Gilbert would have been proud. That's what she'd said to Toby, she remembered, before he'd plunged to his death: dad would have been proud.

BBC South had cornered Reggie ('My brother was that rare spirit that defies the conventions of the world'). Radio Sussex made do with Cissie ('He was a lovely boy, talented too—he understood nature'). Val was being quizzed by the *Sun* about the family mural that had been published in the *Clarion*. She gritted her teeth, charmingly laughed it off as one of

Toby's little jokes and then filled in the reporter on her current and future career plans including the TV show featuring the Mayflowers.

'No one would think the guy was a half-wit the way they talk,' said the *Daily Mirror* stringer who had already made up his story.

Brad was trapped by the Dixons and the Crenshaws who long remembered him and were determined to remind him of his Adelphi triumphs.

Someone from the *Daily Mail* grumbled to Frances, whom he knew in passing, that there wasn't much mileage in all this for him, so he might as well pack up and go back to Kensington High Street and would she fancy a pint at the pub?

'I'm family,' she said frostily. The *Mail* had seriously panned her last TV documentary.

'So, give me a quote!'

She thought. Then: 'It's a great day for a funeral.'

'Thanks a heap!' He called across the street to a youngish man with several cameras who was asking Reggie and Isabel May for 'just one more', out of habit rather than from any real enthusiasm. 'I'm cutting!'

This seemed to be a cue for the rest of

the media to cut as well, although not quite so abruptly. Which was a pity because, apart from Marian Fancey who remained behind and trailed along uninvited to Rushey Green, they missed the closest approximation to a scoop that the day had to offer.

'And what about you, Emmy?'

She started with surprise at being addressed at all when the focus of attention was so obviously on the others.

'Harry!'

'You looked lonely. I thought it was about time someone paid attention to you.'

She smiled. 'You're a good sort, Harry.'

Harry Eardley was a chubby, dapper man with a round pink face that seemed set in an expression of cheerful good humour which never varied whether he was accepting a round of applause for an address to the Institute of Directors, homing in on a hostile takeover bid or convincing a recalcitrant workforce that it was in its own best interests to be made redundant. He used his blunt Yorkshire accent and style as a smokescreen, suggesting a benign competitor, a little slow on the uptake, rather than the ruthless marauder he actually was.

Old-school city gentry who took him at face value invariably regretted it. His brain was razor-sharp, his instincts predatory and his business tactics those of jungle warfare. But he prided himself on being well liked. Even his rivals at the sharp end of his stock market machinations admitted that, for all his faults, he was an amiable cove.

He had decided to marry Penelope May the first time he had seen her on the supporting bill at the London Palladium and he had pursued that aim with the same determination that he set out to score every other goal in his life.

As a boy playing truant from school in Bradford he had spent the sixpence he had pinched from the milk money in the 'Present from Scarborough' jug on the mantelpiece in the family terrace home on a fairground fortune-teller. She had predicted a cloudless future, untold wealth and the ability to overcome all obstacles provided he ate up his greens. He thought about this while licking an ice lolly. Then he went home, took his thrashing for rifling the milk money and thereafter ate up his greens. Years later he insisted, half seriously, that it was the best sixpence he had ever spent. To which Penny, well schooled, would invariably respond on cue that it was probably the *only* sixpence he ever spent. Everyone knew this was a joke because, business apart, he was almost embarrassingly generous to his family and friends.

He started small, buying up surplus army stock with a loan from a friendly and far-sighted pawnbroker, and selling piecemeal at a profit. Having acquired the knack of making money there was no stopping him. As his wheeler-dealing became more and more successful and his fortune grew, he set up his ageing parents in a nice four-bedroom detached on the outskirts of Bradford and helped fund a working-class museum. All his life he ostentatiously voted Labour.

He married Penny May because she was pretty, bright, behaved impeccably and had a stunning dress sense and the figure to display it. In those respects she was an asset like any other and he was enormously proud of her. He also loved her unreservedly (no tasty young secretaries on the side). That she didn't love him back to the same degree didn't seem to matter either to him or to her. They were content with each other.

Their only child Martin was a disappointment, although neither would acknowledge as much. He hated discussing money, probably because there was plenty of it washing around, and had no intention of going into his father's business. He spent most of his time in the London jazz clubs where he sat with the musicians playing a tolerable alto sax. Given his father's drive he could probably have made music his life, rather than merely an absorbing hobby.

'I'm glad Martin came. And Robbie and Deb,' said Emmy. 'Young people are funny about funerals.'

A polite cough interrupted her. She found herself looking up into the brilliant blue eyes of an enormously muscled man in a chauffeur's uniform.

'Excuse me, ma'am.' He turned to Harry. 'Mrs Eardley's waiting.' He spoke in a surprisingly high-pitched Californian drawl which didn't fit his massive shape at all.

'Won't be long, Buddy. Or, better yet, drive her on up to the house. Rushey Green. She knows the way. Emmy can give me a lift, can't you Emmy?'

'If you don't mind my old banger. The undertaker's limousine gives me the creeps.'

Buddy didn't seem happy about leaving his employer. He scrutinized Emmy intently, before reluctantly turning away.

'It's OK, Buddy. She's my sister-in-law. If she'd wanted to duff me up she'd have done it long ago.'

She watched the great bulk of flesh and sinew and muscle stroll toward the Rolls.

347

For a big man he was very graceful and very silent.

'He looks like a minder,' she said.

Harry didn't answer, but screwed up his mouth apologetically.

'Harry, he isn't! Is he?' She burst out laughing, then stopped suddenly, remembering where she was.

'He's a defrocked cop from the Los Angeles Police Department. Used to work out with Arnold Schwarzenegger, too.'

'Harry, you're a *clown!* I'd have thought there were enough British bruisers around.'

'True. But the Yanks have got a lot of style.'

'Who's he supposed to be protecting you from?'

He hunched his shoulders. 'Search me! Maybe the revolting peasants. The security chap in the company thought it would be a good idea. Besides, he, Buddy, is tax deductible. Impresses the hell out of the opposition, too. Makes them think you're more valuable than you are.'

'Well, he certainly impresses me.'

They sauntered toward where her car was parked.

'You know, you should have let me do something for Toby,' said Harry.

'Like what, Harry? He was happy enough. In his funny old world.'

'It would have freed you.'

'*I've* been happy enough. In *my* funny old world.'

He smiled. 'There's still time. Pity about Brad.'

'That's centuries ago.'

'I didn't mean that.'

What an unexpected man he was, she thought. 'How did you know?'

'I've seen enough at the AIDS clinic I support.'

'I didn't know you were involved in anything like that.'

He shrugged. 'Not a lot of people do. Bad for the old cruel despot image. How advanced is it?'

'Not long ago he was diagnosed HIV positive. He's having treatment, drugs. At least I gather so. He doesn't say much about it.'

'I suppose there's not a lot to say.'

'It's a funny thing, Harry. In the last couple of days since I learned from Frances about Brad, he and I have been more—comfortable together than we've been since...' She paused, not sure how to go on and if she wanted to.

'Since Harvey Persky?'

'Do you know everything about everything, Harry?'

'I make it my business to be informed. You see, Emmy, as I see it, you probably only function as a shoulder to lean on. It's tough. Or maybe it isn't. People are what they are. If they try to be something different they're miserable. Toby was your charge. Now he's gone and you've found another.'

'Brad? Don't be absurd. Besides, what right have I...?' No right at all. 'We must stop dawdling,' she said brusquely. 'They'll all get there before us.'

He quickened his step to keep up with her. 'Was that Daniel Boisseau I saw with Marcus Gammie?'

'Yes.'

'So, it's true about the exhibition. Penny and Val were rabbiting on about it but I didn't pay much attention. I think it's a fine thing.' He nodded his head vigorously several times. 'A fine thing. And what about Rushey Green?'

'I've been thinking about that, Harry. Something you said. Not actually. Just a train of thought, an idea. Perhaps we could talk later.' She fumbled with the key to the hatchback, yanked open the passenger door, which tended to stick, then slid behind the driving wheel.

'Comfy?' she asked.

He screwed up his nose, affecting a fastidiousness which was quite alien to his amiable nature. 'I suppose it beats walking.'

CHAPTER TWENTY-ONE
15 JANUARY 1958

Somehow she forced herself to go through the motions of appearing to live a normal life. If she kept very, very busy she found that, for a few rare, blessed moments, the memory of that terrible night would recede, not forgotten but numbed by weariness and exhaustion.

A policeman who knew the family had found her sitting on a bench in the municipal gardens at five in the morning. It was bitterly cold and he was worried that, among other things, she might be suffering from hypothermia. He hadn't known that she was beyond physical distress. The anguish of discovering the truth about her father's past and the certainty that Harvey was a guilty part of it, using that knowledge for his own ends, burned inside her, insulating her from the ravages of the winter weather.

'Are you all right, miss? Emmy—Emmy May, isn't it?' he'd said, concerned. 'You're perished. Here.' He'd taken off his greatcoat and tried to drape it round her shoulders. 'You come along to the station and we'll get you a nice cup of tea and then you can phone your parents. I expect they're worried.'

He knew they were anyway. When Gilbert had got back from the Adelphi that night and realized Emmy wasn't home, he had stayed up waiting for her. It wasn't unheard of. Sometimes she'd stay with a friend and even her mother had now faced up to the fact that she might be with Brad—if it had to be someone it might as well be Brad, whom Madge liked.

For a long time Madge pretended to concentrate on a cushion cover she had been endlessly embroidering for what seemed like years. It was a family joke. No joke now. She looked over at her husband, then looked away quickly, alarmed.

He was pacing the room in a zig-zag pattern, as if unable to control his limbs, his eyes staring. She had never seen this loving, light-hearted man, who had settled on her life out of nowhere like a dazzling butterfly, so distraught. He had thought it had been all right between him and Emmy when they'd parted that evening. But maybe, maybe...

'Is it—is it something—something between you?' she ventured, still not looking at him.

He didn't seem to hear the question. 'I'm phoning the police.'

'It's only three.' She didn't know why she had said that. Only three. *Only* three. And no Emmy. Perhaps she had hoped to calm Gilbert with her reasonable tone. But it had the reverse effect.

'For Christ's sake, Madge, where *is* she?'

She shook her head, then in a small, reluctant voice, 'Why don't you try Harvey Persky? We've already phoned Brad and her friends.'

He turned on her with a rage that made her recoil almost in horror. 'Why did you say that, woman?' He'd never spoken to her like that before.

'No reason,' she gasped. 'It's just—he's the only one left I could think of.'

She'd watched his whole body slump and he fell to his knees in front of her, tears in his eyes. She held out his arms and he sank into them.

'We'll call the police,' she whispered in his ear after a while. 'That will be best. You're right.'

The sergeant on duty had been solicitous and soothing. Of course, they'd find her. Not to worry. Young girls were thoughtless these days. She was probably listening to records with a group of mates and forgot the time. Awful things, like rape and abduction, didn't happen in Clifton Coombe, at least not in his experience.

353

(He wasn't being entirely truthful: awful things did occasionally happen in Clifton Coombe, but not often enough to be an immediate factor in the search for a girl who had been missing a few hours.)

'Can you stand up?' The policeman was debating whether he should call an ambulance, although she didn't look like a stretcher case.

'I'm all right,' she'd said dully, suddenly feeling the cold and shivering. 'What time is it?'

'Five.'

She'd been sitting there for five hours. Five hours in which to think and agonize and arrive at a decision. She would behave as if nothing had happened, although she knew that nothing could be the same again. Between her and Gilbert and Harvey. From now on she would freeze her feelings.

Her mother had asked a lot of questions and her father none. She'd lied about forgetting the time, how she'd walked on the beach and gone into an all-night cafe and listened to the jukebox and got into conversation with a couple of girls who were passing through but she couldn't remember the cafe or the names of the girls. She'd just forgotten the time, like the police sergeant at the station said.

She didn't care if they believed her lame excuse. She was just grateful that they didn't press her further. And grateful even more to Val who took it all with a grain of salt and a jokey insouciance. 'Just give her time,' she had reassured her parents. 'It'll all come out when she feels like it. Probably just a row with Brad.'

'You can tell me,' she'd urged Emmy in private.

'No, Val, I can't.'

They'd insisted she spend the next twenty-four hours in bed, and the doctor had concurred. 'A couple of days and she'd be as right as rain.' And, theoretically, he had been correct. In less than a couple of days she had been as right as rain. Her night on the tiles—as Val described it—might never have been. Except for one significant difference: the old Emmy had died on that park bench during the winter night.

The new Emmy was like a functioning robot, identical in every particular but devoid of warmth and feeling. She involved herself even more efficiently in the administration of the Adelphi, enrolled for evening classes in shorthand, typing and business management and helped around the house so obsessively that Madge complained she had nothing left to do.

'It's a passing phase,' said Penny. 'Maybe,' Cissie doubted.

Dick Whittington was doing roaring

business, the most successful pantomime in the Adelphi's history. 'Another Gilbert May triumph!' the *Clifton Clarion* trumpeted above a feature on the show and the new man, Harvey Persky, who was injecting a slick vigour into the old pantomime formula. In an interview Harvey massaged his past association with Gilbert, in which there was no reference to any third-rate circus, explaining that they'd met in a Broadway show and had gone their separate ways until fortuitously meeting up in this lovely old English town of Clifton Coombe.

Emmy read the piece with blank indifference. She avoided serious conversation with her father, made a point of never being alone with Harvey and cold-shouldered Brad's attempts to draw her out. Even with Toby she seemed preoccupied and uninterested. The boy, more prescient than some in the family, was deeply affected by her remoteness and became even more ungovernable.

When she talked she could be quite animated, as she used to be, but never about anything personal. The flourishing finances of the Adelphi, plans for the next season and who should be invited to a party on stage on the closing night of the pantomime in February, whether Pat Boone was a better singer than Elvis

Presley, the rising cost of living—anything, anything, rather than put into words the hardening sense of betrayal she felt.

Sooner or later, she knew, there would have to be a reckoning. She couldn't wrap herself in a cocoon for ever. But for now it formed a comforting protection, a healing outer skin: until what she had feared happened.

She was studying the proposed poster for the next production to go into rehearsal in February. It had been devised by Harvey: a revue charting the highlights of the musical theatre from Lehar and Romberg and Novello to Gershwin and Jerome Kern and Rodgers and Hammerstein, but—an inspired Harvey touch—elevating it above the routine by introducing a kind of Greek chorus of young singers and dancers giving a sophisticated contemporary interpretation of the familiar numbers between scene changes.

The song copyright would be expensive, but worth it, and it would mean that the Adelphi could keep the company it had employed for *Dick Whittington* with the addition, if Gilbert was successful in calling in a few favours, of one or two star names. Val, Penny and Cissie had not very politely declined, having decided that they had paid their dues in Gilbert's pantomime. Reggie was otherwise engaged rehearsing a revival of *Journey's End* in the West End.

'Emmy, what happened that night?'

She hadn't heard her father come into the office. It wasn't a chance encounter, she realized. He had deliberately waited until he was sure they wouldn't be disturbed.

'You haven't spoken to me since then,' he continued.

She kept her eyes on the sketch of the poster. The names hadn't been filled in yet, but the design was a striking, crowd-puller.

'It's good, don't you think? Eddie's done a great job. Better than the—'

He snatched it out of her hands.

'Listen to me, Emmy. Forget the damn poster.'

She looked up at him and, for the first time, met the pain in his eyes full on.

'Of course I've been speaking to you, dad.' She had an overwhelming urge to clap her hands over her ears. She didn't want to hear, didn't want to talk.

'Emmy, don't lie to me,' he pleaded.

Lie! It was the word that triggered the explosion. How dare he talk to her about lies! Despite the pain in those eyes, the fact that he was her father, she was conscious only of a sense of shock that he could be so duplicitous as to accuse *her* of lying.

'And what about lies? Gideon March!'

her voice sounded shrill and hard to her ears, not her voice at all. 'You thought you could fob me off with half the truth. But what about the rest? What about the rest?' She covered her face with her hands, willing herself not to tax him further, to force him to admit to a crime the confession of which, once in the open, could never be retracted.

'Emmy, I don't know what Harvey told you. But it wasn't how you think.'

'Harvey didn't *tell* me anything.' And that was true. What she had discovered she'd discovered for herself. But Gilbert didn't seem to hear. He was pleading with her, begging. In that moment she grew up, seeing her father not as some sort of god but as a weak, fallible human being, and loving him no less.

'It's all right, Emmy. Harvey's leaving. He's going back to the States. No strings. There's nothing to fear any more. It's over. It's behind us.' He was so eager for her to understand, forgive and forget. Did he really think it was as easy as that?

'Is that how you see it, dad? Harvey's going so it never happened. You, your father. It never happened. Wiped out.'

'Lots of people have things in their past that they'd rather forget. He was a monster, Emmy. I told you. I think if I hadn't gone back home with him, he'd have killed me.'

Just for an instant she wondered whether she was wrong. It wasn't how you think, he'd said. But how else could it have been? It explained so much. The drastic change in him when this man from his past turned up so suddenly. How much had he promised Harvey to keep that terrible secret, maybe to save him from the police who never closed the file on a suspicious death, however many years ago it happened?

'Can't you see? Gideon March is as dead as his father is. He has been for thirty years.' He was shouting at her now, as if the sheer volume of noise might penetrate the implacable certainty of her judgement.

'I don't...' she started to say and then became aware of a keening wail, more heart-rending than a sob, like a small animal in great pain. Neither of them had noticed Toby huddled in the doorway, his undersized body shivering with fear, not comprehending what he had witnessed but knowing only that the two people he most loved were tearing each other apart.

'Don't Emmy, don't daddy! Stop it!' he cried.

Gilbert swung round, too shocked that anyone should have observed a scene he would always remember with shame to realize what he was saying. 'That boy shouldn't be allowed to wander around the theatre on his own.'

'That boy is your son,' she said coldly. 'And it's never bothered you before.'

'No—no it hasn't,' he said contritely. He had looked at the whimpering boy with an expression of such sweet tenderness she could almost bring herself to forget that he hadn't been much older than Toby when he had killed his own father.

She picked up the poster and handed it to Gilbert.

'We'll talk about it later,' he said, not meaning the poster.

'No, we won't, dad. We'll never talk about it again.' She walked over to Toby, took the boy's hand in hers, knelt down, drew out her handkerchief and urged him to blow. 'Silly!' she murmured. 'It was only dad and me discussing a new show.'

'Truly?' he hiccuped, the sobs subsiding.

'Truly.'

'Who's Gideon March?'

'It's just a name your dad used to have. He liked Gilbert May better.' But she saw a great, knowing sadness in his eyes and saw that placating him with meaningless words wasn't the same as allaying his unspoken fears.

'Why don't you go and talk to Alf.

Didn't he say he was going to show you how to work the lights?'

She watched him shuffle off, not willingly.

'I'm sorry, Emmy. I wouldn't have hurt him for the world.'

She sighed. 'Neither would I. But we do. We do!'

She brushed past him, out of the office, down the spiral staircase, past the dressing rooms and into the body of the theatre. It was the time between the rehearsals and the matinée when it would be silent and still and deserted. And that's what she needed: to be alone with her thoughts. She'd meant what she'd said to Gilbert, never to speak of her past again. It was the only way to live in peace with herself and her father. She would never talk of this to Madge or anyone else. What they guessed was their business, but it wouldn't come from her.

Even as she made that resolve she realized she hadn't even begun to confront the greater sorrow. Harvey Persky was going to disappear from her life. Gilbert had said so. It would be best, reason told her. Just as he had changed the Mays since he'd arrived he had also changed himself. She had called him a blackmailer in her unthinking rage and maybe that had been his original motive, but surely not any longer, unless he was a consummate actor.

He would leave and that would be best, she reiterated. But reason had nothing to do with the feeling she still had for him, the loss she knew she would experience when he went away. Reason couldn't dictate emotion or take away the ache of knowing she'd never see him again, or the memory of his touch.

She wondered how she would say goodbye or even whether she would. There would be other men. There was even Brad. But for some inexplicable reason the first—maybe the only—man she would love was a shady, cocky middle-aged predator who looked like a gangster and sounded like a character out of Damon Runyan. It was almost laughable if it weren't so miserably serious.

And then she found she *was* laughing, hysterically. Louder and louder the laughter came, echoing round the empty theatre. It went on and on until she felt drained and exhausted. She sank down into a seat in the stalls, breathing hard.

When it was over she heard a slow handclap. At first she couldn't locate it and then she sensed it was coming from way up in the 'gods'. She looked up, shading her eyes with her hand. Standing above the railing in the gallery was Harvey Persky, looking as if he'd been there a long time. He was drawing on one of those stubby cigars, letting out the smoke in rings.

'That's my girl,' he called down.

'I'm not your girl,' she called back. All the same she got to her feet and made her way up the stairs from the stalls to the circle to the gallery as if drawn by some compulsion beyond her control.

He stood with his back to the railing. 'What is it they say? The Mays can always be relied on to put on a good show.' He seemed somehow different as if he'd come to a difficult but irreversible decision. And she supposed her cold and deliberate refusal to speak to him since that night in his bleak apartment must have hurt him.

'You forget. I'm the other one. I don't put on a show.'

He stubbed out his cigar on the floor: a trivial act but one that made Emmy wince involuntarily. Gilbert always insisted on keeping the Adelphi spotless. 'Oh, I don't know,' he said. 'I guess you've been putting on a pretty good act with me.'

'How do you mean?' She genuinely didn't understand. Her feelings for and about him had, she felt, always been painfully transparent, to him at least, if not to the family.

'I had this crazy idea that maybe you cared for me. Me! A schmuck from Brooklyn, a smart-ass who lived by his wits, old enough to be your father. And you, you with your class and youth and future! That sort of thing doesn't happen, I told myself. But then again, I began to think maybe it could. I was going to be a new person for you, Emmy. And some time you'd even agree to marry me. And, Christ, Emmy, I'd have made you happy, happier than you'll ever be! But you just couldn't believe in me, could you? When the crunch came, you couldn't believe I could do the decent thing. Harvey Persky had to be a bad guy. What did you call me? A blackmailer! Jeez, where did you get that from? The movies?'

She stared at him from the top of the gallery stairs, feeling her heart pounding furiously, her knees weaken. She started to descend the stairs towards him, leaning heavily on the backs of the aisle seats for support.

'I loved you, Emmy. I really loved you. Like no dame I've ever known. Maybe I still do. I thought, maybe I could be different—for Emmy. Nicer, kinder!' he went on relentlessly. 'I always knew Giddy and I could be a team. And it was working, wasn't it? I guess when I first found out that Gilbert May was Gideon March, the buddy I'd bunked with way back, I thought there might be a little percentage in it for me. After all, I'd covered up for him over his old man. The cops thought it was murder and Giddy was the big suspect. It wasn't. It was one of those crazy accidents. The old guy lunged at Giddy, tripped and hit his head on the metal underpinning of a tent pole. I guess if we hadn't panicked the cops would have believed us—maybe. But Giddy was scared, so we hid the body. Giddy took off and I stayed behind. And that was the last I saw of him until—when was it—a month ago? It feels like forever.'

He loomed at her as she continued to walk slowly down the stairs, not attempting to approach her. 'There! Does that satisfy you? Now you know the whole story, the whole goddamned story. What the hell!' He bent backwards looking round the theatre. 'I've just been kidding myself. I don't need this. This cramped little town. When we get the new show together I'm leaving. Back to where I belong.' He did a little jig, mocking himself and her. 'There are plenty of big pickings in the States. Television, movies. There's a guy I know who bought a piece of a real dog of an Italian movie, dubbed it into English, marketed it right and made a fortune. I guess I'll try to get me a piece of that action. If you'd stuck with me, baby, I'd have made you a princess,' he said wryly, discarding the plummy speech he'd so assiduously cultivated as if it were so much excess baggage.

As she listened to him she knew that if he offered only a gesture she would be prepared to go with him anywhere, leaving Gilbert and Madge and the Mays and Clifton Coombe and the Adelphi. It was a kind of madness. A sweet madness.

'Harvey—Harvey, perhaps it's not too late.' She felt breathless and faint. Her feet gave way under her and she swayed toward him.

A flicker of genuine concern, then hope, crossed his face. He gripped her arms to steady her. 'Emmy...!'

But he didn't get any further.

There was a sudden shriek and a whirlwind of fury erupting through the curtains into the gallery. Toby flung himself down the stairs towards Harvey, his head jutted forward like a battering ram.

Harvey just stood there, stunned. 'Punk kid!' he said, amused. They were the last words he spoke.

Caught off-balance, he felt his body pressed hard against the railing and then back over the top into the yawning gap below.

Emmy watched, too numbed to register the horror. She saw his outstretched hands and a look of complete disbelief on his face, as if he were trying to assure himself that this wasn't happening. It was no more than a split second. Then that terrible scream rending the stillness and silence of the theatre.

Soon after the day of the inquest on the death of Harvey Persky at the Adelphi theatre, Emmy learned she was pregnant.

She had given her evidence calmly and coolly. She'd been discussing the new show with Harvey in the gallery. He'd been demonstrating a dance routine. He'd bent backwards over the railing and fallen. She had been momentarily distracted because Toby, her brother, had called to her from the top of the stairs. So she hadn't actually seen him fall.

The coroner hadn't called Toby who was at home suffering, quite naturally, from the shock of witnessing such a tragic occurrence. When he recovered his mind retained such a garbled impression of what had happened it made no sense.

The family testified that relations with Harvey were more than amicable and Gilbert revealed that he and Harvey were drawing up a partnership contract, a fact confirmed by his solicitor, Crawford Ballantyne.

The expected verdict of accidental death was brought in.

They had all lied with persuasive

conviction. Thereafter there was an un-spoken agreement that they would never speak of it again. What was done was done. Harvey Persky, after all, was just an outsider, a brief aberration in the life of the Mays.

Assuming Brad was the father and would do the right thing, they weren't too appalled at learning about Emmy's interesting condition. They were more irritated than shocked when she turned down his proposal of marriage. While neither confirming nor denying that he was the father, she was unbudgeable.

'It's my baby,' was all she'd say. Gilbert and Madge faced up to the prospect of rearing an illegitimate baby in the family home and the ensuing rumour and speculation, and even outrage, that would inevitably provoke in the town. Not long after, a rejected and bewildered Brad accepted a movie offer and left Clifton Coombe.

Gilbert was never quite the same after Harvey Persky's death and people assumed he must be missing his old pal badly. He sold the Adelphi. Four years later he contracted pneumonia and, without even putting up much of a fight, so it seemed to his doctor, he died, having first set up a trust fund for Toby with Emmy as executor. It was a big funeral and the show-business fraternity turned up in force.

Madge followed him not long after. The Adelphi had already started its slow decline as a place of entertainment and a Grade II listed building.

Emmy had Toby and Frances and Rushey Green and in the long years of loneliness she sometimes even allowed herself her memories and her dreams of what might have been.

CHAPTER TWENTY-TWO

'Are you sure this is what he would have wanted?' Daniel Boisseau looked up from the portfolio of watercolours and glanced around the old wooden hideaway, its walls festooned with Toby's paintings. 'There's a terrible clarity about them as if he could foresee the threat to the environment or, at any rate, the recent concern about it. When you think some of these were painted over twenty years ago. And yet...'

He stood back, inspected a surreal image of old Clifton Coombe suffocating under the erosion of what passes for progress— strangling road systems, concrete housing developments with minute windows through which listless faces (all recognizable Mays and their friends) peered, dry parched fields and decaying trees—and lashed by an angry sea battering the coastline like a vengeful God.

'And yet it's so personal, intimate. Everything seems to relate back to the family.'

'I know,' said Emmy. 'I suppose it was the only way he could express himself, by associating everything he felt with the Mays. He didn't know much of life outside the family.'

'Maybe not. But he had all the instincts. It's an extraordinary talent, Emmy. But I remember his rage when I suggested he exhibit a year ago, as if I were proposing to cut off an arm or a leg.'

'Worse than that,' Emmy said. 'A slow death by many cuts.'

'So—are you sure this is what he'd have wanted?' he repeated.

'No,' Emmy admitted. 'But it's what I want. There has to be some testimony to his life. Now that he's gone, no longer exposed to people, however well meaning, I don't think he'd want his work just to rot away. At least I hope not. If I'm wrong he'll no doubt give me a good ticking off when I join him eventually.'

He looked over at her, faintly disapproving. 'You're very light-hearted about death.'

'Well, there's not much point in being otherwise. None of us can escape it sooner or later.'

He took off his pince-nez, which accentuated his otherworldly appearance, and pinched the bridge of his nose. He was something of an anachronism on the modern art scene: a respected expert and dealer who was neither a smooth, tweedy elder statesman with all the proper academic credentials nor a clever, thrusting careerist with a better appreciation of the art market than of the art is was marketing.

He dressed in an Edwardian style that had gone out of fashion twice—once in its rightful time and again in its fifties revival. He wore his grey hair straight and long, flicking up at the ends. Tall and very thin, he had a face that would not have looked out of place in a sepia photograph of a country house gathering before the First World War. What he knew about art he had learned from love, research and meticulous finding out in his own solitary way, fuelled by a family inheritance which had left him enviably relieved of the necessity of having to earn a living. He was also extraordinarily successful 'picking winners', as he put it with a nonchalance which was a total sham. He cared deeply about the young artists he discovered and promoted. He refused to be a party to the greedy trading ('pimping and whoring' he sniffed) in old masters, was derisive about the sums they raised and the collectors who bought them and gleeful when the recession at least lowered the temperature in that area of capitalist acquisitiveness. Like Harry Eardley and Marcus Gammie, with whom he had forged an enduring friendship since their days together at Lancing College, he was a surprising and lifelong socialist.

He turned now to the two men who were perched silently side by side on a wooden bench in a corner of the hut, nursing glasses of good malt whisky which Harry had had the foresight to bring with him, and smoking large Havana cigars. The fragrant smell reminded Emmy of Harvey, except Harvey could never have afforded Havanas—he'd liked, she remembered, his 'stogies' as he called them.

The sudden ache of memory puzzled her. After so long! A stupid thing like a cigar. She shook her head viciously as if to rid it of the thought: a gesture which the others misinterpreted.

'Of course, if you're having second thoughts, Emmy.' Harry carefully deposited a thimble-sized nest of grey ash in an ugly pottery vase where Toby used to house his paintbrushes. He was conscious of Emmy watching him. 'Sorry, if that's sacred.'

Emmy waved her hand. 'Nonsense. Help yourself. No. No second thoughts. I was just...it was something else.'

Outside in the garden, they could hear voices raised, not in anger but in an attempt to override other less intrusive voices. The funeral gathering was obviously looking after itself very nicely as funeral gatherings tended to, in Emmy's experience. She felt no pang of conscience about abdicating her responsibilities as hostess for a while.

The sun was steaming up the lawn and flowerbeds, damp from the recent showers, so there was a chance for everyone to spill out of the house. Thanks largely to Harry and Brad there was plenty to drink. Lorraine's canapés had been a triumph, and plentiful too. Emmy and Val had provided the more workmanlike ham and salmon sandwiches, sausage rolls and vegetable soup.

Yes, indeed, she reassured herself, no need to worry about them yet. She hoped. She affected to ignore a loud comment that floated through the open window of Toby's hut, but couldn't quite.

'The first-born is always a pain in the arse.' It sounded like Val. A Val with a couple of malt whiskies inside her.

Ominous silence.

Then: 'I always think flowering cherries are so vulgar, don't you?' Penny covering up a sister's gaffe firmly, if not graciously.

'We won't have them in the garden,' grunted Reggie. Oh Lord, thought Emmy, how had he taken to being likened to a pain in the arse? He didn't sound too put out, just his usual insensitive self.

'I think they're very pretty, especially the pinks,' Annabel Crenshaw was heard to say, speaking a mind which didn't pretend to be sophisticated.

'Well, if you like that sort of thing,' huffed Reggie clearly more offended that anyone should regard flowering pink cherries as pretty than at being dismissed by Val as a pain in the arse.

'I suppose we should join them,' sighed Harry, comfortable with his whisky, his Havana and Toby's paintings.

'Not just yet,' insisted Daniel Boisseau. 'There's the diary.' He picked up one large battered leather volume from a pile Emmy had taken from a locked drawer in the oak bureau that had been relegated from the sitting room to the hut in a seasonal spring-clean many years before.

'I'm not sure,' said Emmy thoughtfully. 'It's all his thoughts and feelings about us, the Mays, over the years. And those amazing, funny sketches.'

'It could make a book,' said Daniel.

'This history of a family over thirty-five years. The *Edwardian Lady* made a fortune. There's a publisher I know who would jump at it.'

'I'm not looking for a fortune exactly,' said Emmy. 'I don't suppose the family would be too happy. I'd have to edit it. What do you think Harry?'

He drew deeply on the Havana, not much bothered. 'Skeletons in the cupboard! Every family has them.'

'Ours perhaps more than most,' she said quietly. 'I haven't even read all the entries. All the same, the money might be useful. I think I know how I might use it—to do a bit of good.' She looked at each of the three men in turn. Then, tentatively: 'How does the Toby May School for Mentally Handicapped Children strike you?'

Harry nodded. 'I'm struck.'

'Where do you propose to set up this foundation, house it?'

She took a deep breath as if finally facing up to a resolve that had previously been an idle speculation.

'Here.'

'You mean, here, this old hut? Or here, Rushey Green?'

'Rushey Green, of course. I've decided to sell it or, rather donate it to a charity I've worked for. It's subsidiary of Mencap and we badly need a school like that in

376

this area. I was hoping, Harry, that you might bring a little pressure to bear to get planning permission. You know a lot of people and you're good at that sort of thing.'

He grinned. 'It's the least I can do. You refused everything else I offered.'

'I suppose I was just saving the favour until I really needed it. I thought—if the pictures sell and, maybe, the book of memoirs—I could use the proceeds to set up a trust for the school and equip it.' As she related the ideas that had been buzzing around unspoken in her mind since Toby's death, she sounded shy, almost girlish, as if expecting any minute that someone would invade this dream with a bulldozer and destroy it. 'I haven't much of a head for business,' she went on apologetically.

'What does Oliver Ballantyne think?'

'I haven't consulted him. He'd only tell me it was a crazy idea and bound to create a lot of local opposition. You know how people are. They pay lip service and send cheques to help the mentally handicapped, but some of them aren't too keen...'

'Not in my back yard,' Harry elaborated. 'Then it's up to you. You're the one in the firing. Do you feel up to a fight?'

'Yes—yes, I really think I do, Harry. It's about time.'

'More important, Emmy. If you get rid

of Rushey Green where will you go?' It was the first time Marcus Gammie had spoken, unerringly homing in on the crux of the matter.

'Obviously I'd want to keep a watching brief on the project, but I think it's time I left Clifton Coombe.'

In fact she hadn't seriously thought about it and when she had, fleetingly, she imagined she'd probably have to find a little flat in town or join the geriatrics in a bungalow by the sea. But now, quite suddenly, she was very sure. Clifton Coombe had nothing left for her.

'And where will you go?' It was Marcus again.

'To London. Oh, I'm not into a trip round the world or anything like that. I just—I think I'd like to spend some time with Frances. That is, if she can spare any. It's a little late in the day, but maybe not too late.' She remembered the long, comfortable chat they'd had in her bedroom the previous evening after the dinner party. Fanny had been happy to see her mother and Brad so at ease with each other. They finished off the last of the wine and then drank black coffee and talked as she couldn't recall them talking since Fanny had been a little girl. Not about big things like hopes and fears and ambitions, but about the trivia that is the glue of a real relationship—losing weight or gaining it, whether to have your hair restyled or the flat (Fanny's) redecorated, the problem of finding a good chiropodist and a plumber who turned up when he said he would. ('I wish it had always been like this, Emmy.' She'd said 'Emmy', not 'mother', as if they were girl friends who had rediscovered each other, and it had been a good feeling.)

'Also.' She took another deep breath, another resolution arrived at. 'Also I'd like to be nearer Brad. Although I don't want him to think that's a reason. Maybe I could help out in the bookshop, if he'd let me. We spoke of it yesterday. Not seriously. More as a joke. He said he could use a good organizer. Well, I'm that all right. There are some nice places in Teddington, I'm told. I should be able to afford it. That's near enough to both of them, but not—not too close. I can't impose myself after all these years.' She was speaking in a low, ruminating tone, more to herself than to the men who were listening to her.

She felt a hand ruffling her hair, which she hadn't bothered to reassemble in its customary style since it had been blown off course in the churchyard, and looked up into Harry Eardley's good-humoured face. He had stubbed out the remains of the cigar in the paintbrush pot.

'Typical Emmy! Never impose, never expose. Anyway, anything's better than settling for that idiot Oliver.'

She wrinkled her nose, feeling protective. 'He's not an idiot. And I'm not so sure the family will agree with the exposure bit when I tell them about Toby's diary.'

They could hear Val's penetrating voice again from the garden. This time the target seemed to be Cissie.

'The trouble, trouble with you, Cissie, is—out of touch—down there in the wilds commum—communing with nature. The TV show. Bring you out of yourself.' Her words slurred into each other dangerously.

'We'll talk about it later, Val.' Cissie. Placating. 'I think you should come indoors and sit down for a while.'

'Why? I'm—I'm perfic—perfickly—all right.' There was a loud thump and a louder exclamatory expletive.

'Can I help?' A bright, curious voice. Marian Fancey's. Taking mental notes.

'Oh dear!' groaned Emmy. 'I'd better go. It sounds as if Val has had a couple too many.'

She found Val on the lawn, nursing her ankle. Cissie and Marian were bending down on either side of her, trying to hoist her to her feet. Val was resisting.

'I'm perfectly all right,' she enunciated very, very clearly as if picking her way

380

through a minefield. The fall seemed to have sobered her up somewhat or, at least, made her aware of how undignified she looked.

'Come on, Val!'

'Emmy, where—where have you been?' asked Val from her prone position.

'Nowhere,' said Emmy. 'Come on. Upsy-daisy!'

After a couple of attempts Val made it upright, looking around her at several embarrassed faces. She waved imperiously and then leaning heavily on Emmy's arm she minced up the steps to the french windows with great delicacy. 'I think, Emmy, I think, I'm just the weeniest bit squiffed,' she giggled.

'I think you are, too, Val.'

She urged her into the sitting room, settled her on a sofa and went in search of some black coffee.

'Your sister!' said Lorraine, who was piling up plates in the sink. 'She can certainly knock it back.'

'Yes, well, she's probably upset. The funeral,' Emmy lied.

Lorraine looked at her sideways and winked. 'Suit yourself. Here. This should help.' She handed Emmy a tray with a pot of hot coffee and a mug.

Penny was hovering in the door. 'You shouldn't let that girl talk to you like that,' she hissed in passing.

Emmy ignored her.

'I hate black coffee,' said Val, screwing up her nose.

'Drink it!'

'Is that a command?'

'Yes. I want everyone sober before this day's out. How could you get so pissed, Val?'

Val drained the mug and held it out for a refill. 'I know. I've let you down. I just suddenly felt lonely leaving the church. Robbie and Deb. They're a couple...'

'Soon to be a triple.'

'...and they don't want me around. Oliver treats me as if I'm about to *castrate* him or something.' She made a face. 'Toby's gone. You and Brad seem so—so together. Cissie is putting up an argument about the TV show. Reggie and that awful Isabel act as if I'm a has-been who never was. No one cares about me. No one cares about poor old Val.' Tears started trickling down her cheeks.

'Stop it, Val! If there's anything worse than a drunk it's a maudlin drunk.' She gripped her sister's shoulders and shook her. 'Just get a grip on yourself. You've a career, Lord knows how many lovers. Don't kid me that you give a damn about Toby, because you didn't. And as for Robbie and Deborah—when was the last time you gave a thought to Robbie, before this anyway?'

'You're cruel,' whined Val.

'Yes, I am.' But, cruel or not, it had the desired effect. Val had stopped crying and was sufficiently in control of herself to start inspecting the damage to her make-up in the mirror of her powder compact. 'I look a mess.'

'That you do. Go upstairs and tidy yourself up.'

'Hitler!' She looked at Emmy over the top of the compact. 'What did you mean about wanting everyone sober before the day is out?'

'Because I've something to discuss with you all,' admitted Emmy, then corrected herself. 'I've something to announce.' Now that decisions had been made she was in no mood for helpful advice or argument.

'Oliver. I know it's Oliver.' Val sat upright, shooting the compact to the floor where the loose powder spewed over the carpet. 'Damn!'

'You'll hear soon enough. Now be a good girl, Val. I don't suppose I can prevail on you to get a carpet sweeper and brush that up before it gets trodden in.' She shook her head. 'No I thought not.'

On her way back to the kitchen she passed Penny, who was giving her famous imitation of being animated and interested while thinking of six other completely different things from the conversation in which she was currently involved. The Crenshaws and the Dixons were totally captivated.

'Quebec! How lovely,' Ellie Dixon was saying. 'You'll be going with him?'

'Good God, no! If I wanted to be insulted by the French I'd rather be insulted by the French French.' They all laughed anxiously perceiving it to be a joke. 'It's just some deal Harry is closing over there. He'll only be away a few days.' She smiled at the two couples very sweetly. 'I'm really rather a homebody.'

'Pull the other one,' whispered Emmy in passing.

'You *will* excuse me, won't you?' cooed Penny, shooting a hard look at Emmy. 'I just wanted a word with my sister.'

She cupped her hand round Emmy's elbow and marshalled her smartly out into the garden.

'What have you been hatching up with Harry in that shed of Toby's? People were asking—and what could I tell them? You were always so secretive. I got stuck with that vicar and the awful Rose woman for ages.' The hat wobbled in sympathy with her sense of grievance. 'And what's more—what the hell's coming over Val? I know she's erratic, always has been. But falling down drunk at her own brother's funeral...'

'She's not *drunk*. Well, not too much. Just a bit too much. She's upset about the TV show. You know how much it means to her. Apparently Cissie isn't keen. Penny, have a heart, she is your *twin*. You will try to persuade her, won't you?'

Penny looked slightly mollified and even the hat seemed less agitated. Appeals to her vanity and her superior powers of persuasion never failed, as Emmy well knew.

'Persuade me to do what?'

Cissie was walking toward them, a plate of abandoned sausage rolls in one hand a healthy glass of milk in the other. She'd discarded the woolly hat she'd worn in church and appeared pleasantly at ease breathing in the fresh air and appraising her old home afresh. 'It was always such a happy house,' she said.

'Yes it was. Most of the time,' Emmy agreed.

'If it's about the TV show...' Cissie changed the subject. 'I haven't been on television for yonks. It's all right for Val. She does it all the time.' She sighed heavily. 'But I suppose Penny is going to convince me that if we don't co-operate Val will commit suicide spectacularly and leave us all feeling guilty.'

The twins exchanged rueful smiles and then, quite spontaneously, hugged each other. It was out of character for both: but, just for a moment, Emmy felt as if thirty years had been wiped away, dumped in the grave with Toby. Cissie and Penny were again the twins who backed up the star of the Mayflowers.

Emmy left them to it. Thankfully.

'Touching!' said Martin. He nodded toward his mother's reunion with her sister. He said it quite sincerely, with only a trace of mockery for appearance's sake. He was, after all, a member of the younger generation and wasn't expected to be moved by the behaviour of his elders, especially if one of them was a mother who never rated him highly.

He was a nice enough young man, thought Emmy, but somehow unnoticeable. You could easily lose him in a crowd. But he seemed to be comfortable in the company of his cousins, Robbie and Deb, and Flo Gosling who made anyone feel comfortable provided she could categorize them as deprived in some way.

'How did Val take the baby?' Emmy turned to Robbie and Deb. 'Come to that—Reggie and Isabel, too?'

Robbie helped himself to another glass of

hock from the bottle he'd commandeered for his private use.

'Me too?' said Deb.

Emmy was amused by the vehemence with which he turned down her request. 'You've had one. And that's enough.' He was behaving just like any expectant father. In fact, more solicitously than most. Wonders would never cease: except it wasn't a wonder at all, just human nature.

'Val is making a gallant attempt at playing the role of a loving grandmother, but not up to Oscar standard yet,' he said. 'Reggie and Isabel are still in a state of shock, but rising above it, wouldn't you say, Deb?'

She grinned. 'You have to hand it to my parents. There are no two better at keeping up appearances. Putting a brave face on it. All that guff.'

'Maybe not guff, Deb,' said Emmy. 'It's the glue that holds them together, perhaps. There are worse ways of surviving.'

Flo Gosling shook her head in disbelief. 'You always have reasons. I've never known anyone like Emmy for finding reasons.'

'Who's that girl I keep seeing everywhere?' said Martin. 'Nosy bitch!'

Emmy looked across the lawn to the pock-marked garden statue of some unidentifiable Greek god where Marian Fancey was quizzing Oliver, who was silently signalling 'help!' to anyone within eyeshot.

'That's the local reporter. I didn't invite her, but she's quite harmless. All the same I'd better rescue Oliver before he takes a gun to her.'

'Gun?'

'Metaphorical.'

She strode briskly over, wishing she'd helped herself to a glass of Robbie's hock. She needed fortifying. She'd been avoiding Oliver since last night. He'd thoroughly disapproved of all her plans. But it wasn't that that bothered her. It was something else which might be just a figment of her imagination.

'Miss Fancey! I'm so glad you dropped in.'

'I'm sorry...I know I should... But you were so kind the other day. And there's been so many enquiries about the picture of the mural of your brother's we printed in the *Clarion*. Not just from Clifton Coombe, but all over. I was going to get in touch with you about them, after the funeral.' She went on and on, gushing, wheedling, but very decently. She deserved a break, thought Emmy, and made up her mind to give her one.

'Why don't you stay a while, Miss Fancey. I've—I've a sort of announcement to make that might interest you.

Meanwhile, I can see my brother Reginald and his wife Isabel over there. I'm sure they'd love to talk to you.'

'Emmy, you're disgraceful,' said Oliver, watching Marian Fancey swoop down on Sir Reginald and Lady May. 'They'll be furious.'

'No they won't. They'll put up a jolly good show. The Mays always do.'

He took her hand. 'I think I've an idea what you're going to—to announce, as you put it, rather grandly I might say.'

'Oh, with all these egos floating around, I have to assert my own.'

'Emmy!' He seemed lost for words, which was practically unheard of for Oliver. 'Before you get too deep into whatever you're planning, I'd like to make an announcement of my own. Or, more accurately, a proposition.'

Dear Oliver, she thought. A proposition. So much more legal-sounding than a proposal.

'You know how I feel about you, how I've felt about you for a long time. You're an infuriating woman in so many ways. You're secretive, wayward. And—and you've let yourself go to seed with the years. Not a lot, just a little.'

She laughed out loud. Thank you,

389

Ollie, for making it easy. 'You're right, Ollie. That just about sums me up,' she conceded.

He looked contrite. 'I didn't mean to offend you.'

'You didn't.'

'It's just I never quite know what to say or how to approach you. If I'm nice you take the mickey. If I'm helpful you ignore my advice. I get the feeling the only time you respect me is when I'm thoroughly rude. So, that's what I'm being and maybe you'll respect my asking you to marry me.'

She took his other hand in hers and squeezed them both. 'I respect you very much, Ollie. I always have. And I respect your proposal, too. But you know I won't accept. Not because I don't think we might even have a good marriage in our declining years. But I can't exchange one life in Clifton Coombe for another not so very different. In the same place among the same people. Don't you see, Ollie, it's all changed? Toby's death changed it. I have to find out what's on the other side of the mountain.'

He shook his head, smiling. (Was it ungracious of her, she thought, to suspect it might be a smile of relief?) 'Well, it's said. The offer holds. Well'—he jiggled his hand from side to side in a gesture of doubt—'maybe not for ever.'

'You ought to marry Val. She's always been in love with you. And she'd be a damned good wife, too. Play the role to perfection.'

He actually saw the joke, chuckling. Then: 'That's just the point, Emmy. The Mays were always good at role-playing, except for you. That's what I liked about you. That's what made you different.'

'The other one,' she remembered. Perhaps that would be her epitaph.

She prevailed upon Daniel Boisseau and Harry and Marcus Gammie to be with her when, towards the end of the day when the other mourners had left, she gathered the family in the sitting room for a farewell drink and conversation.

It was quite late and humid from the rain earlier on. Through the windows of the old house, the garden assumed that eerie dark greenish-blue gleam that shrubbery, grass and trees take on in the fading light.

'So this is it?' whispered Frances in her ear. 'You're going to tell them?'

Emmy nodded and glanced over at Brad who was leaning against the flocked wallpaper, part and yet apart from the assembled company. He nodded back at Emmy and raised his hands, thumbs up.

'Make sure that girl Marian Fancey

gets it all down,' said Emmy. 'Persistence deserves a reward.'

'Softie!' said Frances. 'Anyway it's hardly earth-shattering.'

It was amazing how quickly it was over, thought Emmy. Ten minutes and a lifetime. The exhibition and sale of Toby's paintings. The donation of Rushey Green to be set up as a school for mentally handicapped children, bearing Toby's name. The trust fund to equip and subsidize it. Her move to London. And, finally, the diary. The memoirs of the Mays illustrated by the author's sketches, although, she conceded, that was up for discussion.

For several minutes there was a deafening silence. Then Reggie raised his glass. 'To Toby! God rest his soul!' They took their cue from him, raised their glasses in turn and echoed the blessing.

She sat down, exhausted but content and not a little amused. You have to hand it to the Mays, she silently repeated to herself. They can always be relied upon to put on a good show.

CHAPTER TWENTY-THREE

It was the night after the funeral that she was roused from a deep sleep by a hammering on her door. At first she thought it was the thunder which, along with the sudden cracks of lightning, had kept her awake earlier. Then, in the calm that followed, she had dozed off to the sound of steady rain as it sought out the weak spots in the guttering and trickled soothingly on the paving below outside her window.

In her dreamlike state, exhausted but subconsciously reliving the events of the past days, she equated the noise with ghosts. Toby. Gilbert. Madge. Harvey Persky. She'd never thought of Rushey Green as a haunted house. But perhaps it was. Perhaps all houses whose walls were riddled with the secrets of past generations were haunted. Some more than most.

But the hammering persisted. Not ghosts. Live people.

She dragged on a dressing gown and opened the door.

Terry and Lorraine were standing outside. They seemed lost for words. Their stricken expressions were eloquent enough. Something disastrous or, at least, odd had been happening.

'What is it?'

Terry swallowed hard as if summoning up reserves of courage.

'It's...Emmy, I'm sorry...'

'It's the Adelphi,' Lorraine interrupted, more in control.

'What about the Adelphi?' yawned Emmy, not really caring much. The Adelphi had done her no favours. But, curiously, people in Clifton Coombe always seemed to talk to her in hushed tones about the old, abandoned theatre as if they regarded her as its last surviving guardian, which in a sense she probably was, although she never felt that way about it.

'It's been struck by lightning,' said Lorraine.

'We were out in the town and saw it. Clap! Just like that. You should have seen it.' Terry had found his voice and was conveying the excitement of a sight worth seeing.

'Terry!' Lorraine reprimanded him. She looked at Emmy anxiously, maybe expecting her to throw a fit or burst into tears.

But all Emmy could think was: What a surprise!

Maybe ghosts *had* been at work, after all. She recalled a watercolour Toby had done once when he was in a paddy at being ticked off by Alf Gravely for messing around with the props backstage. It showed the Adelphi disintegrating under a rain of fireworks. Daniel Boisseau had much admired it.

'Toby *has* been busy,' she murmured to herself.

'Toby!' Terry frowned. He hoped she wasn't going off her rocker.

'Just nonsense,' she assured them. 'Was anyone hurt?'

'Not so far as we could see. There was hardly anyone about. We were in the gardens across the way.' Doing no doubt what people did in the gardens which had survived the years of redevelopment in Clifton Coombe and were still the venue for couples after dark, just canoodling or getting down to more serious business.

'The fire brigade turned up and we thought we'd better come back and let you know.'

'That was considerate,' said Emmy for want of something better to say. What, she wondered, was she supposed to do? The Adelphi had ceased being the responsibility of the Mays years ago when Gilbert had sold it for a nice profit.

It was then that the police called. 'We thought you should know,' the sergeant explained sympathetically as if informing her of a great tragedy.

'What's it got to do with me?' she said irritably.

'We just thought you should know,' he reiterated, sounding hurt that his gesture should have been so rudely rejected.

Oh dear, thought Emmy, the trouble with being beastly is that you have to make up for it with an extra larding of gratitude. 'Of course. It was very kind of you, sergeant. You woke me from a deep sleep and I wasn't quite ready for it.'

He mumbled something about lucky to be able to sleep through a storm like that and put down the phone.

The next morning early she drove down to the town centre to see the damage for herself. It was, she felt, the least she could do. Show an interest.

The word got around that one of Clifton Coombe's important landmarks, albeit a pretty tacky one, had fallen victim to the lightning and there was quite a gathering of early sightseers.

It was only when she faced the wreckage that she was truly shocked. The lightning had struck the already rickety dome and sliced through the roof, igniting the rotting timbers and starting a fire that had gutted what remained of the inside of the building. Two fire engines were still standing by and hosepipes snaked through the gaping entrance.

The chief fire officer recognized her. 'There's no saving her now,' he said. 'She'll have to be completely demolished.'

The fact that he described the Adelphi as 'she' seemed oddly touching, like the captain of a sunken ship referring to his lost vessel, as if he really regarded the old building as a living thing now dead.

'It was high time. She was just a shell of her old self,' said Emmy, adopting his mode of tribute to the Adelphi.

'All the same it'll be quite a blow for you I suspect. So soon after—well, you know—your brother.'

'A blow?' She thought about it for a moment. 'I didn't think it would be. But yes, you're right, I suppose it is a blow.'

But he'd moved on, supervising the withdrawal from the site, comparing notes with the town surveyor and the police who were cordoning off the area.

One last look, she decided. A two-minutes silence in memory of all the shows, all the people, that had been part of the glory that had once been the Adelphi. She tried hard to feel suitably sombre, but all she could muster was a kind of sadness allied to a sense of completeness. The old theatre had given itself up dramatically to a fitting end, a finale that might have delighted Gilbert.

People around her shook their heads in wonder. A bolt of lightning can do a lot of damage but to have achieved this smoking ruin was something special. But the old place was ripe for demolition anyway, a death trap; and they went on about their business in the town.

'Well, that's that then,' volunteered a gruff voice behind Emmy as she stood there silently surveying the scene.

She recognized it as that of Alice Gravely.

'Best thing that could have happened —especially now.'

'What do you mean, especially now?' said Emmy.

'I hear you're leaving Clifton Coombe. Well now the Adelphi's gone there's nothing to keep you. Clean break. Should have done it years ago. Still, better late.'

Emmy smiled. Trust Alice to get to the nub of the matter. 'Didn't you ever want to leave?'

'Every day of my life. But I didn't, did I? So let me be an awful warning to you.'

The old lady turned away abruptly as if fearing that Emmy might engage her in more confidences. The less contact the less grief when that contact was broken. 'I'll probably see you before you go,' she said airily as if it were of no consequence whether she did or not. Then she tottered off on those failing legs to the shops.

The *Clarion* ran another enormous feature about the Adelphi and the Mays at the end of the week. But Emmy refused to be drawn any more on the subject even by Marian Fancey, whose stock on the paper had risen with her coverage of Toby's funeral and Emmy's announcement afterwards. There was surprisingly little interest in the inquest on Toby May and its verdict of accidental death. Perhaps even Clifton Coombe had at last had a surfeit of Mays.

During the next weeks Emmy was kept busy with the legal ramifications of handing over Rushey Green to the charity, battling with the planning department of the council and setting up a fund to help equip and subsidize the school. It was a matter, said Harry Eardley who knew about these things, of setting it all in motion.

'Your pittance won't help much in the grand scheme of things,' he'd explained derisively. 'Unless Toby's paintings make you a fortune. But I wouldn't hold your breath.' Meanwhile he beavered away getting the support of Mencap and a small but useful grant from the local welfare service, despite serious opposition from some image-conscious councillors who grumbled about capping and cutbacks while pressing for a new mayoral Daimler. It was only by chance that she heard from Oliver that Harry was backing her scheme with more than words and effort.

'He's a very rich man,' Oliver dismissed Harry's massive contribution to the fund after inadvertently letting the cat out of the bag. 'And you'd better not mention it to him. It's supposed to be anonymous.'

Emmy grinned. 'Good old Harry! You shouldn't have told me, should you, Ollie?'

Ollie! He grimaced as he always did.

'No. Anyway you can rest assured it won't just fold up for lack of cash.'

'That's a relief. I wondered if perhaps it was all just a pipe-dream. A sort of three o'clock in the morning grand idea.'

'There'll still be a lot to organize.' He had put on his schoolmasterly voice, lecturing the layman on the pitfalls of anything remotely adventurous.

'Some,' she agreed. 'But once it's in place, permits and so on, it's for the experts to take over. I wouldn't know how to begin to organize a school of that complexity. The charity will hire the staff, oversee the structural alterations necessary. I've a horrible feeling I'll be looked upon as Lady Bountiful who comes down on special days to dispense approval, encouragement and support.'

She'd mentioned that to the charity secretary, Mavis Turner, who could be brusque and quite brutal when she needed to be. The endless struggle for donations and help was no job for sensitive souls with weak constitutions and a tendency to give in at the first refusal, or even the tenth.

'Well, of *course,* you are, Emmy, old girl. You always have been. Lady Bountiful. But that doesn't mean you haven't worked bloody hard for the charity and the kids in your time. So stop poncing around being mournful. We'll miss you, you can be sure of that. We'll never get anyone to run a fête better than you. But we'll be a lot more grateful for the school and the money than for a pair of willing hands.'

Emmy had burst out laughing. 'Mavis, I've never known anyone like you for cutting somebody down to size. Thanks for your help but we'd rather have the cash!'

Mavis grinned back. She wasn't at all like the accepted and largely false image of a typical, tireless charity worker. Exceedingly elegant, fine boned, with a classic Garbo face, she was always impeccably groomed. She also had a foul tongue and a foul temper which she used to remarkable effect.

'So, you can sod off to the smoke with a clear conscience, Emmy. Special dispensation from the blinkered misogynist in the Vatican.'

'Mavis!' Mavis, Emmy remembered, was not only agnostic but fiercely anti-Catholic on the subject of contraception and abortion.

'Mavis, Mavis!' Mavis mimicked. 'I hope I'm a humanitarian, but I've never claimed to be holy.'

When they'd parted that day, she had taken Emmy's hand in hers. Emmy was surprised how tough and rough her palm felt. A working hand.

'You won't be a stranger, will you?' she'd said, sounding unusually mellow for her.

'How could I be! Rushey Green is my home.'

'Not any more, it won't be.'

'No,' Emmy agreed. 'Not any more.' She wondered if she were sad or glad. But perhaps only time would tell that.

'You won't be a stranger.'

Emmy started. She realized that Oliver was repeating Mavis's exhortation.

'Of course not.' Her shoulders sagged. 'Oh, Ollie, for God's sake, don't go sentimental on me. We're friends. We'll always be friends. And be honest, you wouldn't want to marry me any more than I want to marry you.'

He screwed up his mouth pensively. 'I

suppose. It's just I'm not very good at admitting failure.'

'I know. Success becomes you, Ollie. It always did. You and Mavis would get along fine. Except she has a nice, meek, dreary-looking little husband tucked away in the background whom she loves to distraction. You see, there's just no accounting...'

That evening she drove to the outskirts of town as she had every month to the municipal cemetery where Harvey Persky was buried. She stood looking at the stark headstone for a long time in the gathering dusk. 'I suppose this is goodbye, Harvey,' she murmured.

A mother and teenage son carrying flowers passed by and smiled, understanding. It was a fallacy that the dead could not answer back, they knew.

When she got back Terry told her that Val had rung to say that the TV show was definitely on, Cissie had capitulated, Penny was agreeable and Marcus was certain it would lead to something juicy for Val. She wasn't to bother to ring back that night because Val was dining at the Savoy.

'Savoy! Classy. I suppose she wasn't about to tell who with. With whom,' she corrected herself.

'Well, she wouldn't tell me, would she? She just happened to mention that she mustn't keep Ken and Emma waiting. So putting two and two together...'

'Let me guess. Ken Smith and Emma Jones?' She laughed.

'No! Kenneth Branagh and Emma Thompson,' he said, annoyed at having his scoop spiked.

'I can't see Val carrying a spear in his next Shakespearean production.'

He looked at her, puzzled. 'Why should she carry a spear?'

'You're quite right, Terry. I'm being facetious.'

He hung around, seeming to have something to say and not quite sure when might be the right moment. 'Me—and Lorraine...' he began.

'You're leaving,' she said with certainty. 'That's what you're trying to tell me.'

He nodded. 'It's not that we want to let you down. You've been good to us. But sooner the better. And you won't be here much longer anyway.'

'No, I won't,' she agreed. For a moment she felt a stab of sorrow. Parting wasn't sweet at all. Flo, too. But she brightened up for Terry's sake. He looked suddenly so distressed.

'No, I won't,' she repeated. 'And a good thing too. For all of us. You'll do fine, Terry. You and Lorraine. And if you don't I'll haunt you. That's a promise.'

Promises, promises! 'You will promise to visit me some time,' Flo had urged her before setting out for somewhere unpronounceable on the fringe of the Brecon Beacons where her women's group was based. She was dressed for hard travelling in a coarse denim skirt, layers of sweat-shirts and a duffel coat spilling out of her canvas holdall. Her only concession to conventional transportation was the train to Cardiff, thereafter she was hitching. She thought she'd pick up a cheap little runabout when she got there.

They'd been squatting on the floor of Toby's old hut, empty now since Daniel Boisseau had arranged for his paintings and sketches to be collected and stored. Even the family mural had been carefully hacked out of the wall.

'It all seems so odd, now,' said Flo looking round her at all that emptiness. 'Almost as if he'd never been.'

'Flo! That's maudlin. The paintings will go on show. They're still alive.'

'Yes. But not *here*. Don't you see? Here is where they're most alive. Where Toby was most alive.'

'You don't have to remind me.'

'Sorry. Careless. What about his diaries?'

Emmy took a deep breath. She'd done what she'd done off her own bat, without reference to anyone. But Flo could be trusted.

'I burned them.'

Flo didn't seem surprised. 'I thought you might,' she said. 'Too personal, too intimate, too many skeletons. Right?'

Emmy nodded. 'That's about it. I've told Daniel Boisseau but no one else. On the whole I suspect they'll be happy to forget the diaries ever existed.'

'Why did you *really* burn them, though? You're not that much concerned about the family reaction, are you?' She put her hands on her friend's shoulders and peered deeply into her eyes. 'It's Frances, isn't it? You didn't want her to guess who her father really was.'

'Maybe. Not that Toby wrote anything explicit. He couldn't have. He didn't know. But Fanny would be smart enough to read between the lines. And it's too late to bring all that up. Let's face it, Brad has been more of a father to her than her real father ever had a chance to be.'

Flo grinned. 'As the dreaded Thatcher said: it's a funny old world!'

'Look after yourself, Flo,' she'd said as they parted. But she doubted whether Flo would pay any heed to such a trivial undertaking as looking after herself. There was a whole world to be set to rights before that.

When they'd all gone she felt oddly comfortably alone in the old house. Already it seemed to be responding to its future usefulness.

Frances took two weeks leave to help her pack. She'd found her a rented flat in Teddington until she could sort out her finances and buy a place, preferably on the river or near Bushy Park where she could walk and watch the deer and cross the road into Hampton Court gardens for the flowering of the daffodils which pleased her more than the great vine or the maze.

'How's Brad?' she said, knowing the answer for she'd spoken to him often on the telephone since the funeral, but knowing too that it would please Frances that she should mention him.

'Not too bad. He's looking forward to you coming up to London. He wants to take you up on your offer to work in the bookshop. But you know that.'

They were piling Emmy's own books into cases for the removal men.

'I hope you can get all this lot into the flat.' She pressed her mother's hand. 'You'll miss it, won't you? Rushey Green. All the things you do in Clifton Coombe.'

Emmy shook her head firmly. 'No, I won't. I won't let myself. It's a far, far better thing that Rushey Green is *going* to do than it ever did after mother and dad died. Besides, there'll be no terms of reference. That, I've decided, is the trick when you move. Pick somewhere and some place that are so entirely different from what you've left that it's impossible to make disparaging comparisons because there's nothing to compare. As for things to do, I can be just as handy in London as I have been here. It'll just take time.'

She picked up a load of schoolgirls' books. Annuals. Angela Brazil. Louisa May Alcott. *What Katy Did.* Books about spunky wartime heroines. And the classics which were a duty that became a pleasure.

'Well this lot can go to the Spastics or Oxfam.'

Frances took them from her. 'Don't be hasty. They must be treasures. Or once were. This—for instance.'

She inspected the slim, vellum-bound volume of Jane Austen's *Pride and Prejudice* and opened it at the flyleaf. '"Emmelyne Disley. 1893. A Lady of Quality. H."' she read. 'It's quite a rare edition, I should think. Who gave it to you?'

'Oh, just some man I once knew.' When Frances had first picked up the book she'd felt her throat contract, but it passed and she found she could talk easily, as if it were a matter of no importance.

'He must have been very fond of you.'

Emmy touched her daughter's cheek and looked into Harvey Persky's eyes. 'I think he was,' she said. 'In his fashion.'

Other MAGNA General Fiction Titles In Large Print

FRANCES ANNE BOND
Return Of The Swallow

JUDY GARDINER
All On A Summer's Day

IRIS GOWER
The Sins Of Eden

HELEN MANSFIELD
Some Women Dream

ELISABETH McNEILL
The Shanghai Emerald

ELIZABETH MURPHY
To Give And To Take

JUDITH SAXTON
This Royal Breed

HRH 10/11
Down 5/12
QAL 6/12
HRH 10/18
HH 3/15